THE EVOLUTION
OF CHARLIE K

THE
EVOLUTION
OF
CHARLIE K

Richard Nye

RICHARD NYE

Matador
9 Priory Business Park,
Wistow Road, Kibworth Beauchamp,
Leicestershire. LE8 0RX
Tel: 0116 279 2299
Email: books@troubador.co.uk
Web: www.troubador.co.uk/matador
Twitter: @matadorbooks

ISBN 978 1800462 830

British Library Cataloguing in Publication Data.
A catalogue record for this book is available from the British Library.

Printed and bound in Great Britain by 4edge Limited
Typeset in 11pt Minion Pro by Troubador Publishing Ltd, Leicester, UK

Matador is an imprint of Troubador Publishing Ltd

For Ann
with love

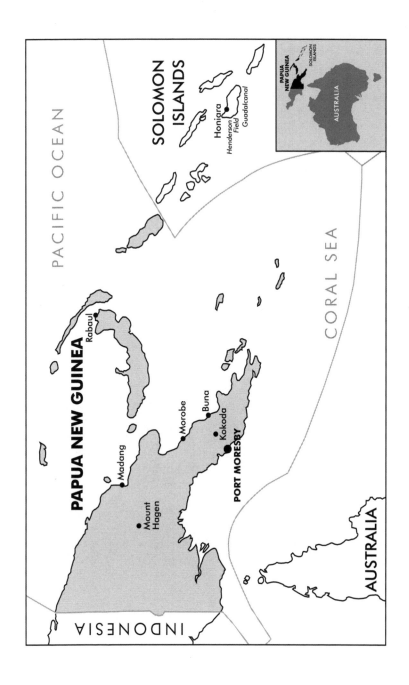

PART ONE
TORI VILLAGE

CHAPTER 1

Squatting in the shade of his uncle's hut, Charlie Kikira was sweating from the exertion of helping repair its roof of plaited leaves. At his side, wizened Uncle Paru was talking of his hopes.

'Charlie, perhaps one day my hut will have an iron roof like those we have seen at some of the big villages. I am getting too old for this work.'

Charlie listened patiently to this favourite topic of his uncle. He was about to reply when suddenly the hot still air carried a shout of 'Hey Charlie!'

It was the voice of his boss, Patrol Officer Bruce Petersen. Charlie rose to run across the dusty tree-lined compound.

A few minutes later, standing before Bruce's desk, a breathless Charlie looked at his boss in disbelief. Anxiety gripped him as he wondered if he had heard correctly.

He knew that white men were prone to making strange irrational decisions, but this one took some beating.

'Tomorrow we'll visit the Hulwari,' Bruce had said. He didn't actually say these words but 'Tumora me tupela lukim Hulwari.'

Bruce had been using Pidgin English or Tok Pisin. Charlie understood perfectly but did not immediately respond, so Bruce repeated himself.

'Yes, Masta', said Charlie who deemed it best to humour his kiap boss. In Papua New Guinea, a patrol officer was usually referred to as a kiap.

What Charlie did not know at that moment, was that Bruce had earlier taken a radio call from his boss, the DC in neighbouring Koroba. A district commissioner was generally referred to as a DC. The call had been an instruction to report on a rumour that the bloodthirsty Hulwari tribe had got new axes and killed some members of a neighbouring tribe.

Visiting the Hulwari, famed for their terrifying wigs and cannibalistic rituals, was considered by villagers of the relatively peaceful Tori tribe to be an act of foolhardiness at the best of times. Now was just about the worst of times since a Tori villager had only last week inadvertently come into possession of a stray pig, without considering that it might be Hulwari property. The man could not believe his good fortune and had promptly slaughtered it for his hungry family. As it happened, this nomadic pig belonged to the chief Hulwari wigman and was highly prized by his owner, a deeply revered member of the tribe. To cap it all, it was a well-known fact that a full moon was considered by the Hulwari to be a particularly auspicious time to be eating human flesh. Tomorrow night, the moon would be at its fullest. Charlie did not know for certain if the fate of the pig was known to its owner. His imagination conjured the effects of an attack by an affronted war party seeking revenge for the creature's abduction.

The year was 1960. Bruce Petersen had arrived two months earlier to take charge of the Tori region patrol office in a remote area of the forested highlands of tropical Papua New Guinea, generally referred to as PNG. Eighteen-year-old Charlie had been recruited as his assistant and general factotum. Patrol Officer Petersen occasionally seemed to forget that Charlie understood and spoke better English than he himself spoke Tok Pisin. He had learnt at his training at the Department of Territories in Canberra that English-speaking natives were virtually unknown in the interior. Petersen had grown up in rural Australia and recently arrived in the territory bringing with him a classification of the human race in somewhat simplistic terms – it comprised Australians, bloody foreigners or primitive natives. Although at heart a kindly man, Petersen's prejudices had been formed at the knee of his somewhat bigoted father.

Unusually tall and slim for a Highland native, Charlie was of a similar height to the burly Australian's five feet ten inches. Otherwise, the contrast between Charlie and Bruce Petersen was stark. Bruce's northern European ancestors had endowed him with pale skin and straight blond hair. The Australian World War Two soldiers' sobriquet of 'fuzzy-wuzzy' for Papuans was earned through the tight black curls of which dark-skinned Charlie possessed a typical set.

On the following day Charlie strolled to the battered government Jeep at the back of the patrol office compound. As he did so he thought about the whole situation. As a Tori he was by nature instinctively cautious in any dealings with the Hulwari. Although traditional enemies of the Hulwari, the Tori had largely given up fighting and cannibalism since the establishment of a government patrol office in the area some five years after the end of World War Two.

Successive village headmen had discovered the advantages of a pragmatic approach in dealing with white men and the benefits of adapting to the laws set by the Australian administration of the Territory of Papua New Guinea. The Hulwari by contrast clung to their old ways and whilst wary of the white man would still indulge in cannibalism when the opportunity presented itself.

In a land of over 1,000 isolated tribes and more than 800 languages Charlie was unusual in so far that he had a working knowledge of the Hulwari language and of a number of other tribal dialects, not to mention the lingua franca of Tok Pisin. Just to complicate things language-wise, Police Motu was also in use but declining. Charlie could also switch to that at will. He was orphaned at the age of nine and virtually adopted by a benign patrol officer, one Philip Smithson, a distant predecessor of Bruce Petersen. Smithson, who had become something of a father figure to orphan Charlie, went on to become a district commissioner before his eventual retirement some eighteen months ago. At that time Charlie went back to his tribe, the Tori, in the foothills of the Owen Stanley Mountains. Smithson's work had led him to travel widely throughout the territory taking Charlie with him. As a result, Charlie as a Highland native, was also unusual to be well-travelled. His linguistic abilities stemmed from times when he would play with local boys at Smithson's new postings. The greatest impact on Charlie of his travels had been the realisation of the existence of a world outside the Tori region where he had spent his childhood. In common with the vast majority of the four million population of PNG, people believed the world comprised an area of a few square miles surrounding their village. If any Tori villager cared to think about it further, the world's population numbered the outlying Tori villages and those distant war-like foreigners – the Hulwari. It was true there were a few white men but somehow, they didn't count.

Also marking Charlie out from the large majority of his countrymen was his ability to read and write. This he had acquired at schools of the London Missionary Society. Access to Smithson's library with its Encyclopaedia Britannica and atlases had furthered his realisation that the world was a very large place. He had started to appreciate that PNG was a country without any notion of nationhood on the part of its inhabitants. He frequently wondered about the fact that life was controlled by white men. His reading revealed that other countries had a ruling class of white men. There were a number of places in Africa and Asia where, similar to PNG, the whites seemed to be in charge.

Never formally adopted by Mr and Mrs Smithson, Charlie's upbringing had been quite unique. In PNG tribal society, an individual's identity is largely grounded in his or her own kin group and rarely extends beyond those of relatives and in-laws. While an individual may share a language and culture with hundreds or maybe thousands of persons, only leaders and other unusual individuals spend time outside their village. Charlie's uncle, Paru Kikira, the Smithson's elderly houseboy was such an exception in the early post-war years. He had travelled with his master for most of the latter's time in PNG. Uncle Paru had manfully taken over the responsibility for Charlie upon his brother and sister-in-law's untimely death. They had drowned during a fishing trip in the turbulent waters of the Ipigi River. Charlie was their only child. Paru's wife was already struggling with her own children and her husband's lively nephew did not readily fit into their family. Charlie found solace with Mr Smithson's kindly but childless wife Pamela. She encouraged the young boy into her house when he tired of his cousins' company. This became more frequent as the years passed although he still resided with his uncle. Despite the daily exposure to the ways of a western household, he had not completely crossed the cultural boundary from a society steeped in beliefs in magic, the powers of ancestors and traditional lifestyles. The latter demanded that at puberty Charlie be initiated into manhood. Initiation ceremonies are designed as preparation for marriage and adulthood. These rites are elaborate, arduous and sometimes frightening. The rotation in Mr Smithson's postings meant that periodically Charlie found himself back in the Tori region and his uncle took care to see that he participated in the tribe's essential rituals. With his fellows on the verge of adulthood he put on a brave face when his time came, but was inwardly terrified.

Many schools of western psychological thought dwell on the significance of earliest memories in the development of the adult mind. Imprinted on Charlie's mind was seeing the body of his Uncle Torea, his father's eldest brother, being brought back to the village after being killed in a fight further up in the mountains with the Hulwari people. Never before had Charlie heard such wailing, which continued through the night. Uncle Torea was set down, daubed with coloured clays and ashes and decorated with sea shells. The following day his body was removed to the forest to be set high in a tree facing west where his spirit would watch out for the tribe and be ready to be called upon in times of danger. Village life then returned to normal, except Torea's widow remained in isolation for months. The men of the village became preoccupied with revenge as their honourable duty. As a result, a cycle of violence would be perpetuated. The death of a family member at the hands of his enemies imbued Charlie with the belief that revenge was the only way of settling scores. The notion of compromise and peaceful settlement did not come naturally.

In common with all his people, for the rest of Charlie's life, he would have a strong subconscious feeling of the importance of his ancestors. After all his presence in the world was due solely to them and he owed it as a duty to respect them. The same logic dictated that the younger members of his tribe cared for and honoured their elders. Much later in his life Charlie was shocked to find the practice in western society of placing the elderly in homes to be cared for by others. There were some things about the world of white men that Charlie found fascinating and attractive, but when it came to the cult of individualism being placed above the needs of the tribe it seemed quite shocking.

CHAPTER 2

Charlie guessed the upcoming meeting with the Hulwari was for Bruce to investigate reports in which Tori village gossip said their enemy had been brandishing strange sharp weapons with great cutting ability. The impact of this was something akin to a western country learning that some unfriendly neighbouring regime had acquired a nuclear weapon capability. Maybe the whole business had a simple explanation. Despite the propensity of the Tori for gross exaggeration, these reports had come from separate sources. The most extraordinary aspect of the stories was that the Hulwari, in common with many Highland tribes at the time, were still largely isolated from the rest of the world. For centuries they, like other remote Highland tribes in PNG, fashioned their weapons and cutting tools from rock. They were literally still in the Stone Age.

The visit the following day would partly be by ancient Jeep, a relic of the war that ended some fifteen years ago. Few patrol offices at outstations possessed a vehicle simply because there were virtually no roads in PNG's rugged interior. The Tori office however had some driveable tracks leading to outlying villages. During the dry season a precipitous drive could almost reach Mt Hagen, the regional HQ of the Department of Native Affairs. Part of the route to the Hulwari village ended at Tori's airstrip. Officially Charlie did not drive the Jeep, he had no licence and the only place to have a test and obtain one was in the capital Port Moresby. This was a two-hour flight away in one of the small twin-engine nine passenger aircraft, which formed the principal means of connecting the territory's network of outstations. His position as a native combined with the logistics involved ruled out him ever being able to drive officially. Nonetheless, Mr Smithson had taught him to drive and his current boss, Bruce, had last week allowed him to drive the Jeep around the compound. The risks involved were virtually non-existent. There were no other vehicles in Tori furthermore Bruce, the only white man resident in Tori, represented the administration, the Australian government, the Governor General and ultimately Her Majesty the Queen. In other words, he was virtually God for the remainder of his posting to Tori. With such blessing Charlie drove to Bruce's bungalow and parked outside.

The journey could only realistically be carried out in the daylight hours so they would leave at dawn the following day. Charlie surveyed the venerable Jeep. Outstations such as Tori invariably had the cast-off transport from a main centre, newer vehicles being initially allocated on the basis of rank. Tori's ex-military Jeep had started civilian life at headquarters in Port Moresby followed by years with the district commissioner in Mt Hagen and now destined to end its days in Tori. A Public Works Department white man visited periodically to service it or carry out repairs. Travelling in the government vehicle, even in a battered heap such as this conferred some status on Charlie and normally, he would have looked forward to a trip. On this occasion however with the Hulwari as the destination, he felt differently with a sense of foreboding. It was customary to take Tori's two PNG policemen on such trips for protection and to help with loading fuel, food, camping equipment and water. Charlie set off to find this escort. As usual they were to be found at the back of the patrol office. Constable Diro was fairly large in height and girth whereas Constable Ona was short and wiry. Diro was asleep and Ona staring into space, slowly chewing betel nut and acquiring the red-coloured gums and teeth that went with the habit. The narcotic effect of betel chewing produces a sense of well-being, even euphoria and was definitely banned to government servants on duty. Charlie felt little comfort in knowing that these guardians of the law would be protecting Bruce and himself from a few hundred hungry Hulwari armed with stone axes.

'Kirap! kirap! yulesbagas!' shouted Charlie, prodding Diro awake and pulling Ona to his feet.

Using pidgin rather than Tori dialect for greater effect, he chastised them for being lazy. He commanded them to present themselves for inspection to Bruce before the following day's trip. Grumbling, the constables ambled off to fetch their elderly .303 Lee-Enfield rifles, relics of World War Two, like the Jeep. In reality Charlie had no authority over policemen, but his natural confidence and assertiveness always made him test his boundaries. Nine times out ten it worked. In a very short time, most of the village believed that some of Patrol Officer Bruce's white godliness had rubbed off on Charlie. Although harbouring some puzzled resentment, few felt inclined to challenge him.

'Where's Laurel and Hardy?' asked Bruce. Tori's police force had been so called by previous generations of patrol officers and the names were now used as a matter of fact.

'They are coming Masta. Do you think they will be sufficient if the Hulwari become dangerous? Is this a good time to visit the Hulwari? Perhaps we should go later. Also, I hear strange noises from the Jeep, perhaps we should go after the Public Works Department man has fixed it next week when he comes?' Charlie ventured nervously.

He knew he was treading on somewhat tricky ground here. It was very unusual for a native to question action decreed from such a great height. Fortunately, Petersen was not burdened by the outsize ego possessed by some kiaps. He took no offence, indeed, he would have been happy to abandon the trip and spend his time on local inspections or perhaps in his office with a cold beer between naps and some undemanding paperwork.

'No chance Charlie, we're going. The DC's here next week and we have to tell him what those Hulwari clowns are up to.'

At that moment, Laurel and Hardy appeared clutching their rifles. They stood somewhat untidily to attention. Petersen looked over his barefoot escorts in their black PNG police uniforms edged with red piping. The uniform comprised a loose one-piece, open-necked, short-sleeved outfit with a skirt just covering the knees. A leather belt and black beret with a badge completed the ensemble. The whole effect was quite distinctive, if somewhat bizarre to the European eye. Men in skirts, known as lap-laps, were quite acceptable to the local population who had no point of reference in terms of dress, apart from traditional native male garb. The Australian designer of PNG's police uniform perhaps wanted to make sure that the native police were totally distinct and identifiable tools of the administration. There certainly could be no link with the traditional khaki-coloured colonial uniforms of the territory's few white police officers.

For the male inhabitants of PNG's remote interior dress varied from tribe to tribe but was often confined to minimal covering of the private parts, derived from strategically positioned pieces of bark, animal hide or even bones. The most bizarre feature to European eyes was the elaborate wigs used on ceremonial occasions. These were decorated using bird of paradise feathers secured in place with dried mud. Faces were painted with white pigment embellished by colourful marks and stripes to produce the desired terrifying effect. Women had an altogether simpler appearance; dress usually being confined to a grass skirt. Charlie had adopted European shorts and shirt since his days with the Smithsons.

Bruce eyed his police escort. He had little doubt that the only protection they afforded was achieved by the psychological effect of the uniforms and rifles. Diro's girth and Ona's betel-induced haze did not inspire confidence. Bruce made a mental note to take his personal Webley .45 as a precaution.

'Yutupela hia tumora wen sun ecum – savvy?'

The guardians of the law nodded uncertainly to the command to be ready tomorrow at dawn. They knew this usually meant a day of having to work as porters, carrying overnight food and camping equipment as well as their heavy rifles. The sinecure of being a policeman suddenly paled. Bruce reckoned that if they left at first light the next day, they should reach the Hulwari before nightfall and in time to pitch camp. Diro and Ona would double as porters for the second part of the journey.

At dawn Charlie stood outside his hut enjoying the brief cool respite from the tropical heat of the day. The smell of smoke from cooking fires hung in the still air of the lush valley. The village was surrounded by dense green forest rising on all sides. The night sounds of chirping cicada bugs gave way to a mix of voices, barking dogs, bleating goats, wood chopping and early morning calls of jungle birds ringing through the valley. This was Charlie's favourite time of day, a time of freshness and contemplation of what lay ahead. He strolled to the Jeep as his lord and master was emerging from his bungalow. Ona and Diri were already lounging by the vehicle having loaded up all the necessities for a three-day round trip.

'You drive, Charlie,' said Bruce.

This was a thrill for Charlie who previously had only been allowed to drive around the compound. His mood lifted. Whatever dangers the expedition held, there suddenly was the pleasurable prospect of a drive beyond the village and particularly of taking Bruce on official business. This public demonstration of trust was most satisfying and undoubtedly accumulated kudos for Charlie in the eyes of the villagers who had gathered to watch the departure. They set off taking an easterly track along a valley hemmed in by green-clad mountainsides. Due to the mountainous terrain, very few roads existed in the territory and almost all were confined to a mile or two from main coastal centres. Australian soldiers had hewn this track during the deadly conflict with the Japanese that had claimed so many lives. The only purpose of the track was to connect Tori's grass airstrip to the patrol office which during World War Two was an army command post. The airstrip was the only practical connection with rest of PNG. It was 1,500 feet of narrow, almost flat ground, a rarity in the interior of the country which ranks as one of the most rugged and inaccessible regions in the world. Flying in PNG was a skilled and hazardous business for the pilots of local airline Patair's tiny nine-seat Piaggio aircraft.

To reach the airstrip from the Tori patrol office was three quarters of an hour's slow drive over a rutted and rock-strewn track, frequently impassable after rains. The track received minimal maintenance and was becoming progressively worse during each succeeding wet season. This had just ended and the drive was slow and bumpy.

They needed two stops to dig the Jeep out of axle-deep mud. Once at the airstrip Charlie parked the Jeep and everything had to be carried from then on. To reach Hulwari village the party faced a six-hour slog on foot though dense rainforest.

Leaving the Jeep behind Charlie led the group single file followed by Petersen with the constables bringing up the rear, Diro grunting under his load. They headed up a rough path that quickly became a green tunnel with occasional glimpses of sunlight through the rainforest canopy. Vines hung, occasionally brushing their faces. Birdcalls punctuated the heavy forest air. A day's ascent lay ahead, punctuated only with an occasional dip in the terrain. The Hulwari village, although in the lower slopes of the dominating Owen Stanley Range, was still over 4,000 feet above sea level.

Each of the party was occupied with his own thoughts. The main focus for Bruce was his forthcoming leave back home in Shepperton, Victoria about one hundred miles north of Melbourne. Apart from the prospect of a reunion with his girl and his parents, the question on his mind was should he shortly renew his contract for another two-year tour and return to PNG. On his desk lay the form requesting a decision. His motive for coming to the territory was twofold. Firstly, it was the relatively generous salary and on the other for a change from the tedium of the Policy Division of the Department of Social Services in Canberra. His cousin had served in the administration a few years back and told tales of an exotic, untamed, tropical country with the longest lizards, the tallest trees and the biggest butterflies in the world. Actually, his know-it-all cousin had only spent a couple of months in Port Moresby as a carpenter with the Public Works Department. At interview Bruce seemed to communicate well with the board, conveying an impression of a man deeply committed to improving the lot of native people. His degree in social sciences from Sydney University was exactly the background they needed. One of Bruce's greatest abilities was to sell himself. He undoubtedly would have made an outstanding salesman. His choice of study had been more influenced by the fact that it seemed one of the easier options, together with the allure of Sydney and its beaches and nightlife. Surfing was high on easy-going Bruce's priorities along with girls, beer and barbeques with his mates. At this stage in his life any form of creative activity or career was way down his list. Most of his tour so far had been spent in a Port Moresby office but now he was in his own little world.

Bruce wrestled with his thoughts about PNG. Here was a country that was probably the most primitive in the world. There were several tribes in the interior that had yet to be contacted by the administration. Headhunting among these folks was still considered a reasonable way of dealing with one's enemies. Consumption of human flesh not only provided a meal, but conferred useful powers in future conflicts. For all these occasional appalling practices, on a day-to-day basis PNG's tribal society was on the whole a structured, peaceful place to be. It lived in harmony with its environment and had survived unchanged for thousands of years. Bruce had started to realise that 'civilisation' was inexorably on its way and would bring uncertainty and complexity with somewhat doubtful benefits. Bruce had a lot of prejudices to overcome, with his dad's xenophobia somehow confirmed by his government's 'White Australia' policy. Nevertheless, university had opened his mind to flashes of liberal thought. Take Charlie for example; he undoubtedly had intelligence, seemed to have a surprising command of English and frequently came up with thoughtful suggestions on how to deal with difficult matters. Sometimes his assistant had better ideas, often ahead of his own conclusions. Bruce occasionally even felt a pang of discomfort at being lord and master of a barefoot native who had only a rudimentary education but with a problem-solving capability superior to his own.

Charlie's thoughts were partly running on a parallel track. He appreciated from his reading that while the whites undoubtedly had by some means achieved great advances in terms of discovery and power over others, they certainly did not have a monopoly over intelligence or insight. He had great respect for the wisdom of Mr Smithson and at the same time was quite aware that his mind worked faster than that of Bruce Petersen. In particular, Charlie instinctively knew better how to manage human relationships given his obviously greater understanding of local culture. Charlie liked and respected Bruce but sometimes despaired of his apparent obtuseness. On a wider front, Charlie wondered what the future held for his country and in particular his own role within it. Mr Smithson's library had given him a glimpse of a bigger, more exciting world. For the moment he could see no possibility of a change from being the gopher of Tori's kiap. White men had this wonderful opportunity to go anywhere, anytime and occupy a privileged status, or so it seemed. He sometimes thought about those who did the menial tasks in Australia – 'land of the dead' as it was known in some of PNG's many languages. Even though he had seen pictures of white labourers in an encyclopaedia in an interesting item about mining, it was still hard to imagine white men digging holes, building roads and herding cattle. Nonetheless, it brought home to him the fact that white men were just another large tribe echoing any PNG tribe; there were leaders and followers. It was just a fact that white men in PNG automatically were leaders, demanding the obedience a superior expected. And that deference had to come from any PNG native, even a wise and respected headman of a large tribe. Charlie thought this was not always true. Mr Smithson, unlike most white men did not expect to be revered. Indeed, he treated all with consideration respect and kindness, paradoxically receiving total respect himself. All would call him 'Masta' because of his colour but without resentment, recognising his true stature. Smithson had been a significant role model in Charlie's life.

Charlie's reveries were interrupted by Bruce who had taken the lead, halting and studying something to one side of the track ahead. The other three caught up with him, instantly recognising what they saw.

'Masta it is a dead bird of paradise; we think it was shot by a Hulwari. Their hunters are very skilled with a bow and arrow.'

Charlie turned the bird over with a stick.

'It is a male, stripped of its feathers to make a Hulwari headdress. It has not been dead long. It will disappear quickly after it's eaten by ants, rats or snakes. We must now be in Hulwari territory,' he explained.

Officially, hunting the protected bird of paradise in its forty odd species had been banned in the country for the last ten years although here in the depths of nowhere no real effort was made to enforce the law. Any effort to stop its killing would have been met with total disbelief and resentment, hindering the authorities' efforts to pacify the more warlike tribes. The law was more directed to stop plundering by voracious white traders who kill birds to supply the European fashion industry. Bruce knew all of this and would ignore this technical breach of the law. Even if the culprit could be identified, to have tried to make an arrest was too nonsensical to contemplate. Native people for thousands of years had used this superb gift of nature for ornamentation. Once again, he reflected on the fact that man and animal here had been in an environmentally balanced state since long before the era of Jesus Christ. Only when the European appeared on the scene, here or anywhere else in the world, did things change - frequently for the worse. But for Captain Cook he would not now have been standing in a rainforest, part of a concerted effort to impose an alien set of values on an otherwise well-ordered system. To what end, he wondered. The three natives stood waiting for Bruce to finish his pondering.

'OK, let's forget the bird and move on.'

He could not sustain this line of thought for long, uppermost in his mind being the immediate task of reaching the main Hulwari village before nightfall. The party continued on its journey climbing steadily through stands of massive agarwood and other native pines. Halfway through the day they paused for rest and food. They shared the same meal, a mush of rice, chicken and vegetables prepared by the patrol office cook. Ona contemplated sneaking a fragment of betel nut into his mouth but resisted the temptation as he knew it would not escape Charlie's eagle eye and disapproval. He did not care too much about Charlie's opinions but guessed that Bruce's attention would be drawn to it. Diro was happy just to stop, eat and doze.

Back on the track, they continued to climb steadily until coming into a forest clearing where one could look up and see a vast expanse of blue sky. The track started to become more clearly defined and was obviously well-used. Charlie had visited the Hulwari before with Mr Smithson and was aware that they were only half an hour from the main village. Instinctively he sensed that the Hulwari would already be well aware of their presence, the party having been detected some miles away. He wondered if they would receive a peaceful reception or whether the Hulwari be sharpening their stone axes? He kept thinking about an ambush reported last year of a party led by a patrol officer at the other end of the Owen Stanley Range. He shuddered, wondering if the fate of the wigman's pig had reached the ears of this notoriously bloodthirsty tribe.

'Masta, I think it would be good if the constables are ready with their rifles in case the Hulwari are waiting for us with their axes and arrows. I will take Diro's load so he can be more ready with his rifle.'

Bruce assented, drawing out his pistol. Charlie took the load off Diro's back.

It was normal for the Hulwari to have several hunters in the area at any time during daylight hours. Such a hunter was Mafongo, tracking wild boar. Like any PNG tribesman he possessed acute senses of hearing, sight and smell. Evolution had ensured that a man's survival depended on awareness of the slightest disturbance in the forest environment. A herd of elephants would have been no more obvious than Bruce's party. The disturbance would require investigation. Mafongo's senses were on full alert. The uncertainty of the nature of the advancing party complicated his decision-making on how to deal with this intrusion into his tribe's territory. Most disturbances could be resolved into potential food or danger. The background of normal daylight forest sounds passed through his aural system without impact, much as traffic noise might do for a city dweller. This was different. The sounds he detected did not spell animal life but men, not stealthy men from an enemy, but men who did not care about detection of their presence. Without revealing himself he approached sufficiently to survey the source of the noise. He saw a white man and three black men that he guessed to be Tori. One of the latter was a tall young man, barefoot in khaki shorts and shirt. The other two were policemen, one fat and the

other thin. He had seen white men before and knew that
nothing positive ever came of their visits. He decided to
warn the village of their approach.

CHAPTER 3

Evening shadows were lengthening as Mafongo arrived back at the Hulwari settlement ten minutes ahead of Bruce's slow-moving party. He went straight to the hut of headman, Mbeki, who also happened to be his uncle.

'Uncle, four are coming. They have sticks that kill. One is a white man. Shall we kill them before they reach the village?'

Mbeki calmly received the news from his nephew. Pensively he continued to sharpen his new steel parang against a stone. He considered the situation. In common with other human beings his thought processes were fashioned by the sum of his experiences from birth. At a basic level his instincts were not dissimilar to a man born into modern western society. Mbeki had to survive whereas his western counterpart was not so much concerned by death or hunger but perhaps preserving his job by satisfying a difficult boss. A business owner might be worried about predatory competitors. Mbeki did not fear death at this moment but knew the power of white men and resented it. Death could come quickly and without warning in a primitive tribal society. He needed to maintain his standing in the eyes of his people. This had grown significantly since the new weapons had arrived at his disposal. These had proved their worth in recent confrontations with other tribes, enhancing the fearsome reputation of the Hulwari. The opposition had been armed with traditional stone axes, blowpipes and wooden shields, but were no match for Mbeki's warriors with their terrifying shiny metal weapons.

Mbeki sensed that his recent activities would have reached the ears of the white men and he knew that, despite the optimism of his warriors, he had no defence against the white man's rifles.

'Tell all men to hide their new weapons. The white man shall not know of them,' he ordered Mafongo. 'Go quickly.'

Mafongo ran from hut to hut spreading Mbeki's order. It was a close-run thing. All metal weapons disappeared from view under piles of leaves or into the undergrowth as Bruce, followed by Charlie and the policemen, strode into the centre of the village clearing. The village was a collection of huts, each built from broad leaves covering a rough frame of wooden poles and creeper twine. The huts were clustered around a central clearing with the headman's hut larger than the others, standing slightly apart.

Bruce stopped in the middle of the village where a crowd of tribesmen gathered with women and children grouped at a distance. A battle of egos now came into play. Mbeki deliberately stayed in his hut to keep the white man waiting. This would impress the village, showing that he was not awed by Bruce's presence. Bruce on the other hand had to look indifferent to Mbeki. Charlie perfectly understood the psychology of the moment and made a suggestion to Bruce.

'Masta, order the policemen to bring you the camp stool and set it down facing away from Mbeki's hut. Sit down and read some papers. I will order him to come and you can ignore him. You will be sitting and he will have to stand before you – it will look good for you.'

Bruce took the point and sat down in a leisurely fashion. Charlie with measured arrogance called to Mbeki that the white master was now ready for him and he should present himself without delay. To make the point he ordered Ona and Diro to unshoulder their rifles and cock them as noisily as possible. This show of strength and indifference had the desired effect and Mbeki emerged from his hut with the whole tribe watching. Attempting to preserve as much dignity as possible Mbeki ambled forward and stood before Bruce. The queen's representative ignored Mbeki as directed and took the opportunity to crack open a precious can of Fosters. Using his best pidgin, Bruce spoke slowly.

'So Mbeki, I come to you for good reason. The all-powerful white queen and her lords wish to hear more of these stories of the wars and killings by the Hulwari tribe.

Do not lie to me Mbeki, for I have ears everywhere and also need to know more of these weapons that you are using.'

A murmuring arose from the watching crowd. Why did their leader allow himself to be insulted? The tribe still rankled from the recent episode in which a Tori had abducted and killed one of Mbeki's prize pigs. Retribution was in the air. There were only four of these intruders and they could be killed at a single gesture from their headman. Mbeki hesitated, contemplating this line of action for a brief moment. He savoured the thought of eating white flesh and the power it would bring him. Yet he was not headman for nothing having sufficient insight to know that such action would bring more troubles. A more prudent strategy would pay off long term.

'Masta, I know nothing of these matters. It is true that from time to time we have been attacked by others and forced to defend ourselves and there have been some unfortunate deaths. We wish only for peace with other tribes. As for the weapons, we Hulwari are the most skilled at making axes from rocks for felling trees and other purposes. We are unlike the weak, thieving and stupid Tori who cannot make anything useful.'

He shot a meaningful look at Charlie who ignored the insult. Mbeki spoke in Hulwari and Charlie although with a limited ability in Hulwari, was able to translate for Bruce.

'We are getting nowhere Charlie,' said Bruce. 'Tell him we are going to search the village and woe betide him if we find he is lying.'

Ona and Diro were then instructed to make a thorough search of each hut. The Hulwari had done a good job at concealing the metal weapons. The policemen found nothing to arouse suspicion, only the traditional stone implements, axes and blowpipes. Bruce was stumped. It was late in the day, soon dark and he was tired from the journey and dispirited at the prospect of facing the DC without insight into the recent reports. He also realised that Mbeki was undoubtedly lying and so far, ahead on points. Bruce would need to find some way of asserting his authority, not to mention finding the weapons and their source. Turning to Charlie he said, 'Tell the lying bastard that we will be back tomorrow.'

Charlie did as bid to a grinning Mbeki, adding that the white master was tired of dealing with a foolish old headman and would require Mbeki's presence early the following day when he would find answers to his questions. They left to pitch camp in a clearing within sight of the main village. As the throng of silent warriors parted to allow them to leave Charlie hesitated. He noticed that one of the taller Hulwari had, together with the usual collection of shells and bones, something unusual suspended about his neck. Before Charlie could collect his thoughts, the Hulwaris dispersed.

He left to follow the others to the campsite where Ona and Diro had started to labour over the erection of tents and other preparations for the night's stay. Charlie had an instinct that what he had seen around the Hulwari warrior's neck was a clue to solving Bruce's investigation.

CHAPTER 4

Ona and Diro had the tents erected just in time before the usual early evening monsoon rain drove the party inside. The Hulwari had disappeared into their huts. As the rain beat against the canvas, Bruce nursed his second Fosters of the day. He wondered what on earth he was doing in this godforsaken place and why he wasn't back home with his girl on a beach. He wouldn't be renewing his contract when he got back to his patrol office. He still had no idea what to tell the DC. He slept uneasily that night under his mosquito net while Charlie, Ona and Diro kept watch in turns and maintained their camp fire.

The next day Hulwari cockerels ensured that nobody would sleep late. Breakfast over, a crumpled and frustrated Bruce stood yawning in the morning's cool air.

'OK Charlie let's get them out of their huts. You,

Laurel and Hardy widen the search for these alleged magic weapons.'

Among the grumbling Hulwaris Charlie saw the tall man with the item he had noticed the previous day. Suspended about the man's neck was a chain with shiny metal squares stamped with English characters. He stopped by the befeathered and painted warrior. Charlie suspected that here was an answer to their enquiries. He also knew enough of human nature that to enlist the man's cooperation he would need to flatter him. He overcame an inborn reluctance to be civil to any Hulwari.

'Mighty warrior, I see you,' he started in Hulwari with a traditional greeting.

'Tori, I see you,' was the haughty reply.

Swallowing his pride with difficulty, Charlie continued in Tok Pisin,

'All Tori know of the great hunting and fighting skills of the Hulwari. I see before me the appearance of a great man of the tribe. We Tori could perhaps learn more from the tribe's wonderful stories.'

The other man softened and started bragging.

'We Hulwari are famous because we are the cleverest, strongest and bravest tribe in the mountains and forests. I have many strong sons who will be famous hunters, like me,' he added immodestly.

Pointing to the metal chain about the man's neck Charlie asked, 'Can I see and hold the magic for an instant so I can tell my village of these wonders?'

The warrior was won over to the point of letting Charlie inspect the necklace. It comprised a metal chain suspending two identical oval aluminium tags on which were inscribed three lines:

Orlowski
Joseph P. 32388720873AF
O+ RC

CHAPTER 5

Some seventeen years earlier the Pacific war was in progress. Lieutenant Jim Fletcher, aged twenty-three, was a seasoned and experienced pilot and navigator in the 13th Air Force of the USAAF. The 13th had played an important role in the Pacific war against the Japanese. Two years earlier Jim had taken part in his first mission in the company of seventy-two other B-25 Mitchell bombers. He was part of a raid on Rabaul harbour on the island of New Britain, north of the mainland. This operation marked a turning point in the war in the region. The Japanese had since been pushed out of Papua New Guinea and Jim Fletcher's B-25 was now reduced to the role of staff transport around the region. Others had the more exciting work of harassing the Japs further north. Jim was bored.

Jim and his crew had been positioned to Henderson Field on the Solomon Islands following the US victory at Guadalcanal. He loved flying but fuel shortages meant sometimes a week or more would elapse before he would climb into his B-25. During these times not only boredom but also homesickness would affect him. He missed his girl, his family and life back home. In more optimistic moods, like most young men on both sides of a war, he was convinced of final victory and his own immortality.

The visions he harboured before his posting to the Pacific were of white beaches, waving palms and friendly natives. The reality of tropical life soon showed itself to Jim after arrival in the Solomon Islands. It was true the beaches were white and fringed with palms but for most of the days they were unbearably hot and bare skin was attacked by legions of sand fleas. A sand flea cannot do much more than hop, so he or she tends to attack feet and ankles causing severe itching, inflammation and general unpleasantness. A bite can even cause infection and worse. Come night-time, mosquitoes take over from sand fleas, also with an appetite for American skin and similar consequences for the victim. At night, Jim's mosquito net offered a sanctuary from immediate attack. When trying to sleep the temptation to scratch the various insect bites delayed slumber for hours. The unit's medical officer prescribed various potions to combat these problems but they had limited effect. Generations of sand fleas and mosquitoes had never had it so good with the arrival of all this soft white flesh.

In contrast to its abundant insect life the expected friendly natives were noticeably absent. The Solomon islanders were not unfriendly but they were rarely seen at

Henderson Field. Jim and his colleagues spent long days waiting for orders. Reading, fishing, poker and sleeping were the main occupations during these times. With flying restricted by fuel shortages, the arrival of a tanker was anxiously awaited. The tide of the war had started to turn with the end of the battle for Guadalcanal but much had to be done to clear the Japanese from the Pacific. Jim and his fellow crew members chafed at the inactivity.

Jim received a summons to the airfield's headquarters. He left the building exhilarated, walking quickly to find his crew. He found his co-pilot, Jack Turner, dozing under a palm tree on the beach, an open book at his side. Jim prodded him.

'Hey Jack, good news. We got fuel and we got orders! It's Port Moresby tomorrow on the New Guinea mainland to pick up some parts to bring back here. We're taking an army passenger and getting that number two radio fixed today. We'll be overnight at Moresby. I hear they've got a great mess there with WACs and nurses on base! Get your ass into gear Jack, go and find Joe and meet me at the plane.'

Jack got up, brushing sand off himself. 'That's great Jim. We'll be at a nice cool 8,000 feet with no mosquitoes!'

Jim's B-25 lifted from Henderson's runway the following afternoon. With no headwind it was three-and-half hours flying to Port Moresby, a more or less straight track mostly over the Solomon Sea. The bomber's crew consisted of Jim from South Dakota, Jack from Idaho and navigator Joseph, a Pole from New York. There was no longer any threat from enemy aircraft so the gunner's position amidships was occupied by their passenger, a serious-looking Major Harris.

Jim's mind drifted back to his home state. A pilot's eye view of South Dakota yielded unending flat geometric farmland dissected with straight lines of roads or farm boundaries. The contrast with flights in the Pacific, with its blue sea and tropical islands, could not have been more dramatic. Jim's hometown of Brookings seemed to be on another planet. Until coming out to the Far East, Brookings had been the centre of Jim's universe. Nothing much else mattered except the economy of the manufacturing companies in which Jim's father had spent his life and where Jim would have probably worked had Pearl Harbour not intervened. His mind was now set on working for Pan Am after the Japanese finally surrendered.

A straight-line flight in clear weather did not make any great demands of Joseph's navigational skill, so he computed a track to steer after taking wind drift into account. He then dozed as the Wright radial engines droned a steady beat. Jim and Jack, having imbibed a little unwisely in the Henderson officer's mess late the night before, were not on top form and like Joseph, drifted in and out of consciousness. Jim's experience did not mean that he could not make mistakes. Inattention could be as much of a killer as an enemy fighter. Nonetheless he too, with the autopilot engaged, could doze a little. He woke suddenly and looking at his watch realised they should be just over ten minutes from their destination. He should be seeing coastline but instead saw only mountainous terrain.

He looked out and realised that the late afternoon

sun was setting to the left ahead of where the plane was heading. He was heading on a more north-westerly track – not westerly! He was suddenly alert and his mind racing. They were over three hours into the flight and he had been on this heading all the time. What the hell had happened? Was the compass faulty? Not very likely. Had that dumbass navigator given him a wrong heading to steer? Were the forecast winds aloft completely wrong? Why the hell hadn't he checked it all himself? Worst of all, the radio homing beacon at Moresby was out of service and he was dependent entirely on the accuracy of his own navigation. Hell, even the Indians or Eskimos could navigate a simple track from A to B simply by using the sun.

Orlowski had given him a correct heading. Unknown to Jim, a spanner had inadvertently been left under the instrument coaming after the radio change that morning. This was directly beneath the compass distorting its reading. Jim looked at his fuel gauges. Due to fuel shortages he had loaded only a marginal extra amount over that needed for the trip. He had less than twenty minutes fuel left!

'Wake up for Christ's sake, wake up!' Jim yelled into the intercom.

CHAPTER 6

Charlie was excited for he knew he had the key to their search. He relayed his find to Bruce who immediately guessed that the Hulwari warrior was wearing a military dog tag, presumably from a deceased World War Two serviceman. He was right. The wearing of tags is required by most nations of its soldiers. US personnel were issued with two identical tags, one worn on a long chain around the neck, the second on a much smaller chain attached to the first chain. In the event the wearer was killed, the second tag was collected and the first remained with the body.

At that time Bruce did not know that the tags belonged to Lt. Joseph P. Orlowski USAF, late of Plainfield, Connecticut, a B-25 navigator. Joseph was aged twenty-two when he died seventeen years previously. His remains lay in thick rainforest with his fellow crew members about five miles east of where Bruce stood. He now guessed the connection with the mysterious Hulwari weapons. It was now a question of extracting the detail from the devious Mbeki.

He of course knew of the presence of large quantities of military objects abandoned after the end of World War Two. There had been no significant military activity in the Tori or Hulwari areas but here was a connection with World War Two which he would now solve. Bruce guessed, correctly as it turned out, that the Hulwari had stumbled on some old World War Two hardware in the jungle and had somehow found a way of converting it to a military purpose, PNG style. He asked Charlie if he had any opinions about the best way forward with Mbeki.

'Masta, pretend you know what Mbeki found in the forest.'

Bruce concurred with Charlie's proposal together with a stick and carrot approach. The strategy would be to allow Mbeki to extricate himself gracefully. Mbeki was summoned to Bruce's presence out of earshot of his warriors.

Charlie's address to Mbeki was along the following lines:

'The mighty government officer has seen and knows you have found some of the government's property in your territory and knows you are using it for purposes which are against the law. He also knows you have found the bones of dead white soldiers. These bones and the property may be old, but there are terrible punishments for not reporting them and giving up the property. On the other hand, there are rewards for those who report what they have found. These rewards could even be to allow retention of some items for peaceful purposes.'

It took about quarter of an hour to get this across to Mbeki who responded with an occasional grunt. Charlie's translation included lengthy references to the powers of the queen's government and its huge armies, weapons of destruction, harsh prisons, etc.

Mbeki considered this at some length. He was impressed at how just overnight Bruce had worked out the source of his treasured metals. He had to decide how to deal with the situation and rescue himself whilst retaining credibility with his tribe, yet still satisfying this nuisance of a white man. He was cautious in his response.

It was true, he admitted, that there were some useless items of metal in the rainforest a day's walk from the village. The Hulwari language did not have a word for metal so this roughly translated into 'hard, thin silvery stone that reflected the sun like water'. The white master would not be interested in these useless items. His clever tribe had used a few of these items for decoration and purely peaceful purposes, he assured Bruce.

Privately, Mbeki had no intention of giving up the weapons his tribe had fashioned from Jim Fletcher's B-25. His most prized possessions were two axes recovered intact. These were part of an aircraft's standard equipment to help the crew to free themselves from a wrecked plane. Perhaps he could give up some of the early, less satisfactory results of the Hulwari attempts to use of the metal skin of the bomber. The soft aluminium was of little use except to make a cooking pot and several had been made by one of the tribe's more accomplished craftsmen. When they discovered slivers of the harder thicker duralumin plates, used as armour around the cockpit, they were able to fashion long sharpened spears and knives. The stone axes of their enemies were no match for these fantastic weapons. Development of these implements had taken literally years of laborious grinding and shaping and Mbeki would not easily give them up. As for the bones, he saw no use for these apart from decorative items of which they already had a plentiful supply. He would take Bruce to the crash site.

CHAPTER 7

That same day, with a group of Hulwari, Bruce and his party tramped through the forest until they came upon the remains of a B-25 bomber. Tragically for Jim Fletcher and his crew, fuel scarcity meant that only a minimal reserve had been loaded for them to reach Moresby. When the plane's engines stopped, it was over a mountainous area and too low for the crew to bail out. Even if they could, a drop into the jungle was probably not survivable.

There had been nothing resembling a patch of clear, flat ground for Jack to land the stricken bomber. At over one hundred miles per hour the aircraft, with its silent engines, cut a swathe into the trees on the hillside east of Mbeki's village. At this speed, thick solid hardwood trunks methodically dismembered the plane. The impact of the negative g-force and destruction of the fuselage instantly killed all four men.

The intervening years in the forest had virtually swallowed up the B-25 and its occupants. The only evidence of the aircraft's existence were occasional large shapes covered in creepers. These shapes would resolve themselves into an engine or section of fuselage. One particular shape turned out to be the aircraft's tailplane assembly which was largely intact. This comprised two large, vertical fins joined by the horizontal stabilizer. Bruce noted down the numbers 43-24576 and made a sketch of the striking crest painted on the fins. He knew from his interest in military aircraft as a boy that this aircraft was a US machine. Only the Americans had this predilection for adorning their military aircraft with elaborate crests comprising bolts of lightning, arrows, Indian heads or other symbols of aggression. Frequently the nose of an airplane would, in contrast, portray a naked woman or maybe comic characters. He had wondered before at this flamboyant side to the American character. He compared it to the more prosaic attitude of their European allies who did not seem to see a bomber as anything else but a war machine, never as a canvas projecting some kind of aggressive phallic symbolism.

He realised there would be many days' work to try and find any human remains, let alone any evidence of Mbeki's pillaging of the wreck for objects having the potential for making weapons. He photographed what he could amid the remains. They returned to their overnight camp at the Hulwari village and prepared to leave early the following day. Bruce summoned Mbeki and Charlie translated.

'Other white men will return in the future and any

person who removes or even touches the war machine will be severely punished, perhaps with death.'

This was language that Mbeki understood, but he was not particularly concerned, he already had his axes and spears.

Before they left, on Bruce's instruction, Charlie was able to relieve warrior Gubag of one of Joseph Orlowski's dog tags in exchange for a small hand mirror and a box of matches.

The return to Tori was a silent affair. Witnessing the remains of the crashed aircraft gave each man much food for thought. Bruce found himself in a sombre mood. He reflected on his fortune at being too young at the time of World War Two to suffer the horrors endured by those Australian troops who fought and died in the jungles of south-east Asia or those captured by the Japanese. He was sober at the thought that there were the remains of young men lying in the Hulwari forest, their whereabouts unknown to their families. Another thought was how invaluable Charlie had been. Not only had he been a key to the success of the trip, but also an intelligent companion. Over the campfire Charlie had been able to provide a perspective on Papuan village society, its attitudes, customs and rituals.

Charlie was also in a thoughtful frame of mind. From Mr Smithson's library, although he knew of World War Two, he suddenly was struck by its enormity and the scale of wasted resources, human and material. He asked himself what good had come of it. He could not imagine the reasons for embarking on destruction on such a vast scale. It had to say something about the wisdom of these apparently all-wise white men and their society. The reality had to be that they were similar to the warring Papuan tribes. The contrast was in the scale of their conflicts. The two policemen were less affected by the experience but relished the thought of impressing their fellow Tori with tales of the escapade and their heroic leading roles. Without Ona and Diro, Bruce would have undoubtedly been lost or killed. Charlie had played no significant role in the adventure.

Bruce's written report on the discovery of the B-25 crash site inexorably wound its way through bureaucratic channels. First to his DC, thence to the Governor's office in Moresby, the Home Office in Canberra, the US Embassy in Canberra, the State Department in Washington, finally to the Pentagon where it landed in the Department of Defense POW/Missing Personnel Office (DPMO).

CHAPTER 8

In the early 1950s more than 80,000 Americans still remained unaccounted for from World War Two. Following the war, the US government mostly had access to former battle areas. This significantly assisted the recovery of the war dead although some, particularly those lost at sea, would never be found. The Department of Defense created two military identification laboratories, one each in Japan and Germany. Those laboratories worked only on World War Two cases where recoveries had been made in all parts of the globe from 1945 to 1951. Bruce's discovery of the B-25 was a new site that required investigation. The US military have a strong tradition of returning the bodies of fallen soldiers to their homeland and to this end, a team of three USAF airmen was detailed to do just that.

Three months after Bruce and his party found Jim Fletcher's B-25, Captain Thomas Paul, Sergeants Tony

Oakes and Jack Brjeski arrived in Port Moresby. With them they had detailed records of the crew of B-25J No. 43-24576, its passengers and the aircraft itself. They also had bags to collect remains plus other paraphernalia usual for such tasks. Tom Paul was a pilot who had served in Korea and had experience of visiting crash sites, but for the others it was a new venture. A day later they landed at the Tori airstrip in a chartered Piaggio to be met by Bruce and Charlie.

Charlie had only ever had contact with Australians and was interested to see what differences existed between white men from what were essentially different tribes. He immediately liked them. All three came from northern states with a more liberal outlook on skin colour than their southern countrymen. They were friendly, full of bonhomie and clearly made no social distinction between Bruce and himself. Tom was a tall, well-built man in his mid-twenties, full of confidence and quiet authority. His companions were older, in their thirties, each with technical training in their field. Tony from Brooklyn was a communications specialist and Jack from Spokane an airframe and engine mechanic. All wore their drab USAF work fatigues.

There seemed no question of Charlie calling them Masta, they insisted on first name terms. The plan was to set up camp at the crash site and collect any human remains, try to find reasons for the crash and fully record their findings. Bruce detailed Charlie to accompany them for the duration of their stay, to help them with translation and negotiations with the Hulwari, organise logistics and be a general helpmate. The Americans looked with some amusement at Bruce's Jeep – they had not expected to travel in a museum piece on a serious mission. Nonetheless, they accepted everything with good humour and eventually set off. Porters had been sent ahead with Constables Ona and Diro to set up camp at the crash site.

The search of the B-25 wreckage involved methodically searching a wide area. The main object was to find any human remains for return to the US. The team set out to locate the parts of the aircraft where the crew would have been at the point of the crash. The front part of the fuselage had been completely dismembered and it was probable that the bodies would be in several pieces. With the team were five Hulwari who were familiar with the site. These included the warrior Gubag who had found Joseph Orlowski's dog tag. Gubag led them to a marshy area from which projected a creeper-covered unnatural shape. Several days of digging revealed a crumpled and compressed cockpit section.

In a tropical environment decay of a body occurs very rapidly. Apart from attack from carnivorous creatures, a whole range of bacteria, flies and other organisms reduce a body to just bones in a matter of months. Tiny moths and bacteria feed on hair. Mites in turn feed on these micro-organisms. A dead body is therefore an ecosystem of its own in which various fauna arrive and depart from the corpse at different times. The arrival time and growth rates of insects inhabiting corpses are often used by forensic scientists to determine times and circumstances surrounding death. Bone decay takes place over a much longer period depending on the environment.

The only Catholic in the party, Jack Brjeski, crossed himself when two barely recognisable skeletons were found on the debris and plant growth in the shattered cockpit. The Americans stopped in reverent contemplation at the discovery of their fellow airmen. The phlegmatic Tori and Hulwari members of the party continued to chatter until silenced by Charlie. Discovery of a body or old bones was almost commonplace. The intervening years of decay and predations of nature meant that in a few more years there would be nothing left at all. The US team were looking particularly for teeth from which positive identification could be made. In the case of the two B-25 pilots, they found dog tags. They separated and bagged the human remains as carefully as possible. Thereafter they continued the search of the area and eventually found some further fragments which evidently belonged to Joseph, the aircraft's navigator, and the B-25's army major passenger. No other dog tags were found which made Charlie suspect that the major's was adorning one of Gubag's fellow tribesmen. A comprehensive set of photographs was taken for DPMO records. The team made an examination of the aircraft's scattered remnants to try and establish what caused the B-25 to crash so far from its expected track. Tom noted the exact coordinates of the site before leaving.

The whole mission took some three weeks to complete during which time Charlie formed a close rapport with the three Americans, particularly with Tom Paul. Tom quickly came to appreciate Charlie's intelligence and longing to gain first-hand knowledge of a world beyond PNG. He asked searching questions touching on politics, religion and world affairs. Charlie had a remarkable thirst for learning.

For his part, Tom was curious and eager to learn more of this amazing country and little-known tribal cultures. From Connecticut, Tom had a liberal education. Over campfires he tried to paint a picture of life in the USA, not just the everyday physical world but also the attitudes and values of American society. Tom was proud of the many positive aspects of his country. As a liberal northerner he did not hide the bigotry and resistance to black/white integration in the southern states. The books in Mr Smithson's library did not deal with the American civil rights movement and Charlie had many questions. He was amazed to learn that here was an educated Christian country in which black people were considered inferior to white. His mission schools had taught him that God loved everybody and that in His eyes, all men were equal. Charlie had always wondered about this but had grown to somehow accept that God must have some special set of rules for PNG. As a child, white men seemed cleverer than black men. This was the natural order of things. However, as he matured into adulthood, Charlie had come to realise that this was not necessarily so and that being black meant that he had drawn a short straw in life. In no way did he feel inferior, indeed he was proud of his tribe and had emerging positive feelings about his PNG heritage. On the one hand, the visit of the Americans had stimulated an even stronger desire to see the world outside PNG, on the other, America seemed less attractive. Tom's picture of a country with a white majority and underprivileged black minority shocked Charlie. At least in PNG Charlie knew that the vast majority of the population lived in self-governing villages, owning their own land with little interference from the Australian colonial government.

Two days after their arrival back at the Tori patrol office a Patair aircraft had been chartered to take the Americans back to Moresby, en route to Washington. Charlie was sad to see them go, having made firm friends with Tom and his companions. Even after such a short visit Tom had formed an attachment to Charlie with almost an older brother concern for his future.

Charlie and the Americans stood on the Tori airstrip awaiting the flight. Tom said,

'You know Charlie, America is so unlike life here. I'd love for you to come and see it for yourself. Though I'm not sure if you'd like it. Here it is so peaceful and life is unhurried.'

Charlie did not reply. To him, Tom as a white man was returning to an exciting world full of what seemed limitless opportunity and freedom. As a black man he was not sure what the world offered. He had become unsettled, thinking he was destined to a lifetime as the gopher to Bruce Petersen or some other itinerant Australian civil servant. As they all shook hands before leaving, he felt sure he would never see his new friends again.

Chapter 9

Copies of Tom's report on his assignment were sent to the US Embassy in Canberra and various other State Department offices in Washington. The Royal Australian Air Force which helped facilitate the logistics of the recovery operation also received a copy, as did the district commissioner who would forward a copy to Bruce. So far as the PNG administration was concerned that was the end of the affair. No inquest would be carried out as war dead are not required by law to be investigated. The Pentagon would contact the next of kin and ascertain burial requests. The late occupants of the B-25 would receive burials with military honours wherever requested. In the absence of any directions from family the remains would be interred at Arlington Cemetery. Since 1864 this has been the last resting place of some quarter of a million US service personnel.

As a pilot himself, Tom Paul felt an emotional attachment with the B-25 crew. Although he had been on other crash recovery missions, this one seemed unique. The length of time the men had lain undiscovered without closure for their grieving families was one factor. Another was his personal role in their recovery and the mere fact that he himself had brought their remains to their homeland. The trip had also been special because he had come into contact with a primitive population whose lifestyle could not have contrasted more with that of those living in the US. For all this, his observations of the people of PNG found them to be apparently content with their lot. This was an acute contrast to some sections of US society who resorted to drugs, alcohol or crime to overcome unfulfilled needs in their lives, resulting in a complex criminal code and employment of numerous law-enforcement agencies. He laughed to himself when he thought of Ona and Diro, but most of all his mind turned back to Charlie making the contrast even starker. Charlie was less than ten years younger than himself, yet destined to live a totally different life. Although intelligent, ambitious and personable his future seemed destined to be little more than a lowly servant in a colonial administration.

Tom resolved to attend the burial of Jim Fletcher and his application to be the official USAF representative at the funeral was approved. Jim's parents were alive and living in Brookings, South Dakota. They had informed the Pentagon that they wished their son to be buried in his hometown. A month after his arrival back in the US, on the day before the funeral, Tom flew into Brookings via

Minneapolis from Washington where he was attached to the aforesaid DPMO office. He had previously phoned Jim's father who met Tom's commuter flight. Jack Fletcher was a thickset, balding seventy-year-old whose lined face spoke of a lifetime of hard work at the car part manufacturing plant. He felt a pang of loss at seeing Tom, handsome in his uniform and not unlike his son whom he had last seen alive nearly twenty years ago.

'Good of you to come captain,' Jack greeted Tom.

'It was my duty sir, and please call me Tom.'

'And call me Jack,' said the father.

Jack's wife, Wilma, was filled with emotion when she saw Tom at the door of their home. There was an aura about him and she somehow imagined he was a friend of their son's who had recently seen him. The Fletchers insisted Tom stay with them that evening. They wanted every detail of his mission to PNG and he was able to show them photographs of the crash site, omitting the pictures of their son's remains. Wilma was racked with grief and sobbed at the sight of the pictures. Jack was too choked with emotion to speak. Tom himself was moist-eyed.

Jack said, 'Tom, I had a call from the editor of our local newspaper, the Brookings Register. They want to run a story about our Jim and the recovery operation. As he put it, the town will want to read about one of its heroes of World War Two. They want you to get in touch.'

'I'll be glad to Jack. I'll call them first thing tomorrow.'

He did as requested, also called the local office of the National Guard who were to provide the honor guard. He needed to liaise on the detail of the ceremony.

Local dignitaries turned out in force for Jim Fletcher's funeral at Brookings Greenwood Cemetery. As well as family and friends, the mayor attended with other civic leaders and even the state governor who happened to be in town that week to open a new wing to the State University, Brookings main claim to fame. The attendance of the governor ensured TV coverage to show on the evening news. After a moving eulogy by Jim's older brother and the customary firing of a salute over the grave, there were few dry eyes. The funeral party finally withdrew to the Brookings Inn for a wake hosted by the town. The story spread beyond Brookings and as well as the local press, it appeared in the papers of Sioux Falls, South Dakota's largest city. Always one for a photo opportunity with a uniform alongside, the governor arranged for a picture featuring himself with Tom and Mr and Mrs Fletcher.

The picture in the local newspaper's next edition appeared with a whole page story of Jim Fletcher, the family, the B-25, PNG and the crash recovery. Tom had also managed to get across the story of Charlie and his key role in finding the crash site. It was all very exotic to the South Dakotan readers and others further afield. One of these phoned Tom Paul in Washington a few days later.

'Captain Paul, this is Joanne Bickford of the Valodis Foundation in Washington DC. I followed up on a brief report I saw in the New York Post and have now read a fuller account in the Sioux Falls newspaper. One of our trustees was very interested to read of your adventures in the Pacific and the recovery of the bodies of World War Two airmen. One of the aims of this foundation is the promotion of American values in the third world by sponsoring foreign students through our educational system. Our trustee, Mr Nevern, was wondering if you thought that the young man mentioned in your report might be an appropriate recipient of an award. We have never sponsored anybody from Papua New Guinea and look constantly to spread our work as widely as possible throughout the world.'

Tom hesitated. The phrase 'American values' disturbed him. He would have loved to help Charlie maximise his potential in life and satisfy some of his thirst for knowledge. But he was not certain if this way would be a positive influence. Would Charlie succumb to the culture of a consumer society or would he rise above it? His feelings were decidedly ambiguous. Since leaving PNG he had strange feelings of envy of the briefly witnessed, simple lifestyle. The respect for the natural environment and strong ethos of community life contrasted abruptly with the isolated lives that many lived in large urban areas of the US. He was thinking enviously of Charlie's life in his village. Had he known, Charlie often thought about Tom, yearning for his apparently exciting and stimulating life.

'Miss Bickford, perhaps it would be best if Mr Nevern and I were to have a discussion here in Washington?' It was agreed that a meeting would take place at the Valodis Foundation offices.

CHAPTER 10

Frederick Nevern was a man of about sixty, distinguished by a distinct Ivy League look to his dress, manners and accent. At least this was Tom's assessment on first meeting. Nevern opened the meeting with a description of the foundation of which he was managing trustee. It seemed that the late Caspar Valodis' life was a rags-to-riches story of a Latvian immigrant. Valodis had made a considerable fortune setting up bottling plants which he eventually sold to one of the country's soft drink manufacturers. He decided to show his appreciation to his host country by funding foreign students through US schools and universities. Valodis' idea was that the values that had enabled him to succeed would spread to other, apparently less fortunate countries. His intention was that recipients of his awards would not remain in the US. They would return home to spread his belief in the system that so freely rewarded vision and hard work.

'You know Mr Nevern,' began Tom, 'I have travelled to many parts of the world and I sometimes wonder if Mr Valodis' belief in the virtues of our culture necessarily applies worldwide. The people of Papua New Guinea live a life almost free of concerns for material possessions. They live in perfect harmony with their environment. It is true there are fights between neighbouring tribes but by and large, crime as we know it, is unknown. Folk put loyalty to tribe and family as their priority in life. They don't lock their doors at night – in fact, they mostly don't have doors to lock. Their moralities may look a little skewed to us but who is to say we've got it right? Maybe a dose of those Christian values which respect human life more seriously would not go amiss, but do they really need supermarkets, cars and Coca Cola?'

Nevern considered this unexpected piece of philosophy from the young air force officer. He sometimes felt himself a little ambivalent about his role in distributing the Valodis millions.

'The fact is Tom, there is nothing we can do about the march of human progress, if that's the right word for it. It is going to catch up with the Papuans sooner or later, whatever you and I decide here today. Change is going to happen and the tribes are going to have to cope with these changes, for better or worse. If we can select the right people and if nothing else, send them back to their country armed with some of the Christian values you mention, we will be doing the right thing. Mind you,

Mr Valodis never thought of his money being spent in spreading religion, but I think he would have approved of what we are saying here. Anyway, tell me all you know about this young man.'

'Well sir, Charlie is a very unusual young man from a very unusual country. I spent a few weeks in his company and came to admire his intelligence and maturity. He is thoughtful and has an enquiring mind. He has benefitted from the patronage of one of the local expatriate officials from whom he has learnt a good deal but he is still a man of his native culture and traditions. Despite this there is a certain charming naivety about him. He makes friends easily and I admit I have missed his company despite our short time together. I would like to help him in his future life if that is possible. Would he benefit from an American education? Possibly. Would it benefit Papuan society in the future? Again, possibly – I think he has some natural leadership qualities and will probably anyway rise to importance in his society. My main worry is whether he would be corrupted by some of the negative aspects of life in our world.'

'Such as?'

'This country's consumer and drug culture.'

'And the positive aspects?'

'This is where I think a liberal education would benefit him. He would gain skills in dealing with the pitfalls that a young country may encounter and, as a future leader, learn to cope with them. He would recognise the benefits of democracy and good government and for that matter, the dangers of bad government.'

The two men continued to discuss the whole idea of influencing Charlie's future and what might be the most appropriate plan. They agreed Charlie would benefit from some form of high school education before entering university. Tom found that he and Nevern had similar ideas on the subject. Nevern favoured a preparatory period at a community college. Such an institution would need a strong record of preparing more mature international students for a university degree course. International clubs at such colleges are fairly common and are great places for new students to meet others who share similar interests and challenges. Such clubs offer their members a variety of social activities as well as special assistance in navigating American college culture.

Nevern did not have to consult anyone else on the sponsorship of Charlie's education. The board of trustees usually rubber-stamped his recommendations. Nonetheless, in the absence of a personal interview, he always tried to have face-to-face contact with somebody with personal knowledge of a potential award recipient.

Experience had shown that written recommendations were not always to be relied on, as was the case in his early days with the foundation. On one occasion, such a proposal from a senior US Embassy official had resulted in an unsuitable young Eritrean becoming a victim of American drug culture. Nevern's judgement after listening to Tom was that Charlie was an ideal candidate upon whom to bestow Caspar Valodis' benevolence.

CHAPTER 11

Nearly four months elapsed and with the memory fading of the Americans' visit to Tori, Charlie's life settled back to its usual routine. In his official report of the discovery of the B-25 crash site and origin of the Hulwari weapons Bruce gave generous praise to Charlie's role in the affair, nothing changed in his assistant's daily life. This however was not without distractions as Charlie was starting to take an interest in Beida, the Tori headman's seventeen-year-old daughter. He had known her during his childhood as a noisy, unruly distant cousin but found her on his return to the tribe to be a comely, beautiful young woman.

Now at the ripe age of nineteen, Charlie was already old not to have a wife – not even one. Polygamy in PNG's interior was relatively commonplace and some of Charlie's contemporaries had more than one wife and several children. Once again, he found himself puzzling over the apparent inconsistencies in the teachings of his mission school education. The latter definitely condemned polygamy as a sinful practice but without any explanation why. Several of Charlie's relatives were in polygamous marriages and none seemed the worse for it. Charlie was unusual in his exposure to western culture in that he did not relate completely with traditional village life. He felt that he needed not only a mate, but a spiritual and intellectual companion. He also wanted to have a role in the life of his children. As in most highland villages, the Tori had separate unmarried men's and women's houses with men's ceremonial houses off-limits to all women and uninitiated males. In Tori society women were the primary caregivers to children and the primary food producers. Men would traditionally spend much time in the large ceremonial house where matters of importance were planned. Men would also often take their meals here, only returning to their huts at night. Food for the day was often placed in a woven basket that was suspended from the ceremonial house rafters. People simply ate when they got hungry. Family life, western style, by and large did not happen. Charlie lived in a house with the other bachelors of the village, as he would have even if his parents had been alive.

Courting rituals varied from tribe to tribe. These rituals usually involved the young couple, dressed in ceremonial attire, meeting at the tribal ceremonial grounds to sit cross legged, side by side, or rub their faces together. Charlie's interest in Beida had not reached the point of this formality but they would meet out of the gaze of others and flirt. This was not the usual pattern in a society where the choice of a marriage partner is rarely left to the individual. After initiation into adult society, young men and women would more often spend time with the opposite sex in supervised courtship sessions. Charlie's attentions to Beida had already been noticed and were drawing disapproving comments, particularly in view of Beida's status as Headman Bao's daughter. Charlie found himself having unusual feelings, which he found difficult to share with his peer group. He strongly identified himself as a Tori and had pride in his people but felt in some sort of cultural no man's land. His difficulty in integrating totally with his tribe and settling down was due to a nagging feeling of wanting to see something of the world he had learnt about from Mr Smithson's library, and more recently from Tom Paul and his companions. These thoughts had started to give way to Beida, now uppermost in his mind, and planning their next tryst. He planned to speak with Uncle Paru to initiate a formal request to Tori's headman to court his daughter.

He and a dreamy-eyed Beida were sitting close together on a fallen tree trunk at the edge of the village while he related facts he had learnt of English kings and queens. Suddenly, Constable Ona appeared and smirked at the sight of the couple.

'Masta Bruce em laik tok tok yupela,' he nodded at Charlie.

Although annoyed at this intrusion, Charlie nonetheless obeyed the command to attend Bruce in his office.

'Charlie, I have a letter from Canberra about you and what's more you have a letter from America.'

He handed both to Charlie, who for the moment forgot Beida. He was overwhelmed with curiosity. Apart from Mr Smithson who had written just once since his retirement back to Sydney, this was only the second time he had received post in his life. He put aside the large envelope with its blue airmail stamp and stamps depicting American presidents, first reading the letter addressed to Bruce from the Department of Native Affairs. The enormity of its contents left him speechless for several minutes. He felt confused. His life had suddenly become complicated. For the moment he simply sat and read and reread the letter informing Bruce that his assistant, Charlie Kikira, had been nominated to receive education in the USA. Bruce would therefore need to find a new assistant. It went on to say that Charlie's travel would be arranged by his US sponsors, a mysterious Valodis Foundation. He would later be advised when he was required to travel to report to his school for the beginning of the next semester. Finally, Charlie opened the envelope from America. It was from a Mr Frederick Nevern, describing the Valodis Foundation and its offer to fund Charlie's education in the US. The foundation hoped Charlie would accept the offer. Upon his acceptance the foundation would make all the necessary arrangements. His employers had already been contacted and indicated their approval to release him. This was another first for Charlie. He was being consulted on his future. He could actually refuse to go. The Australians obviously saw the whole thing as a fait accompli and had not dreamed of asking Charlie's opinion. They simply didn't do consultation where a native was concerned. Charlie showed Bruce the letter.

His mind was reeling with the implications of it all. Before today he had started to dream of a future in his village as a married man with Beida, maybe with children. He had already had talks with Uncle Paru about some long-neglected land belonging to his late parents. Headman Bao had no sons and if Charlie married Beida he might even be a future Tori headman.

Bruce handed back the letter from America.

'Well Charlie, are you going? If you don't I'll ask them if they'll take me instead,' said Bruce with a laugh.

Charlie did not laugh. He looked serious.

'Masta Bruce, I don't know the answer to that question. I must think about it.'

'Say if you want to talk with me Charlie.'

Charlie left the patrol office and suddenly remembered he had left Beida sitting alone. He went back to where she was sitting.

'Beida, white men want me to go to school in America.'

Beida stared wide-eyed at Charlie. She could not immediately grasp the meaning or implications of this statement.

'Are you going to leave Tori?'

'I don't know. I must talk about it with Masta Bruce.'

Charlie did want to talk to Bruce, but first needed the thoughts of his uncle as the senior male member of his family. If only he could talk to Mr Smithson whose opinion he would value above all others.

That evening he sat outside Uncle Paru's hut with some of his cousins. In the Tori dialect he related the contents of his letters. His uncle looked dubious.

'Why do these white men want you to leave our village? I don't understand. Many here will believe you will be going to the land of our ancestors, never to return. I am not sure about that but we both know that Masta Smithson went to live in Australia and that is where all old white men go. And where is America? Is that part of Australia? I don't believe your father would want you to leave your life here.'

There were murmurs of agreement from the other men sitting around the flickering flames of Paru's fire. The discussion continued until the late evening hours. Certainly, the letters made no attempt to explain why Charlie needed further education. He was already the best educated man in Tori. One of his cousins voiced a suspicion that it was a white man's plot to get rid of Charlie because he was too clever.

'Uncle, I have listened to your wise words. I will speak with Masta Bruce to better understand why I should leave Tori.'

The following day he sat with Bruce in his office.

'Masta Bruce, why do you think these people want me to go to school in America?'

'You know Charlie, all over the world white men are starting to leave countries that they have ruled over for many years. Local native people will be ruling themselves. This has already happened in India, over ten years ago – one of the biggest countries in the world. It is possible that some long time in the future it will happen here. If it does, the country will need some educated leaders. You could be one of these.'

Charlie struggled with this radical concept. Even if Bruce's scenario was true, it surely would not happen to him. He saw no need for change. Nationalism was an idea that had no meaning for him.

That night he slept little. The letters didn't specify how long he would be away. He had long dreamt of exploring the world described in Mr Smithson's encyclopaedias and now he was hesitating. What would Mr Smithson say?

The following morning, he stepped onto the veranda of the patrol office. Bruce looked up enquiringly from his desk.

'Masta Bruce, I am going to school in America.'

A grinning Bruce rose and shook his hand.

'Hey Charlie, you're going to have to wear shoes now mate,' then with a pause said,

'You are doing the right thing.'

Bruce had never called him 'mate' before or shaken his hand. Somehow Charlie sensed that in an instant their relationship had changed. As time passed Charlie would find that not all white men would possess Bruce's generous nature. He would be entering a world taking his place alongside others able to assert their full rights as human beings. But he later found he would encounter resentment and prejudice for no other reason than tiny genetic mutations had occurred tens of thousands of years ago, before which all the world's people had dark skin. Just one letter of DNA code out of the 3.1 billion letters in the human genome, the complete instructions for making a human being, was responsible for one of humanity's greatest sources of strife. But this was in the future and for him to discover in his life's journey.

CHAPTER 12

Little did Charlie know that just a few months before, he had been discussed at the highest levels of the federal government in Canberra. A request from the Valodis Foundation had been received via the US Embassy. After percolating up through layers of federal bureaucracy the request landed at the top. The foreign minister called a meeting which the Director of Native Affairs attended together with numerous representatives from other interested departments. A briefing paper spelt out the subject of the meeting. Some American charitable foundation had taken it into its head to educate a native from the interior of PNG. This was ground-breaking stuff. Under its UN Charter to administer PNG, successive federal governments had done nothing to advance the lot of the native population. There was no interest politically to do anything, any more than there had been any willingness to treat its own Aboriginal population as anything but third-class citizens. In 1960 the 'White Australia' policy was still entrenched in the country's political and public consciousness. It would remain in place for another fifteen years until the Australian government passed the Racial Discrimination Act. The Minister and most of those present were thinking along the same lines – in a country where virtual apartheid reigned, it went against the grain to see a 'PNG blackfella' go off to university. It would set a dangerous precedent with a consequential awakening of political consciousness among the natives. Why, even their own aborigines could get ideas above their stations.

The more insightful at the meeting knew full well that sooner or later they would have to face the inevitable and grant autonomy to this land of primitive people. Already there were national and international pressure groups demanding changes in Australia's official discriminatory policies that applied to the mainland. Equally, the worldwide movement after World War Two to dismantle colonialist regimes was well under way. The UK's post-war Labour government had a firm policy of giving independence to most of its colonial territories. PNG was an Australian colony under another name but given respectability by its UN Charter. The Minister opened the meeting.

'So gentlemen, as we all know, while official policy would not encourage this situation, I cannot see that we can refuse the request. It would look bad for us at the UN. We are already getting enough stick there for our immigration policies.'

The Minister for Territories spoke.

'This was inevitable in the long term, we just didn't expect it so soon.'

There followed discussion over the implications of the prospect of this first PNG citizen to receive a tertiary education. The towns of Moresby, Madang, Rabaul and Lae had administration funded schools but these only provided education up to Elementary Certificate level and were only producing a tiny number of literate children. Christian missionaries were introducing education in the interior where the government had notably failed to act. Charlie had benefited from such mission schooling. Things were changing, but universal primary education was a very long way off. Secondary education was non-existent. The education of Charlie being sponsored by a foreign organisation would undoubtedly receive much media attention and only serve to highlight the Australian government's desultory approach to improving the lot of PNG's population.

The Minister started looking at his watch. 'Gentlemen, we could sit here debating this issue forever. It is quite clear. We will cooperate, albeit reluctantly, with the request from this Valodis Foundation. The matter shall be kept as low a profile as possible. Any press statements will talk more about the government's vigorous efforts in development of a widespread educational programme for the country and the identification of future leaders. Any such statements will be cleared by my office before issue. I need to be advised of how we propose to deal with nationality issues and passports to PNG citizens. There are lessons to be learnt from some of the difficulties the UK is facing by having an open immigration policy for the populations of its colonial territories. The Prime Minister has asked to be kept briefed.'

The meeting dispersed. It had not occurred to anybody to suggest asking Charlie if he wished to accept the Valodis offer. If he refused it would solve the government's problem.

As it was, a telegram from Bruce to the Department in Port Moresby confirmed Charlie's acceptance and a month later he set out on his life-changing journey. Bruce drove Charlie to Tori's airstrip. A large crowd of villagers had assembled, among them Uncle Paru and Charlie's cousins. As they stood awaiting the aircraft's arrival the crowd was silent, aware of the huge significance of the occasion. Many were anxious for Charlie at the news that he was going to white man's land, inhabited by everybody's ancestors. A dot appeared in the sky.

'Charlie mate, it's been great knowing you.' said Bruce as the aircraft taxied towards them.

The pilot flung open the door. Charlie was the only passenger. Bruce pumped his hand.

'Come back sometime.'

Charlie was too choked to reply. For him, leaving Tori village was to experience an extraordinary range of emotions. He knew he would not be returning for a long time. Though a confident young man, he nonetheless already felt homesick and lonely for the first time in his life. 'What on earth made me decide to go?' he asked himself as he looked at the forest below from the aircraft's window.

This was his first visit to his country's capital. The new experience of a bus journey took him from Port Moresby's airport to a large government office in the town. Here he was to collect his air ticket to travel to Sydney the following day.

During his brief stay in Moresby, he was witness to the marvels of buildings over twenty feet high, tarmac roads and the sight of large numbers of white men and even some white women. He had been to Madang, an important regional centre but nothing on the scale of Moresby. He was diverted seeing the roundabout in the centre of town. He stood watching a constable with outsize white gloves who stood under an umbrella-like structure. His function was clearly to direct the sparse traffic. A slow-moving car would cautiously approach and be allowed to proceed with much white-glove waving. White men did not make eye contact or acknowledge him as he walked past. Even fellow natives often ignored him. It all seemed quite alien to Charlie.

After staying overnight in the police barracks, a bus took him back to the airport to start his journey into the unknown.

PART TWO

ANOTHER WORLD

CHAPTER 13

As he was about to climb the steps to the enormous silver airliner Charlie looked up, overawed. He had seen pictures of large aircraft – indeed, seen the wreckage of the bomber near Hulwari village – but nothing like this. He had flown to Moresby in the tiny Patair plane but it seemed almost impossible that this huge shining machine could take flights full of people all the way to Sydney. At the end of the runway, he gripped his seat as the engines roared and the aircraft vibrated. As the noise lowered, he opened his eyes to see Port Moresby below, slowly receding on his way to his first destination en route to the USA. With his face pressed to the window he became totally absorbed by the blue ocean below with tiny white specks on its surface. Suddenly, a voice made him start.

'What would you like to drink, sir?'

He turned to see a smiling blonde apparition bending

towards him. He was momentarily stunned, never having been so close to such beauty or been called 'Sir' before. Neither had he drunk anything other than water in his entire life.

'Some water please,' he eventually responded.

He knew he was now in a white world where people drank all manner of liquids. The Australian administration banned the consumption of alcoholic drinks by natives, whereas some patrol officer's almost entire liquid intake seemed to be beer from cans. His boss Bruce in Tori was one of these.

Very few Papuans had travelled outside of PNG. Some had assisted Australian forces during the war and had been on ships, but hardly any had returned. This reinforced old beliefs that the lands of white men were inhabited by the dead and that white people in PNG were in fact returning dead people. In Moresby, Charlie met a man from Kerema who had been to Fiji to train as a medical assistant. Apparently, he had stayed for a few days in Sydney and been embarrassed at having to travel wearing a lap-lap. In Charlie's case he was spared this, having been given European travelling clothes. He was used to these as Mrs Smithson had given him khaki trousers and shirts which he had worn since his teenage years. One new thing was his most uncomfortable, extra-wide shoes.

Despite his extensive reading, Charlie was unprepared for the even greater shock of Sydney's huge airport terminal full of white people rushing about. He had never seen so many white people at once and felt self-conscious as the only black face around in his new clothes and large shoes. It was a huge relief to see smiling Mr Smithson amid the crowd of faces meeting his flight. With Philip Smithson was a white man introduced as Mr Wells from the American Embassy. The two men steered him through the terminal to a waiting car.

'You are staying with me tonight Charlie,' said Smithson. 'Tomorrow Mr Wells here will take you to the US Embassy to go through some formalities and issue you with a US visa for your new passport. There is also a press conference. You are famous now, you know.' He laughed.

Later that evening, sitting with his hosts, Charlie said, 'Mr Smithson I have to thank you for helping me while I am here. I must ask you if you think I have made the correct decision to go to America? I had almost decided to marry Headman Bao's daughter and lead a life like any Tori man.'

'Charlie, you will not regret it. When you return you will understand how you can help both Tori village and the rest of PNG to cope with the changes that are coming. It is almost certain you will have a position of responsibility as a well-educated man. You will later find another woman you can marry.'

The conversation followed similar lines to those Charlie had with Bruce Petersen. It helped relieve his worries but did nothing to lesson his homesickness for Tori village.

Staying with the Smithsons was another new experience. Although he had become familiar with a western lifestyle in their household at their various postings in PNG, there was nothing to compare with the luxury of their Sydney home. That night after suffering the discomfort of a bed with a mattress, he decided to sleep on the floor.

He lay awake, thinking about his situation. He kept thinking about Mr Smithson and Bruce's predictions that PNG one day would be ruled by its own people and that Charlie could be one of the country's leaders. He was not sure even what being a country's leader involved. A village chief had a clearly defined role in which he was the final arbiter when arguments arose between villagers. Occasionally a kiap with authority would appear, but the country had functioned quite well before these white foreigners were imposed on them. The chief made all important decisions and had a role in seeing that tribal customs were observed and followed properly. These were supremely important matters. He was responsible to no one else and he knew everybody under his rule on a personal basis. Delegation of authority simply did not happen. How on earth could a leader be responsible for thousands of people, most of whom he would never meet, maybe not even share a common language? Charlie had a glimmer of understanding when he considered the role of the Queen of Australia, who did not even live in Australia, but appointed wise men to rule PNG and Australia for her. So, who would he be as a leader? Just a servant of the Queen? Just as he was a servant of Bruce Petersen? The whole notion of nationhood simply did not make sense. Why not just keep the whole of PNG exactly as it was, just on a local village basis? It had worked for generations back, as far as anyone could remember and nobody complained. Certainly, nobody wanted anything to do with the neighbouring villages some of whom were traditional enemies, let alone fellow citizens. If Charlie had any role in the future, he would keep everything exactly as it was.

The following day was spent in a whirlwind, the necessity for which Charlie could not comprehend. Visits to the US Embassy, form filling with the aid of Mr Smithson, being photographed for his visa, medical tests at a hospital and finally a press conference late in the day. As well as newspapers, ABC TV cameras were there. The reporters asked Charlie a variety of questions about himself, his country and his ambitions. He could frame simple replies about lifestyle and what he had learnt from encyclopaedias,

'Mr Kikira, do you think that Papua and New Guinea will one day want to be independent from Australia?' asked the Sydney Morning Herald. His thoughts while on the floor of Mr Smithson's guest room returned to him.

'Sir, I do not know, I cannot answer that question. It would have to be asked of all the people of PNG.'

Another asked, 'We understand you are going to study at an American university, the first Papuan to do so and the only native person to go to university anywhere for that matter. Do you think that there is any point to this given the nature of your country?'

A more patronising question Charlie could hardly imagine, he even felt Mr Smithson bristle alongside him. He thought for a moment and framed what he hoped was a suitable response.

'Well sir, it seems that the Valodis Foundation thinks so and the US government has just given me a visa for the purpose, so they appear to think so too.'

As he left the media conference, Charlie was pleased and relieved as Mr Smithson at his side said, 'Charlie, you did very well at replying to the media. I think you made an excellent impression. You already have the makings of a politician.'

He laughed as he said it. Charlie did not reply – he really didn't know what a politician was.

What he had already seen of the white man's world in the last twenty-four hours looked completely alien. People certainly did not look any happier as they rushed around, mostly not talking to or even looking at each other. In PNG it was unthinkable not to talk to or at least acknowledge somebody if you passed by them on a path. Mr Smithson apart, Australia already seemed an unfriendly place and Charlie certainly drew some strange looks and could not tell if they were friendly or not. Something that amazed him was the shops crammed with cargo, the PNG name for manufactured goods. He also remarked on the extreme orderliness. He concluded so far that the rest of the world had little to offer PNG. Charlie nonetheless was now looking forward to learning more about it and seeing the contents of Mr Smithson's encyclopaedias for real.

The series of aeroplane journeys that a week later took Charlie to his destination in the USA were a further revelation to him of the size and variety of the world. Despite his awareness of a world beyond PNG through reading in Mr Smithson's library, nothing prepared him for the actual thing. As he gazed down, mesmerised seeing the endless waters of the Pacific between Australia and the USA, he unconsciously came to place PNG and the Tori region into another context. It was still the centre of his world and way more precious. Encouraged by Bruce and Mr Smithson, Charlie held no fears of the unknown, but as the plane droned on he was still wondering if coming to America was such a good idea. He could not imagine what he could possibly learn that would be relevant to his life in a PNG village. So far, the white people that he had seen on his journey had looked serious and evidently with thoughts elsewhere. Take for example the frowning man seated in the opposite aisle. He was busy writing and moving papers in and out of his briefcase when not tapping away at a little box, later known to Charlie as a pocket calculator. The man was dressed in a beautiful suit, a shining watch on his wrist and a wonderful leather briefcase in which to keep his papers. Yet the man was not happy, thought Charlie; how could he be, with that look on his face. He must miss his village, his family, his parents and friends.

'Say, Mr Kikira, where is Papua New Guinea – is it part of Africa?' asked the US immigration officer at Honolulu Airport. He was looking at Charlie's brand-new passport, the issue of which had been the subject of numerous meetings in Canberra. Bureaucracy eventually decided it was to be an Australian document endorsed, 'Resident of the Mandated Territory of Papua and New Guinea – Permanent Residence in Australia not permitted.' Charlie was going to need to explain where his country was many times over the next few years.

The official was curious in seeing Charlie. It was unusual at that time to find a black person on an intercontinental flight, but sure enough he had a visa issued by the State Department in Washington DC. The plane had stopped for refuelling at Hawaii and had been Charlie's entry point into the USA.

The next leg of his journey ended in Los Angeles. There he was met by a white lady, an agent arranged by the Valodis Foundation to guide him through a dizzy complex of corridors to check in for his next flight. By the time he was seated on the aircraft his head was spinning.

CHAPTER 14

His journey finished in the nation's capital where, waiting at the gate, he was relieved to see the friendly face of Tom Paul who shook his hand.

'Welcome to Washington Charlie – you've shown me your country, now it's my turn.'

Fortunately, Bruce Petersen had schooled Charlie before he left in some of the niceties of western behaviour. Hand shaking was one of these. In the traditional PNG greeting, one person extends a bent forefinger which the other person pinches between his fore and middle fingers. Both hands were then rapidly pulled apart, causing the fore and middle fingers to make a 'snap' sound. The process is then repeated with the roles reversed.

The next few days were a blur of yet more new experiences as Tom took his guest on a whirlwind tour of local sights. Charlie was impressed by the sheer enormity of downtown Washington; its soaring buildings and busy streets thronged by a mass of mostly white faces surging back and forth. They would emerge from or disappear into buildings or even below ground into some mysterious subterranean world. Looking down from a tall building, he was reminded of a species of ant that travelled along the forest floor. The ants were apparently purposeful but Charlie could never work out where they were coming from or going to, they just kept going in an unending stream that had no start or finish. Washington was a forest with buildings instead of trees. Charlie felt as if he was on another planet.

Tom showed him the White House on a conducted tour. They also visited Arlington Cemetery and Charlie saw the headstone engraved with the name of Lt. Joseph P. Orlowski USAF. A flashback took him to first seeing the name whilst standing in the Hulwari village some six months earlier. He stood silently for a while, back in PNG, engulfed in homesickness.

Later in the day he was introduced to Tom's parents. Edgar and Ann Paul lived in a comfortable middle-class home in a leafy suburb. Not unlike Mr Smithson's Sydney home Charlie thought, but even more luxurious. He was not yet aware of the differences in western society and for the moment assumed everybody must live like this. Eventually he would come to learn of the gulf between rich and poor. Such differences simply did not exist in PNG. Primitive societies could not exist with such divisive arrangements. What struck Charlie most forcibly was the isolation that this lifestyle produced, both physical and personal. He did not really think in those terms, but knew that his identity came from being a member of a tribe with whom he interacted almost continuously on a day-to-day basis. He knew every other member of the tribe and all social interaction depended on that knowledge and their common problems and traditions. He could not see how this happened when everybody seemed confined to their brick and tile boxes and only moved about in cars, again isolated from each other. People rarely seemed to walk, except when they were in the big city when generally they did not speak with others. He felt concerned that Tom and his brother and sister lived a long way from their parents. How could they care for each other from miles away? What was even more puzzling was the fact that Tom's surviving grandparents, although in the same city, lived ten miles away in a home with a lot of other old people. Again, how could the family fulfil its obligations to each other in this situation? Although his parents were dead, Charlie knew that if they had been alive, he would not have left them unless he knew that his brothers or sisters were living with them and looking after them. It was all a simple matter, not just duty but an instinct as the only way to behave. After all, parents did everything for you as a child when you could not hunt or fish or build a hut. After adulthood, when previous generations became unable to do these things, it was only natural that the roles would reverse. The tribe could not function in any other way.

Charlie's curiosity was overwhelmed by a sense of alienation. He was longing for the simplicity of life in Tori village.

CHAPTER 15

Charlie had been enrolled in Osterley Community College in Ohio. The Valodis Foundation had sent overseas students there before with favourable results. The plan was that Charlie would complete his secondary schooling thereby enabling him to attend a suitable university for degree study. His education at the hands of the London Missionary Society was somewhat rudimentary by US standards. Nonetheless, he had achieved a great deal more by his voracious reading of Mr Smithson's Encyclopaedia Britannica.

Normally Mr Nevern would have met Charlie but he was overseas on the latter's arrival. He had asked Tom Paul to unofficially represent the foundation and see Charlie safely installed at the college. Tom happily assented, even taking some overdue leave to cover the period. He felt a sense of responsibility for Charlie's well-being. He was starting to feel misgivings, having been instrumental in Charlie being plucked from an almost stone-age society into a totally alien environment. They arrived at Osterley together, Tom leaving an uncharacteristically quiet and reserved Charlie with the dean's secretary.

'Goodbye Charlie. Don't forget I am your friend here in America, who you can come to anytime you need anything – and I mean anything. Just think of me as your brother.'

After Tom left, Charlie suddenly felt alone. Tom, with his knowledge of Charlie's world in Tori village was somehow his only link to home. Charlie started as the door opened and a smiling, white middle-aged lady entered the secretary's office.

'Hello Charlie, my name is Mary Holden. I'm your pastoral carer and your sponsor, the Valodis Foundation has asked me to meet you.'

She handed over a business card. Charlie looked at it and saw the strange word 'Psychotherapist' on it.

'Just think of me as a friend here to help you adjust to living in what must seem a strange country where everything is unfamiliar. If you ever need advice or want to discuss any aspect of your life here, please contact me. We'll shortly go and meet the head of college, Mr Dyment.'

Having a woman in authority was yet another culture shock for Charlie. Although he had seen from Pamela Smithson that white women had a different place in society to their PNG sisters, he could not adjust immediately to the idea of a female authority figure. He was overwhelmed with all the attention this lowly kiap's assistant seemed to be getting from all these important white people.

With Mrs Holden at his side Charlie was ushered into Mr Dyment's office. After the customary handshaking Mr Dyment spoke, 'Welcome to Osterley Community College, Charlie, we hope you will be happy here. Tell me what you hope to achieve during your time in the United States?'

Charlie still had to restrain himself from addressing white men as 'Masta'.

'Well sir, I hope to learn things that I can take home for the benefit of my people.'

'And what do you think of what you have seen in the few days you have been here?'

This stopped Charlie in his tracks. So far, he had seen nothing that appealed to him, in fact quite the contrary. It was all engrossing but he thought he could bring a few ideas to America from PNG to make people look a little more relaxed and happier. Giving a satisfactory answer was going to be difficult. In PNG society you tell it like it is, without thought of offending. On the other hand, together with the experience of long chats with Tom and Bruce, he already had an instinct that over here one tended to say what the other person wanted to hear for risk of causing offence. These foreigners were so generous, though even now he had not worked out why they were doing all this. Tom and Bruce's projections of the future PNG ruling itself and needing the likes of Charlie to play a role didn't add up. Why did anybody need to come to America for this? Most of the headmen that he had encountered in his brief life had not been outside their villages let alone out of PNG, yet they all seemed to be doing a reasonable job. As he saw it so far, the very last thing his country needed was to emulate the USA. He had put this to Tom who said he agreed, but PNG was going to have to adapt and life there was going to change. For the life of him Charlie could not see why. There was silence while his mind wandered trying to think of a response. Mary Holden came to his rescue.

'Maybe Charlie needs some more time here to decide what's good and what's bad. Let's hope he finds something good to say about us when he returns home.' She laughed.

Charlie could only nod in agreement.

'Fine,' said Mr Dyment, rising. 'Let's leave it at that. Please remember that Mrs Holden and I are always available if you have problems or questions. Perhaps these can't be answered by your teachers, or matters that you would like to talk over in confidence.'

Not understanding what that these matters might be, Charlie thanked Mr Dyment, relieved that the meeting was over.

In the following days and weeks, Charlie compared notes with other students at the college. He discovered that, as well as Americans, there were other foreigners sent from their homelands either by wealthy parents, governments, or recipients of scholarships like himself. One was another black student, Maxime Dupois from Haiti, sponsored by an American charity. Maxime also spoke good English as a result of having been in America for the past two years.

Charlie and Maxime sat together in the college library. Earlier, Maxime had pointed out Haiti on a map of the Americas.

'Tell me more about your country, Maxime.'

'We were a colony of the French until winning independence in the last century. Ever since, we have had a succession of corrupt violent dictators. We just don't seem to be any good at ruling ourselves.'

'So how did you get to be in America?'

'My family decided to escape the oppression and cruelty. My father and brothers stole a Haitian coastguard boat and sailed to Miami,' Maxime said simply. He went on to tell Charlie how the immediate reaction of the US government had been to return the family and boat to Haiti. However, it had relented after a public outcry and media campaigns highlighted the certain fate of the family if sent back.

'We were very lucky. If we had gone back, we would have been killed,' said Maxime.

Haiti, it seemed, was a chaotic corrupt mess. Maxime assured Charlie that black men were in charge although they were no good at running the country, in fact there were many Haitians who would welcome a takeover by America to bring order. Charlie was becoming more confused than ever with regard to the natural order of things. He had started to think that the inequalities between black and white were unnatural and unfair, but here was evidence that sometimes only white men were capable of being the ultimate masters. He was starting to speculate how PNG would fare if it ever could shake free of Australian domination. He decided there was much to learn about the world at large and the history of Haiti in particular.

The one thing that Charlie did realise was that he needed a better understanding of the origins of racial conflict and why the white man always seemed to have the upper hand. It was true in PNG and true here in the US. So far as he could tell it was true nearly all over the world. India seemed something of an exception, having gained independence from the British after World War Two. There were few countries with a government of local men of colour. He'd tried to find out something about black independent Liberia. It was not a very impressive story from what he could glean from the college library. Maybe the answer was that white men were just more capable of running the affairs of a nation.

Chapter 16

A year after Charlie's arrival at Osterley Community College, Frederick Nevern sat in his office reviewing reports on the progress of the ten young men on whom the foundation had bestowed Caspar Valodis' benevolence. So far there had been no women. Most of the ten or so seemed to be progressing well in adapting to life in the US educational system. There were a few problems, mostly connected with homesickness, complications from love affairs and other minor problems, but nothing serious apart from one case of an incident with drugs. Nevern would wait to see if this could be resolved by college authorities before getting involved. He dreaded the thought of sending a student home, with a possible consequence of the foundation having damaged an individual by exposing him to the worst rather than the best of American values.

Charlie Kikira from PNG was definitely one of Nevern's success stories. After starting to adjust to his new surroundings, he showed academic ability and was socially adept. Mary Holden was most impressed with his maturity, reporting, 'definitely a natural psychologist in the making.' John Dyment recommended Charlie for university, suitable for degrees in law or maybe philosophy. 'A born leader, but let's preserve his clarity of thought and not confuse him with the complications of political science,' was his comment. Nevern wanted to meet this exceptional protégé of the foundation. A decision had to be made as to which degree and university would be appropriate for Charlie in a year's time. Doubtless he had ideas of his own by now but also was receiving advice from all quarters. John Dyment's opinions were valued by Nevern, but he felt a special responsibility bearing in mind his ambivalence towards the foundation's terms of reference. These feelings were amplified after his original meeting with Tom Paul regarding Charlie's selection and having conducted some research of his own into PNG. The worldwide export of American culture and lifestyles had started in earnest in the fifteen years after World War Two as US economic power and that of its multinationals had grown. The influence of US popular music, Hollywood, Coca Cola, to name but a few, would surely arrive in PNG at some point in the future and Nevern's private opinions certainly were not going to change anything. Even the US government's establishment of the Peace Corps was surreptitiously aiding the process, and now he, Frederick Nevern was part the export of USA Inc. As in his meeting with Tom Paul, the best he could do was rationalise the reasons for Charlie's US education. The die was cast and he could only try to help make the best of it.

After receiving the college reports, Nevern arrived two weeks later at Osterley, having arranged a meeting with Charlie and to spend time with Mary Holden and John Dyment. He chastised himself that he had not previously made contact with Charlie. He first saw Mary and John alone during which time they merely elaborated on their written assessments.

'He is one of the most mature twenty-year-olds I have ever met,' said Mary. 'He seems to have so much common sense. He arrived overawed, but after a few weeks started to display a level of self-confidence that I only wish I could impart to many of my therapy clients.'

John Dyment was impressed with his academic ability.

'He is so hungry for learning it is almost hard to believe. His big interest is in world history; he seems to want to know what made today's world, everything from early European history to our civil war to World War Two. I felt a little concerned to learn that he has been asking questions about Malcolm X and the Nation of Islam. On the other hand, he apparently has been finding out about Martin Luther King's civil rights movement. I hope he is intelligent and objective enough not to become unhealthily radical.'

Nevern reflected on this over lunch with his hosts, having arranged to see Charlie in the afternoon, after which he was to see other Valodis students at Osterley. He did not want to send Charlie back to PNG as a violent revolutionary. Over lunch he also learnt that Charlie had taken an interest in Maria Littuma, the sister of Ruben, a privately funded student. Maria was an eighteen-year-old from Ecuador studying at a women's college nearby who frequently came to visit her brother. Such liaisons were commonplace but they were of interest to Nevern with his vicarious parental responsibility for his charges so far from their homes.

Charlie had been anticipating the meeting with Mr Nevern with a mixture of curiosity and trepidation. Nevern was an important older man who had to be accorded considerable respect. This was the first time he had come face to face with his benefactor and he wondered if his performance at the college was adequate. He still had questions in his mind about the motives behind showing so much interest in him. Why bring him to America and provide him with an education clearly designed for a westerner, not an obscure PNG native? On entering the room, Charlie saw the friendly, smiling face of an immaculately dressed white man probably old enough to be his grandfather. Nevern was a medium height, slim, fit man with an impressive mane of grey, almost white hair. His suit probably cost more than the annual income of the entire Tori tribe. Charlie still had some difficulty in correctly guessing the age of white people. A Tori man in his sixties would certainly have been considered very old, whereas an American of this age might still be working, looking remarkably young, vigorous and playing sports. His sedentary PNG counterpart would more likely to be whiling away his closing years chewing betel, engaged in endless gossip and discussions with his peers on matters of feuds, rituals and past glories. Possibly one of the few benefits of living in America might be the prospect of a longer, healthier life. Having said that, on excursions out of college Charlie had been amazed to see some people who were grotesquely fat, presumably suffering with some terrible disease. Only later did he discover that in most cases the name of the ailment was gluttony.

For his part, Nevern took in the vision of a dark-skinned, well-proportioned, pleasant-looking but slightly anxious young man.

'Charlie how nice to meet you at last. Do come in and sit down. First, let me say how pleased I am to receive very complimentary reports about you from the college.'

Nevern wanted to explore Charlie's feelings about his presence in the US. After all, the whole project was only going to be a success if the student took home something positive that he could apply there. After a hesitant start Charlie found his usual confidence and, with his customary directness let Nevern know his doubts about the value of his scholarship to PNG.

'Sir, it is not that I do not find my studies here very interesting, they are extremely so to me personally and I am enjoying life here and have made some good friends. I am treated very well. America is an impressive country and I want to see more of it, as I would the rest of the world. I think there are some problems that I do not completely understand. There seems to be a lot of unhappiness among black Americans, which I read about in the newspapers. It seems they are not always treated fairly. In your history you had a great war over this unfairness, thousands died, yet the unfairness is still there, is that not correct?'

He had already asked this question of one of his teachers, but not received a satisfactory reply. Without waiting for Nevern, who started to ponder an answer to this difficult question, Charlie continued.

'I would like to take home some knowledge that will help my people but a year later I am still not sure what this knowledge will be.'

In the silence that followed this statement, Nevern was uncharacteristically stumped for words that could serve as a satisfactory answer. In PNG, old men were supposed to be full of wisdom and while Charlie had already realised that in fact some were foolish, one always took their wisdom for granted as a starting point.

'You see Charlie,' Nevern started, 'Every society has good and evil within it. I am sure that even in your own country there are people, maybe even tribes that behave badly. This is driven sometimes by greed, sometimes envy, even fear. In this country many white people, mostly uneducated and particularly in the south, have unfounded feelings of superiority over black people. History tells us that often minorities are persecuted just because they are different. This happened to the Jews in Germany before and during the last world war. I am ashamed to say that not only do black people suffer in our country, but there is also a sad story for you to learn about the treatment of Native American Indians. Difference can cause fear and suspicion. Is there no animosity between some tribes in your country? As you have learned, in the last century

President Lincoln started the process to ensure there are equal rights for all Americans irrespective of their colour and to encourage integration between races. Sadly, his vision has not yet been fulfilled, but we are making progress and in a few more generations, who knows, one day we could even have a black president?'

Later Charlie thought about Nevern's statement and while it confirmed his own suspicions, he was still shocked. He had not yet learnt of the history of the American Indians which curiously seemed to be lacking from the lessons he had received on American history. On the one hand, he admired Mr Nevern's frankness, but could not think why so little progress had been made to make everybody equal. Could PNG ever become an integrated nation rather than a loose collection of isolated tribes? And was there any point anyway? In simple terms, America seemed to be mainly two tribes, black and white, and they were having problems and still fighting each other after over a hundred years. PNG had over eight hundred identifiably separate tribes with their own languages, customs and beliefs! This matter of racial difference bred prejudice and was at the root of many of the world's problems. He resolved to learn more about the matter. He had heard other students talking about the civil rights movement and the activities of black groups with militant agendas. While still excited by America, the more he learnt the more he was becoming disenchanted by it. If you were black there was so much unfairness, cruelty and prejudice. His initial fascination with America was starting to be coloured by doubts.

It all seemed a million miles from Tori village. There apart from rare spats with the Hulwari, everybody enjoyed a more or less peaceful existence. The main concerns of most villagers were the state of their families, crops and animals.

Nevern returned to New York later that day. As his flight droned on he was thinking what he might say in his next report to the board of trustees. Should he allude to his misgivings about the ethos of the foundation? At first sight, educating young people from third-world countries had seemed a worthy enough objective but since meeting young Charlie he was starting to have doubts.

Chapter 17

Charlie resolved to find out more about America's black leaders. He had heard about a Dr King and a curiously named Malcolm X. Both seemed to be trying to address what appeared to be America's biggest problem. Mr X was giving speeches in New York, the nearest big city to Osterley. Would his Haitian friend Maxime come with him to hear this black leader? Maxime looked dubious.

'You know Charlie, I don't think the college will approve of us going to New York for the weekend to go to a Nation of Islam meeting. The whites hate Malcolm X and think he is inciting blacks to violent revolution.'

Charlie understood Maxime's reluctance. He was instinctively truthful yet determined to see this important black man.

'We could say we will be sightseeing and visiting your cousin Jean-Claude and staying with him. This will be true and we don't have to say that we will be attending a meeting, anyway that will be kind of sightseeing.'

Two Saturdays later on a cold winter's day, Maxime and Charlie descended from the Greyhound bus station near Harlem, the venue of Malcolm X's meeting. Charlie unused to such low temperatures, was shivering and couldn't wait to get inside. The weather was just one of the many adjustments Charlie had to make. Before coming to America, he had only known tropical heat and humidity. After a year, he was starting to enjoy the changing seasons but still found winters a challenge.

At the hall's entrance, two very large black men in dark suits peered down at the two individuals standing before them. Their orders were simple. Keep out any whites, known trouble-makers for the Nation of Islam, any other undesirables and if in doubt, anybody else. Neither of these two looked as if they fitted into any of these categories and appeared harmless. Although undoubtedly black, the taller of the two had features that made one of the Nation's gatekeepers curious.

'What state are you from, brother?'

Normally Charlie enjoyed describing his country, although on this occasion he was anxious to get inside from New York's cold December air and warm up, not to mention see the object of their visit, the famous Malcolm X.

'From Ohio,' he explained simply and the big man stood aside, wondering at the diversity of appearances that originated from African slaves.

Charlie experienced a frisson of excitement as the tall physically imposing figure walked on stage. Malcolm X had an electric effect on the large crowd who rose with a shout. Charlie was surprised to see he looked almost like a white man, having pale skin and reddish hair.

'I want to thank Allah for coming and giving us our leader and teacher here in America, the Honourable Elijah Muhammad,' he started. Charlie had already learned that Elijah was leader of the Nation of Islam.

As Malcolm continued, it sounded like a religious sermon working up a theme to imply that Christianity was a religion for white people and Islam for black people. It sounded convincing and Charlie found himself becoming mesmerised by the power of Malcolm's oratory. Maxime was becoming more excited as the evening progressed.

'Hey Charlie,' he said afterwards as they walked down the street on their way home. 'This is what my country needs, a new religion. This is our problem. Malcolm is right – the whites are a race of devils and we are bound by the wrong religion.'

Although still reeling from the impact of the evening's speech as he had never heard before, at first Charlie said nothing. After thinking for a while, he said, 'I'm not sure if Islam could solve Haiti's problems or America's for that matter. In fact, it seems unlikely that any religion could sort out answers to poverty, political unrest, human greed, bigotry and all the other ills in any country.'

Charlie had read about conflicts and human cruelty down the ages and so often these had some religious basis. Charlie's beliefs in right and wrong were derived from unwritten tribal rules which dealt pretty well with most situations. Everybody understood these rules. The fact of the matter was that for the most part nobody would risk the opprobrium of the entire tribe by crossing the line. Here in America everything was quite different. Except in remote rural areas, one lived in the midst of thousands of strangers who mostly didn't know or care what you did or thought. Right and wrong were defined in writing at great length in law books, the Bible and elsewhere. Certain bad behaviour, such as having relations with another man's wife or rudeness, was frowned upon but nobody did anything about it. Really bad things were dealt with by policemen who had guns and rode around in big cars. Admittedly Tori village had two policemen but they never seemed to do anything except hang around the patrol office, sleeping and chewing betel nut. Their sole function was apparently to help white kiaps keep warring tribes apart. This happened only very infrequently and in most people's view, matters sometimes had to be settled directly until both sides were satisfied, policemen or no policemen. In PNG they were mostly seen to be superfluous members of society.

On that particular evening Charlie had an unexpected and first-hand experience of American police. As the two friends neared the street where cousin Jean-Claude lived, a large black-and-white car drew up alongside them.

The contrast between the two officers in the car was apparent in more ways than one. For years, Eddie Shipp had trouble keeping his weight down in line with the New York Police Department guidelines. These had recently been issued by the Commissioner, stung by media comments about corpulent officers. Eddie's stomach still hung over his belt. Only three years away from retirement, Eddie just wanted a quiet life and was happy to doze in his patrol car until the end of his shift. By contrast his junior partner, Stan Bachmann, only a year out of training was lean, fit and eager for action. This had been a quiet night; a minor domestic altercation two hours earlier was extremely tedious in Stan's book but ideal for Eddie. Their prescribed beat covered a mainly Latino precinct comprising ten-by-ten blocks of mostly brownstones, run-down retail and some deserted workshops on the south side.

A few snowflakes drifted down onto the deserted streets, starting to whiten the surface. Two figures had passed their car and the streetlight allowed Stan to catch sight of dark faces, one talking animatedly, the other listening intently.

There was no real reason for Stan to stop alongside Charlie and Maxime. The radio was quiet and he was bored with doing nothing. Who knows, these black boys might just be up to no good, maybe carrying drugs or weapons? In Stan's mind, black meant suspicious, he would not have dreamed of pulling up alongside two white men without good reason.

Stan, leaning from the open window, called out, 'Where you boys going?'

This was Charlie's first encounter with American police. Perhaps this guardian of the law was just interested in him and his friend. Officer Stan's question was usually one of the first asked on meeting another person on a path back home. Why, maybe they were about to be offered a lift home. To Maxime the uniform and a white man equated to a threat. He was still fired by Malcolm X's tirades against white rule. Fortunately, Charlie was the first to respond,

'We are going to my friend's cousin's house.' As an afterthought he added, 'I am Charlie and this is Maxime.'

Stan was a little disconcerted at this. Blacks he accosted more often gave a sullen response and never volunteered anything. Also, this guy had a strange accent and was unexpectedly friendly. Maybe let them go.

'Let 'em go,' Eddie intervened. 'They're harmless.'

Hissing over the black tarmac, the police car moved off without another word. In later years, Charlie reflected on this incident and was able to put it into a more realistic context of police attitudes towards the black population. Upon his return to Osterley after the Malcolm X meeting Charlie started spending time on researching the whole question of race relations in America. From his evenings with Tom talking over campfires in PNG he learnt that there was a movement called the National Association for the Advancement of Colored People, known by its initials NAACP. He found he could join and accordingly sent his membership fee. The very existence of such an organisation confirmed to him the second-class status of black people.

Back home, there was a clear distinction in PNG between the status of black and white people. The whites were held as different or even superior in some way, but did not belong in PNG. They were from some distant land to which they all eventually returned. One never saw an old white man. White women were a rarity and nobody had seen a white baby. How or where they were born was something of a mystery and the subject of much speculation. Here in America, blacks and whites were all Americans, theoretically with the same rights and privileges. Whites however, always seemed to have the upper hand. There seemed to be something basically unfair, mused Charlie. Maybe Malcolm X was right.

CHAPTER 18

Towards the end of his first year in the US, Charlie started to notice Maria Littuma. He was not the only one. Maria's dark, striking Latin looks and curvaceous figure had attracted many overtures from young men at Charlie's college. Maria was the sister of Ruben Littuma who was in the same year as Charlie. She was staying in student accommodation at Ursuline, a leading women's college, where she was studying to become her country's first qualified female pharmacologist.

Maria and her brother were from a wealthy Ecuadorian family where their father was none other than the Minister of Justice. They belonged to one of the most influential families in a country ruled by an oligarchy.

Ruben and Charlie usually spent time together at the weekends. In their second year they both found themselves in the college's basketball team. Charlie really enjoyed basketball. It just might be one of those things that he would introduce back home. After a match they would sometimes hang out at a local coffee bar with other students. Eighteen-year-old Maria often joined them and was drawn to this young black man with his tight curls. Her dark sensuality and vivacious personality held a reciprocal attraction for Charlie. He had certainly noticed others, but since leaving Beida, he had not made overtures to a girl.

Although supremely self-confident in most situations, for weeks Charlie found himself wrestling with shyness before inviting Maria to go out with him. Charlie was quite inexperienced with the opposite sex compared to most of the young men around him of his age.

He decided to broach the subject to her brother.

'Why don't you ask her yourself?' laughed Ruben. 'She won't bite you!'

A few days later Charlie still had not summoned the courage to approach Maria. Ruben decided to speak with his sister.

'What do you think of my friend Charlie?'

'I like him a lot – so do some of the other girls. He hardly ever speaks to me. Maybe he doesn't like me, or thinks I am ugly.'

Later that day Ruben went to find Charlie.

'I spoke to Maria about you.'

'What did she say?'

'She's waiting for you to ask her out, you fool!' said her brother, laughing.

Thereafter, on Saturday evenings Charlie and Maria could be usually be found together at one of the town's cafés or coffee bars. Other times they might meet in the student lounge or in fine weather, walk along the banks of the Olentangy River. Their more intimate moments were in Ruben's car when thoughtfully loaned to the couple. As months passed, Charlie became more entranced with her and started to count the hours until they met. One weekend they had arranged to meet at Osterley's stadium after a basketball game against a neighbouring college. Ruben and Charlie were playing for their college. Waiting near the player's entrance, Charlie scanned the dispersing crowds. Maria appeared, aglow with pleasure as she saw her beau hurrying toward her.

After a warm hug, hand in hand they took the walk into town with the intention of stopping at their favourite coffee bar. On such occasions they would take a quiet route through the town park. This offered an opportunity for passionate embraces in a shaded spot. They had not noticed a large, dark-coloured car following them. As they entered the unlit road towards the park the car drew up alongside them and two men jumped out.

'Señorita Littuma?' asked one.

'Si,' replied Maria.

'Ven con nosotros ahora por favor.'

She could not think why this strange man would want her to go with him. His manner was threatening enough to frighten the young couple and they froze and gripped each other's hands more tightly. The man took Maria's free hand and started to pull her towards the car.

'No, no voy a ir contigo,' she screamed.

Charlie was taken aback by the suddenness of it all. Although he didn't understand the Spanish, the situation and the body language were clear – Maria was going to be taken from him by force. Charlie attempted to wrestle Maria away from her assailant. He hit out at the man with his fist but failed to connect. Instead, a blow at the back of his head caused him to see a blinding light then darkness.

Maria was forced into the car and locked inside. She heard the men debating what to do with the inert Charlie. As he would raise the alarm when he came to, they decided to buy time. They loaded him into the trunk.

After some miles the car turned down a narrow lane for a few minutes, stopping outside what appeared to be a large farmhouse building with a number of barns and outhouses close by. A man appeared from the house as Maria's captors dragged her protesting, from the car.

'Señorita, I apologise for this inconvenience, but if your father loves you and does what we demand, you will be released unharmed,' said the man in Spanish. His accent was from her home country, the same as her abductors. The man had an educated presence with an air of authority.

One of her abductors spoke.

'We also have her boyfriend.'

'What?' shouted their boss. 'You idiots, the last thing we need is another hostage.'

'If we left him there, he would have identified us and described us and the car to the police. He's in the trunk.'

Maria was bundled into a room and locked inside. It had boarded-up windows and no natural light. There was an ensuite bathroom and no furniture except for a mattress on the floor. An inert Charlie was dragged from the car's trunk and dumped in the basement.

Maria was frightened but decided not to show it to her captors. After a few hours, the oldest of the three entered with a tray of bread and cheese and a bottle of water. She decided to act friendly.

'I know of your cause and agree there are things wrong in our country but locking me up won't help.'

This little statement produced no reaction. The man leered at her and she smiled back, deciding to encourage him to win some concession, although quite how she hadn't figured out. He left and she heard the door being locked.

Meanwhile Charlie started to recover, finding himself with a blinding headache. He did not know how long he had been unconscious. As his memory returned, he tried to account for the events leading to him lying on a hard floor in a windowless basement. He felt a tender swelling on the back of his head. He didn't know if Maria was nearby. He was disorientated, frightened and totally confused. After a few hours, a door opened and a light went on from a single electric bulb at the top of wooden stairs leading to the house above.

'Hola negro,' called a figure on the top step.

Charlie at first blinded by the light, recognised one the abductors. As he started for the stairs a bottle of water landed at his feet and the man withdrew, slamming the door. The light was left on. Locks or bolts operated noisily.

Later that evening, at the Community College, Ruben noticed that Charlie had not returned to the student residence. He assumed that he and Maria were still together. Although pleased that his sister had found a nice guy like Charlie, he wished he could find a girlfriend for himself. The following day Ruben was surprised to find Charlie had not returned from the evening before. His imagination took over. He knew his sister was close to Charlie but this was carrying things a bit far. He was worried as to what his parents would say if they found out. Colour prejudice ran deep in Ecuador's white families, just as much as in all but their most liberal American counterparts. For your daughter to be seeing a black man was unthinkable, let alone spending a night together. Ruben phoned the student residence at his sister's college. It transpired that Maria had left her dorm early the previous day, saying to her friends that she was meeting Charlie after the afternoon basketball game. But she had not reappeared. Had she run away with Charlie? It seemed unlikely and completely out of character for both of them. Ruben was starting to worry. He dialled 911 to report Maria missing.

Sitting in his squad car, Officer Seth Weschler of Osterley Police took a call. 'Got a missing person report,' crackled the radio.

He took the details down and took off for Ursuline College.

Damn, he thought. The girl's spent the night with her boyfriend I bet. She'll turn up any moment, and I'll miss my coffee break.

At the college he was met by the warden's wife, known by the girls as 'the Dragon.' The Dragon was not amused thinking along the same lines as Officer Weschler. She did mention that she had had a call earlier the day before from a man with a Latin accent. He claimed to be a relative and wanted to confirm that Maria attended the college, as he was planning to visit her. The Dragon also had had a call from Maria's concerned brother.

'Does she have a boyfriend?' asked the cop.

'Yes, an African student at the Community College, called Charlie I'm told.'

With still no appearance from Maria, it was now confirmed that Charlie was also missing. The case was passed to Osterley PD's one detective, Ed Mendoza.

Jack Gower had been Chief of Police in Osterley for the past twelve years. Due to retire next year he just wanted a quiet life. Once a keen young cop, now overweight and out of shape, he spent most of his days in his office dealing with routine paperwork. Osterley was a quiet town with few problems; some drunkenness on Saturday nights, an occasional burglary, car accidents, but nothing by way of big challenges to the Police Department. Detective Mendoza reported to his boss.

'Chief, I've interviewed everybody who knew the girl. The boyfriend comes from New Guinea, wherever that is. They were last seen together outside Osterley Stadium. We don't even know if there's been a crime, maybe she's just got tired of Osterley and ran away with the boy and they are shacked up somewhere. She's a grown woman. Don't think there's anything we can do.'

The Chief scratched his nose.

'Tell the school and the brother we are looking into it.'

Ruben was becoming increasingly frustrated at police inaction. He could only think it was something to do with his father. From a young age he had been aware that his father's importance in Ecuador's political life generated enemies. His home country was riven with intrigue and conflict between the ruling right-wing politicians and communist activists in the labour unions and universities. The American government was violently anti-communist and the CIA was employing all manner of underhand tactics to attack communist sympathisers. He decided to call his father to say his sister was missing.

Sitting in his office in Quito, Ecuador's capital having just received a call from his son, Maria's father was handed a note by an aide. It simply said he was to order the release of two high-ranking communist party members from Quito's high-security jail. They had previously been arrested on multiple charges, including conspiracy to overthrow the government. The note told him to cooperate. Failure to do so within twenty-four hours would result in him never seeing Maria again. The source of the note was unknown and untraceable. He directed his secretary to call the US Ambassador. He also called for his head of security, an obsequious Señor Chiriboga. He explained the situation.

'I suggest we release the communists and then follow them wherever they go. They will have to contact their compatriots in the US to order the release of your daughter and we will allow this and then rearrest them once we know she is safe. Give me authority to release them,' Chiriboga purred.

Minister Littuma weighed the situation. He loved Maria, as would any father. He saw little alternative to Chiriboga's plan but did not underestimate his adversaries. Ruben had mentioned a boyfriend who had also disappeared. Perhaps he was one of Maria's abductors. Whatever the outcome, if the plan failed and the communists were not recaptured, he dared not guess the consequences. He also had to tell his wife. She had opposed him over the idea of Maria going to America. Her reaction to this situation was beyond his imagination. He would not tell her for the moment. How could he be sure that Maria would be released anyway?

Chiriboga interrupted his reverie. 'Excuse me, Minister, but what are your instructions?'

'If we release them and you lose them, to put it mildly, your career and mine will be over. We will wait for a few hours to see if the FBI can find Maria. I will call you later.'

That same day, Police Chief Gower was dozing at his desk, having contemplated a quiet afternoon when his secretary buzzed.

'A call from the FBI in Washington on line two,' she announced.

Jolted from his postprandial torpor, he grabbed the phone. Clearing his throat and trying to sound alert and business-like, he said.

'Chief Gower.'

'Deputy Director Hammersley, FBI. How's your investigation of the Maria Littuma kidnapping going, Chief?' growled the voice from DC.

The chief didn't know he was investigating a kidnapping. He took a moment or two to connect it with Detective Mendoza's report that morning. He replied trying to sound confident.

'We're working hard on it sir, I've got my best men on the case. We're following leads as we speak.'

'Good,' growled the reply. 'I'm sending two agents down today. Also, our Columbus office will be contacting you to provide any help or further manpower you might need. Chief, the case has attention at high levels here in DC and needs resolving quickly.'

'Got it, sir. I'm sure we'll soon have it nailed down.'

The phone clicked off at the other end. Chief Gower wished he hadn't said that as he buzzed his secretary.

'Get Mendoza in here. Now!'

Ruben was surprised to receive a visit from Detective Mendoza to inform him that the full force of American justice had been mobilised to find Maria who had been kidnapped by some communist gang. Mendoza also wanted more information about Charlie.

That evening, two large men, together with Detective Mendoza, presented themselves at the Community College asking for Ruben. Flashing badges, they gathered yet another statement then left to visit Maria's college and interview her friends. Unknown to Ruben, agents were visiting Ohio airport car-rental companies for lists of recent renters. Any with Latin names would be investigated. Immigration lists of recent arrivals with Ecuadorian passports were also being scrutinised.

CHAPTER 19

His head still throbbing some hours later, Charlie started to calm down and think how he might escape and find Maria. He was still alive and so far, it didn't seem as if these people wanted to harm him. He drank some water then explored his surroundings. The basement was almost empty, no tools or implements with which to force the door. He found a derelict washing machine, a sack of rags, empty paint cans and some odds and ends that looked like the typical remains of building maintenance and assorted junk. Nothing immediately useful, although he desperately needed a toilet. Among the trash, to his relief, he found a metal bucket.

He finished the water then sat on the floor trying to work out why he and Maria should be attacked and abducted. Presumably Maria was nearby. He needed an escape plan.

With his interest in Maria, he had already been researching Ecuador. He had learnt it was politically unstable. Popularly described as a banana republic, it suffered frequent revolutions and changes of president. Ruben had explained upheavals and occasional violence was a feature of political life in Ecuador. In America, violence against innocent persons usually occurred only in big cities with robbery as a motive. Charlie was poor and as far he knew Maria did not carry much money with her. He was only just starting to comprehend the differences between various political ideologies. Political parties just did not exist in PNG. From the exchanges in Spanish when they were captured, he assumed this situation had a connection with Maria's important father. He found it hard to believe that it could give rise to the kidnap of an innocent eighteen-year-old girl. In PNG wars happened and occasionally people died but these were rare tribal affairs and never against individuals. It was all quite beyond his comprehension.

Charlie knew he had to escape from these people, find Maria and take her to safety. Casting his eyes once more over the basement's junk, an idea came to him. The washing machine had what he needed for his purposes. It had a mains power cable which with some difficulty, he wrenched free. He imagined he was trapping an animal by getting it to fall into a pit dug in its path. The stairs were the animal's path and the basement was the pit. At two steps below the top, he tightly secured the cable to run across the stair just above ankle height. He armed himself with a broken broom handle and took out the light bulb at the top of the stairs. Would the animal see the cable? He started making as much noise as possible, banging the side of the washing machine with his broom handle. Armed with his weapon the hunter crouched. The door to the basement opened and the same man as before appeared at the top of the stairs. Charlie hid from view under the stairs and groaned as if in pain.

'Que pasa, negro?' called the man.

Charlie kept groaning. The man started to descend then yelled some obscenity before crashing to the floor below. Charlie was upon him immediately and delivered a hard blow to his head. The man was motionless but still breathing. Charlie hesitated. In a PNG forest he would not have hesitated to kill an enemy, particularly one who had kidnapped his mate. But something made him pause and leave the unconscious man, stepping over him for the stairs. Only later did he wonder at this hesitation at not killing his enemy. Back at home this would have been an instinctive act, almost a duty to his tribe. Killing a white man was something outside the bounds of his culture, almost unimaginable.

Cautiously Charlie ascended the basement stairs. The house seemed deserted. There were no voices, no sounds. He looked out of the front of the building. There was no car. He explored the house and found nobody although there was one locked door. Maria had been asleep on the mattress when awoken by the rattling of the doorknob and hearing her name called out. Charlie's voice was unmistakeable.

Maria joyfully responded. Charlie repeatedly threw himself at the door until the frame splintered. After a quick embrace the pair ran up the track from the house until they reached the main highway. Several vehicles passed them until a friendly black truck driver stopped on his way to Columbus dropping them at a police station. They soon found themselves in a government office, answering a barrage of questions from serious men in dark suits.

Two hours later, before Chiriboga's plan could be put into effect, Maria's father received a call from the US Ambassador to the effect that his daughter had been rescued and was safe under the protection of the FBI.

CHAPTER 20

A tearful Maria was speaking by phone with her father. She was able to tell him of her dramatic rescue by a young student named Charlie.

'I must meet this young man and thank him personally for saving my precious daughter,' said her equally emotional father. 'I had never thought that you would be in danger from our country's enemies in America. I must now consider if I want you and your brother to stay there.'

'But Papa, Ruben and I are very happy here. One of the federal agents here tells me they have located these men and are about to arrest them.'

Her father hesitated, he needed to be convinced of the security of his children.

'We shall see,' he said.

After the call, he ordered Chiriboga to fly to the US to report on future security arrangements for Ruben and

Maria which if unsatisfactory, would require them to return home without delay.

Two weeks later from his hotel in Columbus, Chiriboga had a long phone call with Minister Littuma.

'Sir, I have done as you have instructed. The FBI here is quite positive they've arrested all the members of the communist cell responsible for Señorita Littuma's abduction. They see no repeat of the episode, although have detailed regular checks on all Latins in the state who might be sympathisers. In fact, the whole business surprised them and some FBI heads rolled as a result. I have interviewed the local police who are unimpressive, but they maintain they will now keep a close eye out for your children. Having said that, I would not employ the local police Chief except maybe as a car park attendant. You get the picture. I do not think you need to worry about their safety here. As instructed, I rewarded Maria's young rescuer with money. Although he is poor, he refused, but I kept insisting until he accepted with great reluctance. I judge him to be very decent. Having said that, there doesn't appear to be any further threats, but there might be another reason for you to bring Maria home. The young man who saved her is more than just a friend, he is a boyfriend and a pretty serious one at that. His name is Charlie Kikira – intelligent, and a very pleasant personality. He is from Papua New Guinea and is coloured. He has dark skin with tightly curled hair. I am not sure if you would approve of their relationship. Should he visit our country, I think he would find it difficult to be accepted in our society.'

Maria's father did not respond immediately. His mind was turning over Chiriboga's news. Although shocked that his precious girl had a black boyfriend, he was of a slightly more liberal disposition than his wife. He could only imagine the hysterics that news would produce. Chiriboga was right, this Charlie would never be accepted either by his wife or the entrenched racism of the upper echelons of Ecuadorian society. Maria would have to come home.

'Thank you, Señor Chiriboga. You've done well. I will deal with the matter from now on.'

On their return to Osterley, Charlie and Maria were greeted as celebrities. Nothing so sensational had ever happened in the town. The whole episode was headlines with pictures in the Osterley Citizen and even two columns in the Columbus Dispatch. Charlie was the hero of the moment and readers not only read of the adventure but also the background of Papua New Guinea, previously unknown to most of them. In interview Chief Gower managed to convey an impression of having played a leading role in the whole affair. Charlie with his distinctive appearance, was now recognised whenever he ventured into the town. He became totally embarrassed, having only done in his eyes what anybody in his tribe would have. He wondered what had happened to the man that he had almost killed, learning later that he had lived to be arrested. Another consequence of the affair was that Charlie suffered some remorse at not having been able to protect Maria from the abduction. He had seen advertised a course in unarmed combat conducted by an ex-US Marine. He would investigate and sign up.

The furore started to die down when, two weeks later he found Maria in a flood of tears.

'I hate my father,' Maria cried. 'He is ordering me to return home. He says it is not safe for me here and yet he is allowing Ruben to stay.'

Charlie was equally devastated. Maria had become part of his life. He had started to fantasise picturing a life together in PNG, even to the point of asking her if she would return with him when their studies were complete. He had never voiced these thoughts except to himself or even considered whether they were realistic.

I want to be with you Charlie. What can we do?'

He tried to collect his thoughts. In his society, a woman had to obey her father at all times until she married. She then had to obey her husband. A woman was subservient to the dominant male in her life, without question.

'When I have finished my studies in America, I will come to Ecuador to ask your father if I can marry you,' he said simply.

This evoked a further flood of tears. Charlie too was becoming moist-eyed. Two days later, Maria left for Ecuador with a security escort sent by her father. Charlie would never see her again.

Ruben secretly relieved at the turn of events, tried to cheer up his inconsolable friend. His relief stemmed from the certain knowledge of the complications that would have followed if his sister and Charlie became a permanent item. Over the following months, Charlie was eventually persuaded to accompany Ruben to dances and social events at Ursuline College. Charlie was now well-known at the college and attractive to several of the girls there. Despite their unsubtle overtures and Ruben's encouragement he did not become involved. His torch for Maria was still shining brightly. Ruben had meanwhile acquired an American girlfriend by the name of Lucy. Charlie would often make up a foursome with one of Lucy's friends when he would remain polite but distant company. Maxime similarly tried to cheer up his friend by suggesting outings. On one such outing, Charlie did find a distraction, which was to attend an NAACP rally in Chicago led by the Reverend Martin Luther King. Standing in a huge crowd he was spellbound by King's oratory speaking of a 'dawn of new hope for the negro'.

Would black people the world over ever see the Reverend King's visions, Charlie asked himself. It seemed a distant hope. The longer he was in America the more his disenchantment grew.

Chapter 21

The following month Charlie was summoned as a witness in the trial of the three men who had abducted him and Maria. Conducted by a bailiff into the Columbus courtroom, he was awed by its scale and atmosphere of formality. The whole room from the black-robed judge, lawyers, jurors and public stared at the young black man as he entered. The prosecuting lawyer approached the witness box. A tall man in an immaculate dark suit gave Charlie a friendly smile displaying a set of teeth reminding Charlie of a billboard advertisement for toothpaste.

Charlie's views on religion caused him to hesitate before placing his hand on a Bible and swearing to tell the truth. He confirmed his name and his presence on the day of the abduction. He identified the men in the dock as his abductors.

'Mr Kikira, please tell the court exactly what happened on the day of your abduction.'

This elicited an objection by the defence that the question presupposed that abduction had taken place. The prosecutor repeated the question and just inserted the word 'alleged' before 'abduction.' Charlie gave a simple account of the events. It seemed to him there was little more to say. His questioner still decided to have every small detail described to the court, together with a description of the whole episode up to the time he and Maria escaped.

The defence lawyer, a swarthy man with piercing eyes was also dark-suited like his opposite number. Charlie noticed that all the lawyers and their assistants at the front of the court wore dark suits. Maybe it was a kind of uniform for the legal profession. The man struggled to find any alternative version of events and tried to infer that it was not an abduction or kidnapping, both very serious federal offences.

'Mr Kikira, how long have you lived in the United States?'

'About eighteen months, sir.'

'Is English your native tongue?'

'No sir. My native tongue is spoken in the Tori village in Papua New Guinea.'

'My clients are accused of abduction and kidnapping; do you know the meaning of those terms?'

'Yes sir, they mean the taking of a person against their will, usually for ransom.'

'Were you taken for ransom?'

'I certainly was taken against my will. They had to hit me on the head to make me go with them.'

There was a titter of laughter from the spectators. The

judge tried not to smile as he rapped his gavel and ordered silence.

'My friend Miss Littuma was taken for some kind of ransom. I think the court has heard her written statement.'

'Mr Kikira, you are here to answer my questions, not to make voluntary statements. Please just answer my questions.'

It all seemed a bit pointless to Charlie as the defence probed with further questions which just seemed aimed at discrediting Charlie and Maria's statements. Eventually the defending lawyer realised he was going nowhere and Charlie was excused from any further questions. Fascinated by the whole process, Charlie left and sat in the public gallery. Then the FBI agents and Osterley Police Chief Gower were questioned.

Finally, both lawyers summed up before the jury retired.

During the trial Charlie started to reflect on the motives of the three men in the dock. Their leader was allowed to make a statement. He seemed to be an intelligent, educated man who spoke with great passion. If he was to be believed, Charlie was disturbed to hear of the treatment of political prisoners and the harsh arbitrary justice meted out by the Ecuadorian authorities. Up to that point his knowledge of Ecuador was mostly founded on what he had learnt from Ruben and Maria. He realised that Maria's father must have been compliant with these injustices. Charlie also started to appreciate that the United States connived with Ecuador to suppress freedom of speech. Despite his experiences at their hands, he started to feel sympathy for his abductors. The jury returned half an hour later to find the defendants guilty on all charges. The judge adjourned the hearing until the following day for sentencing. Kidnapping is viewed as a serious offence by the federal authorities, carrying a maximum of a life sentence. Charlie subsequently learned that this penalty was applied to his kidnappers.

CHAPTER 22

At the end of his second year at Osterley Community College, Charlie sat for his Scholastic Aptitude Test, or SAT exam. He was a diligent student who found the tests straightforward. His results found him with well above average marks.

'Hey Charlie, how did you do in the SATs?' asked his friend Ruben on the morning the examination results came through.

'I did OK in all three sections. Guess I could go to university now. But I really don't want to. You know all I want to do now is to go home. Maxime is happy too. How did you do?'

Ruben pulled a face. 'I bombed in math. Guess I'll have to take it again to get into a decent college. My Dad's not going to be too happy. Let's go into town, I want to drown my sorrows.'

Charlie demurred. 'Thanks, but I've got stuff to do.'

He went to his room as he needed to think how he was going to tell everybody that he was going to leave America and return home to PNG.

There were aspects of America that greatly troubled him. He had come to realise that the embedded prejudice against black people existed in large sections of the population. Even here in the more liberal north he found prejudice. Once he overheard somebody referring to him as 'that nigger'. He had been ignored in a shop as he waited to be served. He and Maria went into a restaurant and were refused service, being told it was full when it clearly wasn't. He had read that in the South there were marches protesting the inequality that existed in areas of housing, education, jobs and just about every area of life. He had been mostly isolated from this in the more liberal, multicultural atmosphere of the college.

The time had come to discuss his future with Mr Nevern who was paying for everything. Charlie also wanted to talk with Tom Paul. Tom after all was the reason he was here in America. From time to time, he had meetings with Mary Holden. He had told her his misgivings about continuing his education in America. She sympathised but asked him to reconsider after discussing his decision with his sponsor. He had also confided in her his distress at Maria's departure and found a calming and sympathetic ear. She knew that as time passed the passion would cool and cease to dominate Charlie's life. She knew the truth in the old adage that, 'Love feeds on the presence of the beloved.'

Charlie's unexpected windfall from Minister Littuma enabled him to travel to Washington DC to see Tom before his next meeting with Mr Nevern. He confidently negotiated his travel, still amazed by the facility with which the population seemed to be constantly on the move. Tom met him at Washington Dulles airport and had secured accommodation for his friend near his current posting at Andrews Air Force Base. Tom immediately noticed the confidence displayed by Charlie in his surroundings in contrast to the overawed young man two years previously.

The two friends sat in a café talking over coffee. Charlie had acquired a taste for coffee since arriving in America. He somehow associated coffee with Maria, recalling the many hours they spent together in their favourite coffee shop in Osterley. He still missed her and felt a pang of nostalgia.

'You know, Tom,' Charlie started, 'I don't want to stay in America any longer. I've had an interesting time, although with ups and downs, but I don't see anything I can take back to benefit PNG. In particular I hate the racism here. Change may be inevitable, but I want my country to hold back from so-called development as long as possible. All I see here are people with their minds seemingly centred on acquiring money and what to spend it on. And once acquired, is it making them any happier? Happiness comes surely from having close friends and family and feeling a sense of belonging, like being part of a tribe in my country.'

Tom had already learnt of his friend's affair with Maria and her departure. Charlie's sadness was still visible and Tom felt this was possibly something to do with his negative feelings, wishing to put things behind him by going home to PNG.

'Charlie I quite understand everything you are saying and maybe if I were in your shoes I would feel the same. Though please realise how far you have come. Others will follow, but at this time you are the only person from your country to achieve your level of education. And there is so much more you can achieve for PNG. Learn more before you go back. Only a privileged few will have open to them the possibility to be in the rank of a professional teacher, doctor, lawyer or whatever you choose now. As such you will command much respect and influence when you go back and people will look up to you. You will be a force for good. As a true friend I implore you to stay to complete your studies at one of our wonderful universities.'

Charlie listened in silence. Although he had respect and affection for Tom, his negative feelings about America remained.

A few days later after Charlie had returned to Osterley, he again found himself sitting opposite Mr Nevern.

'Charlie, I congratulate you on your successes in your two academic years here at Osterley. What are your plans now? I can tell you that the Foundation will be more than happy to fund further study here at one of our fine institutions.'

Both before and since returning from Washington and listening to Tom on the subject, Charlie had spent many hours pondering this question.

Ever polite, Charlie replied, 'Firstly sir, I thank you for the generosity of the Foundation in helping me. I feel ungrateful to sit here and criticise America, but I know I'd never feel I belong here. Sometimes I have found certain people judge me because of the colour of my skin. I see the looks I get in the street and experience the reception I get in stores. I know this would be an even bigger problem if I lived in the South.'

Nevern, not entirely surprised at Charlie's response, was embarrassed at trying to defend his country. Wanting to encourage him to stay, he replied after a silence, 'I cannot defend the racial prejudice that exists here and the many problems that materialism and greed bring with them. I have never expected you to stay here after completing your education. Think of what you can do for Papua New Guinea and the respect you will have when you return home. I am not saying your ego needs this, but the recognition of your achievement should help you be in a position where you can help your country. OK, you have seen the worst that economic success brings but, in a way, you will have an awareness of its dangers. As a person of influence, perhaps you will be able to help avert some of these negative consequences.'

Charlie realised that the conversation was following similar lines to his meeting with Tom.

'Sir, I feel a strong urge to return home and resume life with my tribe. I think you call this homesickness, even after two years. But I do know if I did this, I would miss the stimulation offered by life here. I had made up my mind to return but I suppose I am hesitating.'

This was not the reply Nevern was expecting.

'So, have you considered the alternative to returning home?'

Charlie hesitated. He wanted to see more of the country, but could not countenance be spending another three years here before returning home. He had started to hate some aspects of life in America. He had been affected by knowing the injustice directed towards its black citizens. He was starting to feel militant on their behalf.

'Not really, sir. I have to think about it.'

'Charlie let us meet again before the end of this semester and we will discuss this.'

Nevern was sitting with Mary Holden and John Dyment at their joint annual review of Valodis Foundation students at the college. Eventually it was Charlie's turn to be discussed. His grades and all the standard topics were quickly covered. Nevern spoke first.

'If I may start, Charlie is one of the most impressive Valodis-sponsored students I have had the pleasure of reviewing. Having said that, he is proving most difficult to convince that he should stay in the US after leaving Osterley. Some of his fellows even enquire if they could stay permanently, having been seduced by the apparently easy materialistic existence. Unlike them, Charlie has become disenchanted with our country. He is not convinced that holding an American university degree will be particularly helpful to his people when he returns. He quite understands that vocational training would be helpful, but he has no interest in being a doctor, teacher, engineer or studying a practical vocation. He has a passing interest in law but sees our system as overly complicated and cannot relate that in any way to Papua New Guinea. At the moment he is focussed on returning there.'

Mary Holden related her many meetings with Charlie since his arrival at Osterley.

'I have grown to admire his exceptional insight for a young man of his age. Looking far ahead, I think he would make a wonderful ambassador for his country. He has a thirst for learning about other countries and cultures. Although not much travelled he has an impressive world view. I think he gained this at an early age, living with his adoptive Australian family. Another thing I have learnt is that he has an acute sense of injustice. We know he has attended a Malcom X meeting and is following the desegregation campaign of Martin Luther King. He has been shocked by the level of bigotry in our society. Also, from his exposure to the harsh sentencing of some individuals who had fallen out of favour with their country's regime, he has a view, which I happen to share, that the US government itself is totally intolerant of ideologies not aligned with its own—'

John Dyment noisily cleared his throat and interrupted.

'Mary, I think we are starting to get away from the point of the discussion, which is to advise Mr Nevern of our views on the best next steps for Charlie in an educational sense.'

Mary Holden had been warming to her theme. She frequently had spirited political discussions with Mr Dyment, who had somewhat divergent views to her own. Deferring to him – who after all, approved her invoices – she continued,

'I have to admit some professional bias here, but I believe Charlie would benefit from some training in psychology. He is always interested in people and often instinctively tries to deduce motives from their behaviour. If he is to be a future leader in his country, what better qualification could he have but to understand the agendas of those around him, not to mention the aspirations of his people?'

'So how do we convince him to stay for a further three years for his Bachelor's? Does he even need a degree at home where he is probably already the best-educated citizen?' asked Dyment.

The discussion of Charlie's future went on for another hour. It was agreed that Mary Holden had the respect and confidence of Charlie and should try to influence him into staying for at least one more year, possibly studying either psychology or political science. Nevern had influential contacts at Stanford, his alma mater. They would almost certainly agree to Charlie attending foundation courses in these subjects, hoping that his taste for university life at one of the country's foremost universities would tempt him to complete a degree. Nevern felt sure this was politically essential in PNG for Charlie's prestige and influence in the future, not to mention his personal development.

On his flight back to Washington, Nevern yet again reflected on Charlie's situation asking himself if the work of the Valodis Foundation was really advancing the sum of human happiness. His thinking had a recurring theme. Would it not have been better if countries such as PNG had been left alone to pursue their traditional lives? Of course, the rot had already been started centuries ago by early colonialists. There was little he could do to stem the tide of another form of colonialism imposing damaging cultural change on an innocent people. Each time he had these thoughts, he rationalised his misgivings by telling himself he could only endeavour to do his best for the likes of Charlie and other protégés of the Foundation.

Two days later after his arrival back at his office, he took a call from Mary Holden.

'I have had a long meeting with Charlie and he has agreed to spend one more year over here before returning home. He took a lot of convincing. We discussed a choice of subject and, of the various options, a foundation course majoring in psychology was his choice. Of secondary subjects he wants to see what might be on offer. He would like to see some of the country before starting at university.'

Nevern thanked Mrs Holden profusely. He would look up his contacts at Stanford.

CHAPTER 23

From the bus window, the Kentucky countryside seemed to go on forever. There were about another two hours before Charlie would reach Nashville. Mr Nevern had offered to send him an air ticket to San Francisco but he'd asked to go by bus so he could see some more of America on his way to Stanford. Listening to the radio in his room in Osterley, Charlie had started to acquire a taste for American music, particularly country and Dixieland jazz. He and Maria had been to dances at the college students' club and, to the amusement of her brother and others, he had attempted to adapt a PNG 'sing-sing' dance to country music beats. Nashville, the home of country music was a definite choice as a first stop on his American tour.

He had been advised to join the YMCA as a cheap accommodation choice and one where a person of colour would be admitted. Finding somewhere to stay would always be a problem when travelling in the American South. Someone gave him a copy of the Green Book, a guide to services and places relatively friendly to black Americans, for whom Charlie was usually mistaken. He was warned by everybody that accommodation would be an increasing problem the further south he travelled. The Green Book reassured him that Nashville's YMCA would be black friendly.

Eventually, he climbed down from the Greyhound bus at their central depot and found his way to the nearest YMCA. Here he received a slightly guarded welcome from the very large white woman in reception. Since his arrival in America, he was getting used to seeing very fat people but until now had not had to deal with one at close quarters.

'Six bucks a day in advance. You gonna be here long?' she asked. Her chins wobbled as she spoke.

'Just two days ma'am,' he replied with his usual disarming smile.

He sensed that she hoped he wouldn't be staying very long. Reading the ledger upside down in front of her massive bosom he could see that there were very few guests at the moment.

He knew from his reading that there had been a Civil Rights Act in 1875 which outlawed discrimination against black Americans in public accommodations and transportation. In practice this had been largely ignored with many states and cities passing local statutes. These so-called Jim Crow laws effectively enforced segregation. Jim Crow was a mythical black slave who figured in a popular music hall act early in the previous century.

These laws allowed 'separate but equal' accommodations, which at first sight appeared constitutional. In practice however, facilities for blacks were anything but equal. Charlie wondered if his cramped and unclean room in an annexe at the back of the building was reserved for black travellers.

Later over a sandwich in a nearby café, he met a friendly white student also staying at the 'Y', looking for work during the summer recess. Josh was as blond as Charlie was black. His physical appearance and laid-back manner reminded Charlie of Bruce Petersen at Tori's patrol office.

'So Charlie, what are you doing in Nashville?'

'I'm on my way to Stanford for my first year.'

'Where are you from? You sound like a Brit.'

Charlie briefly told his story, adding that he was drawn to Nashville's music scene.

He had fallen on his feet meeting Josh who immediately took to this man from PNG. From Washington DC and a big country music fan, Josh was hoping to find employment at one of Nashville's one hundred-odd music venues for the next two months. He had a car and already knew his way around the city and its high spots. He said he normally wouldn't be staying at a 'Y', which was little more than a place for down and outs, but it was cheap and at the moment he was short of cash.

'OK Charlie let's check out some places. One of the best downtown honky-tonk bars is Tootsies. Tootsie Bess, the owner, will be there tonight and I want to see if she'll hire me. We can stop and have a coupl'a beers there anyway.'

Charlie assented and for the next two days followed his new friend around the city's music haunts. Each night they would arrive back at the YMCA slightly the worse for wear, each bar visited often entailed downing more than 'a coupl'a beers'. Charlie was not accustomed to alcohol in such copious amounts and Josh was well under the influence during each day's driving. It seemed a miracle that they had not crashed or been arrested. Neither Ms Bess nor any of the other bar owners seemed to need Josh as a potential bartender, waiter or even dish-washer. Nonetheless the pair had enjoyed the music at the various bars, not to mention chatting up unattached girls. Charlie frequently noticed that his was the only black face among the bars' patrons. He occasionally caught looks of hostile, white male faces.

'Take no notice Charlie,' said his friend. 'They are just bigots – too stupid to cause trouble.'

Many girls were attracted to Charlie and had he been staying in Nashville for longer, there evidently would have been great potential for dates. His earlier shyness when first at Osterley had worn off and he was now totally at ease with the opposite sex. His depression at parting from Maria was starting to lift. PNG, the Tori tribe and Beida seemed to be on another planet.

On his third day and with a sore head, Charlie bid Josh farewell and after pledges of keeping in touch, he made his way to the Greyhound terminal for his southbound bus to New Orleans.

The journey was scheduled to take thirteen hours with stops for bus changes, passengers and refreshment breaks. He had his Green Book and a history of the Civil War to keep his mind occupied. He also had some preliminary reading sent to him by Stanford's psychology faculty. He looked at his map and wondered if he might stop at Birmingham in Alabama, half way to New Orleans. Consulting his Green Book, he found three potential places to stay, one of which had the promising name of Fraternal Hotel.

Getting off the bus he asked a passing white man, 'Excuse me, sir, could you direct me to Fourth Avenue?' – the street address of Charlie's hotel.

The man stopped, frowning, and stared open-mouthed as if surprised by some strange and unpleasant event. He quickly turned and strode off without a word.

Charlie was by now used to cool reactions from white people to his presence but this surpassed anything so far. He spotted a black woman standing on the opposite side of the road. He crossed over and repeated his question to the motherly looking lady in a colourful headscarf.

'You got a two-hour walk 'bout six miles to other side of town. Where you f'om?' was the friendly response.

Charlie had long found not to say Papua New Guinea to this frequent question. He might as well have said the moon.

'I am living in Ohio, but my home is near Australia.'

'You staying long in Birmingham?'

'Just a couple of days, my Green Book says there is a Fraternal Hotel there that takes black people.'

'That's true but you kin stay with me an' my family, if you want?'

Her simple hospitality in contrast to the reception he had experienced a few moments earlier restored Charlie's spirits.

'I'd like that very much, thank you.'

He learnt that his new friend was called Martha and that she was going home from her job as a cleaner in nearby offices. Her husband, Clement, had a gardening business working at the homes of wealthy white clients. He would be along shortly.

Charlie found himself on the back of a pickup among a pile of garden rubbish and tree branches. After about twenty minutes they arrived at a small house in what Charlie learnt was an exclusively black neighbourhood.

He was to find out that Birmingham was probably the most segregated city in the USA. Martha, Clement and their children lived in the middle of black Birmingham's area of social, business and cultural life.

That evening he listened to the family as they recounted their experience of life in Birmingham. It seemed as if the city and its officials were totally complicit in retaining the status quo. The all-white police force took little or no action in investigating abuses of the city's black population which included killings by the Ku Klux Klan. Frequent bombings of black homes and businesses resulted in some calling the city 'Bombingham'.

A horrified Charlie decided then and there to cut short his stay in the city and asked Clement to drop him off at the Greyhound terminal the following day. Perhaps he should have accepted Mr Nevern's offer of air tickets for a direct flight from Ohio to California. A year later he was to read of a KKK bombing of a Baptist Church not far from where he had been staying. This resulted in the deaths of four little girls. Perhaps he should not have allowed Mrs Holden to talk him into staying another year in this cruel country.

CHAPTER 24

Charlie continued his reading after he boarded the bus for New Orleans. As he was to find out, the Civil War finished around a hundred years ago with over two hundred battles resulting in more than a million deaths and the abolition of slavery. The war did little to end white prejudice against the country's black population, which although illegal was still alive and well in America's south.

'What are you reading, my friend?' asked the friendly young white man sitting at his side on the bus.

Charlie named his book and soon found himself explaining where he came from for the umpteenth time. Conversation developed and it seemed Terry Mason was a student from Tennessee University. He was one of a group of young white activists calling themselves Freedom Riders. Mostly students, they were protesting against segregation on buses by sitting with non-white passengers on routes throughout the southern states. Historically, buses had separate white and coloured sections. The actions of Terry and his colleagues had so enraged white mobs near Anniston, their next stop, that a few months back a bus was attacked and set on fire. Highway patrolmen had intervened by firing in the air, but not before some of the riders were injured. A similar incident had occurred in Montgomery, Alabama.

'These events became national news and the President sent in the National Guard and federal marshals to restore order and enforce the law,' said Terry proudly. 'Soon after, the bus companies removed the separate sections.'

Charlie sat silent. After Birmingham he was appalled once again that this had occurred in a so-called civilised country.

'Where are you staying in New Orleans?' asked Terry.

'In the YMCA I hope, if they take me.'

'Come and stay with my folks, they'd love to have you. The Y is a long way out of town and it's really just a shelter for the homeless. Stay with us and I'll show you around.'

This was the other face of white America, friendly and hospitable. Mr Mason was a newspaper proprietor and as Charlie came to appreciate, liberal minded and something of a rarity in the south. He ended up staying nearly five weeks in New Orleans, much longer than he had planned and for the most unexpected of reasons.

Terry's family comprised his parents, two sisters and an eighty-three-year-old alert grandmother. They were absorbed by Charlie's accounts of his homeland, his tribe and its customs and the events which had led to his being in America.

'This is a wonderful story,' said his host. 'I would like to include it as an article in my paper.'

'Certainly sir, if you think it would be of interest to your readers.' Charlie ever diffident, had never imagined that he could be of interest to anybody.

During his stay, Terry took Charlie on several forays into New Orleans nightlife and music. He found himself excited to be in the birthplace of jazz with its black musicians making sounds that instinctively touched him. All the city's best jazz performers seemed to be black. He had never related to the dominant western musical tradition of following a composer's music precisely. Music to a PNG native had to follow emotion or feeling and was always dominated by improvisation.

During the daytime the two friends toured the city's sights which included several monuments dating back to the Civil War era. Confederate heroes and champions of slavery were much in evidence. Feelings for those days and opposition to the union were clearly still strong – Confederate flags flew everywhere.

On Charlie's third day in the city, Terry's sister Sylvia and his girlfriend Mary accompanied the two men for an evening out together. Sylvia had taken a shine to her brother's new friend. She had been captivated by his accounts of PNG and his exploits. They went to one of the many venues renowned for its jazz. At the end of a great session the group went to eat in a small intimate Greek restaurant and Sylvia sat close to Charlie. Terry's father had instructed his son to pay for everything. He realised Charlie was of limited means and southern hospitality insisted anyway. Although the evening started as a foursome, the group quickly became two couples. As they strolled back to Terry's parked car Sylvia slipped her hand into Charlie's. He did not resist becoming used to American girls often taking the lead in a way alien to a young unmarried Papuan girl.

Four white men on the opposite side of the street were staring.

'Hey nigger and you, white bitch,' came the shout as they crossed the street.

Terry said, 'Let's get out of here,' but it was too late, the men were already upon them and standing menacingly in their path.

Charlie felt a sense of déjà vu as the attack on him and Maria flashed through his mind. The aggressive body language of the men in front of them clearly signalled an attack.

'Nigger, you're gonna get a beating you ain't gonna forget, if you ever wake up that is,' snarled the same one who had shouted across the street and seemed to be the leader. 'And bitch, you are going to regret letting the nigger touch you.'

About the same height as Charlie, the man carried around fifty pounds more weight, although most of it looked like beer gut. The three others were not dissimilar and seemed to follow his threatening pose, arms hanging at their sides with clenched fists. Terry was of slight build and although squaring up with Charlie, did not look a particular match for their aggressors.

'These guys are just a bunch of idiots, Charlie. Let's make them regret this,' he said, somewhat unconvincingly.

Although he had never expected to put his lessons into practice, Charlie had been an apt pupil of his unarmed combat tutor in Osterley. The words of ex-Marine Sergeant Owen came to him, 'Sometimes it's better to run than fight, but if you need to, take the fight to the enemy and defend by attacking.' There was nowhere to run. Charlie also remembered his tutor's words in the Osterley gym, 'Keep moving, keep moving.'

The girls stood by their men.

'Run ladies,' said Terry. 'Go back inside the restaurant – use their phone and call the police.'

Before the girls could run, one of the men moved to grab Sylvia. This put him within kicking distance of Charlie who did just that, delivering his hardest to the assailant's crotch. The man went down gasping, doubled with pain. Sergeant Owen would have been proud. The normally mild Charlie was now enraged – he was facing an attack by the Hulwari on the Tori trying to kill them and steal their women. Tribal honour was at stake. He would be merciless and fight to the death.

Taking the fight to them he rushed the men, lashing out at the leader although landing only a glancing blow and receiving a painful punch to the kidneys in return. Meanwhile, with great presence of mind, Terry had picked up an empty Coke bottle from the gutter and joined the fray, hitting one of the attackers hard on the side of the head and suffering a hard right to his face from another. Although in pain from the kidney punch Charlie found himself facing the gang's leader and gave him a full-on head butt to the bridge of the nose. Pulled to the ground from behind Charlie fell heavily on top of Terry, lying there with blood pouring from his broken nose. He then collected a rib-breaking kick before one of the assailants punched him in the side – only later did he find out that he had been stabbed. At that point he lost consciousness. The last thing he heard was the girls' screams mixed with the sound of sirens.

He awoke later in hospital to find Terry's father and Sylvia sitting anxiously at his side. He was in much pain from the stab wound and felt bruised all over. His head throbbed from butting his opponent. He had sustained a skull fracture and broken ribs. It emerged that their assailants had fled before the police arrived. Apparently they were known to the authorities as troublemakers and one as a Ku Klux Klan member. Charlie was gratified to hear that bystanders had confirmed not only their identities, but the fact that two seemed badly injured. They were bleeding heavily and had to be helped from the scene by their fellow thugs.

Considering the two to one odds Charlie felt that he and his friend had acquitted themselves well. Terry was at home recovering but unable yet to visit the hospital.

'Charlie I am so sorry that this has happened you. I have of course always been aware of the open discrimination in our society but never ever been so exposed to this mindless brutality,' Mr Mason had become quite emotional. 'The doctors here tell me that you are exceptionally lucky to be alive. The knife just missed your vital organs although you did lose much blood. You were first taken to a public hospital where the care standards are not always the highest. I have had you moved here to one of our fine private hospitals. Your doctors tell me you will be here for at least another two weeks. I have taken the whole matter up with the Chief of Police who happens to be an acquaintance. I told him I expect to hear of arrests. There is a report in my paper and there is a leading article calling for a rejection of these bigoted values. I fear this will largely fall on deaf ears but change has to come. Not only were you attacked for your colour, but my Sylvia would have been injured but for your brave defence of her.'

Sylvia spoke. 'Charlie what can I say, you were wonderful and I thank you from the bottom of my heart,' at which she burst into tears.

Charlie was starting to feel embarrassed at all the emotion. He smiled and stayed silent. He knew whatever he said would sound trite, besides which his heavily bruised face made speaking painful. He felt relieved when the visitors left. He wondered what he should tell Mr Nevern who had voiced misgivings about the trip. He regularly wrote to Tom Paul, so word would probably get back. He would write but make light of it. Despite the attack and injuries some reward came from being the hero of the moment. He told himself the look in Sylvia's eyes would surely be enough compensation for any man.

Once again in his life he had become an object of public attention. Assaults of Negro citizens in the city were frequent but rarely reported. However, none were upon a guest of the proprietor of the town's principal newspaper.

Mr Mason's newspaper carried a front-page account of the attack. The banner headline carried the words: 'ATTACK SERIOUSLY INJURES FOREIGN STUDENT', with a picture of a heavily bandaged Charlie. A leading article called for federal law to be enforced, repeal of Louisiana's Jim Crow laws and Christian values to be upheld. Only later did Charlie find out that Reuters had picked up the story, which appeared in some northern papers.

It took three weeks for Charlie's injuries to heal sufficiently for him to be discharged. The Mason family insisted he should stay with them for a time before continuing his journey to California.

'Great to see you back,' said Terry. 'I gather you needed a lot of transfusions. You've got white blood in you now,' he joked.

Apparently, no arrests were made after the affray.

'The police weren't trying too hard,' fumed Mr Mason. 'There are KKK sympathisers in the Department, even at senior levels.'

Charlie enjoyed the attention he was getting both from the family and from Sylvia in particular. He and Sylvia would take walks in a local park, but the intimacy of these occasions was spoilt by an armed bodyguard who followed them at the insistence of Mr Mason. There were visits from curious colleagues of Mr Mason, neighbours and the president of the local NAACP chapter.

A week after leaving hospital Charlie announced a desire to resume his journey westward. With invitations to return and pledges of eternal friendship he bade farewell to the family and a tearful Sylvia. Even Grandma Mason looked ready to cry. Terry drove him to the downtown Greyhound terminal.

'Goodbye my friend, take care of yourself. Sit in the back of the bus.' Terry laughed as they hugged.

CHAPTER 25

Charlie had studied maps of the South and read about cities that looked interesting. He planned his next stop on his bus journey to California. This would take to him to Texas. He had chosen San Antonio to visit as it was there that he could visit the Alamo. He learned that it had become almost a place of pilgrimage for many Americans, symbolising pride and sacrifice in a fight for freedom. These were strange ideas for Charlie from a country that had no concepts of nationhood. A man might fight to defend his family or his immediate tribe but nobody else. In America national pride seemed to be an important part of life. This was manifested by national or state flags everywhere from car dealers to public buildings. PNG didn't even have a flag. America also seemed to wear its spiritual beliefs on its sleeve. He noticed religious symbols on the many large and small church buildings wherever he went. He even saw biblical quotations on the walls of a café where he managed to get served.

After the Greyhound bus had delivered him to San Antonio, Charlie again met the full force of southern attitudes.

'Excuse me sir, how do I get to Schnabel Park? Is there a bus service?' he politely asked a white clerk behind the Greyhound counter.

'Nigger, you got legs – you walk,' snapped the clerk.

He arrived at the YMCA in Schnabel Park. It was now dark after walking for two hours. There he had an even more uncompromising encounter than at the bus terminal. As he walked into the reception area, the woman there simply got up and pulled down a blind with 'CLOSED' on it. A light switch clicked somewhere, plunging the area into darkness. He walked out, deliberating what to do: walk back to the terminal and wait for the next bus west or find a park bench for the night? There was one thing of which he was sure. He would not remain an hour longer in this country than he had to. He had been wondering for the past two years about what brand of religion really operated here in Christian America. Would Jesus have approved of it? Perhaps Malcolm X had got a point. Blacks in America had the wrong religion – white man's Christianity.

'Hey brother,' said a voice behind him. The voice belonged to an elderly black man who had been sitting on a bench outside the building.

'Son, this here hostel is fo' white folks only.' He had evidently witnessed Charlie's reception. 'I'm waiting fo' my son to pick me up. Y'all can stay at my place if y'all want?'

During the wait for his son the old man introduced himself. His name was John Fraser. He explained he tended the gardens at the 'Y'. His son was a carpenter working on building sites.

A rusting pickup pulled up and a relieved Charlie happily climbed onto the back. The Fraser family lived in a poor area on the fringes of San Antonio.

'Only black folk live around here,' explained Joseph, John's son. A fascinated family listened to Charlie and his story. None of them had ever met a foreigner or even been outside Texas. They had little comprehension of foreign lands. Similar to most of PNG's population, Charlie thought. Hospitable and friendly, they included him in the family evening meal and insisted he use Joseph's brother's bed. Brother Mark would sleep on a couch that night.

The following day he awoke with spirits restored. Lying in bed his thoughts reviewing the events of the last weeks, he found himself once again thinking about the seeming acceptance by black people of being second-class citizens. He knew that movements for change were afoot. He had seen and listened to the Reverend Martin Luther King and Malcolm X, but here in the south there was little evidence of any influence of these charismatic individuals. He asked himself how long, if ever, it would take for this deep-rooted problem to disappear from America.

He still hadn't visited the Alamo. Joseph Fraser dropped him off near the city centre on his way to work at a site where a large hotel was being built. Joseph kindly lent him a bicycle he kept in the back of his pickup. He had learnt to ride on another student's bike in Osterley. Charlie had read that the Alamo had been a mission – a church building. There were three other former missions in San Antonio. These were founded by priests, early settlers who established not only churches but places of teaching agriculture and practical skills. To Charlie it seemed their religious influence remained to this day, permeating American life.

Charlie was disappointed with his visit to this poorly maintained old building. He appreciated the significance of the Alamo but did not find it inspiring or of particular interest. He used Joseph's bicycle to get him to Mission San José which was in better repair and with a small visitor centre that explained the history of the eighteenth-century settlers. Charlie admired the doggedness with which these outposts were maintained by Catholic religious orders to spread Christianity in the native population. As he pedalled back to the Fraser home, he started to think about the activities of missionaries in PNG with the agenda to usurp local spiritual beliefs, a religious thin wedge of colonialism. Charlie's thoughts and resentment about the white man's domination of the world were starting to mature. As often in his quieter moments, his thoughts went back to life in his country. In his mind he drew one of his many comparisons between PNG and America. The big difference racially was the origin of black people here and at home. His people, although subjugated by the whites, had never been slaves. PNG truly belonged to its people who owned their own land and would always be the majority. Gaining independence from the Australians should be straightforward if ever PNG gained any sense of national identity. With these thoughts spinning around in his head he arrived back to the Fraser home.

'Hey Charlie, did you have a good day?' enquired Joseph, home early from work.

'It was good, I learnt a bit more about Texan history. Joseph, as you are accommodating and feeding me, is there anything I can do to help you or the family if I could stay a few more days? Maybe there is some paid work around here - I'd like to pay for my keep'

'Come with me tomorrow to the site where I work. You can speak to my boss.'

Charlie was thinking that it would be interesting to experience everyday life as part of the black population. Until now he had had a privileged life in America, courtesy of the Valodis Foundation. It was another two months before he had to present himself at Stanford University.

Joseph had already thought about this. He been wondering how long his brother Mark was prepared to give up his bed. As if reading his thoughts, Charlie spoke up.

'If I stay, I insist on sleeping on the couch. Mark should have his own bed. As it happens, most of my life I have slept on the floor of a hut. I'm still getting used to lying on a soft surface.'

The next day, Charlie faced Jack Pelosi, a white, barrel-chested, hard-bitten foreman. From under his black ten-gallon hat, he surveyed the young black man standing alongside Joseph.

'What work y'all bin doing before?'

'For two years I was assistant to the patrol officer in charge of the Tori region of Papua New Guinea,' said Charlie proudly, 'I'm here in America to study at university.'

Pelosi tried to grasp the meaning of the reply that he barely understood, it sounded a bit like a Brit speaking. He had been in the US infantry in Germany near the end of the war. His company had fought alongside some British troops while crossing the Rhine. This was the strangest black he had ever come across. What's more, he didn't look as if he would survive for very long carrying bricks, toiling under the blistering Texan sun in temperatures sometime over one hundred degrees.

'So y'all kin read an' write?'

'Yes, sir.'

Pelosi had just fired a white clerk from his site office for incompetence and turning up for late, drunk and barely able to stand. If this boy could deal with the routine paperwork, reports, invoices and workers' payroll it would solve an immediate problem. It probably wouldn't work – he didn't believe blacks were able to do a white man's job but this one looked a bit different. He'd try it for a day.

'I'll try you in the office. If y'all kin do what I want y'all is hired. It rates one fifty an hour.'

This was a generous rate, given that the minimum wage dictated by Federal Government was a dollar ten an hour. Charlie found himself working in an office for the first time in his life. The previous occupant had left a state of chaos; papers and files which demanded to be sorted into a semblance of order. Pelosi told him to compile lists of suppliers, site equipment, numbers of workers onsite and their jobs. He needed this for his weekly report to the site owner.

Charlie shared an office with a white woman whose sole part-time job was to oversee payments to the site workers and suppliers. Her name was Doreen and when she arrived in the office later in the week, she stopped at the door staring in disbelief at a black man seated at the desk opposite hers. Charlie smiling, rose politely.

'Good morning, ma'am. My name is Charlie.'

Doreen's strident, high-pitched voice filled the office.

'What you doing here, boy? dis here is the office. Git outside where you belong. Ah's gonna speak to Mr Pelosi about dis crazy business.'

Her ample figure shook with chins quivering. Before Charlie could speak she stormed out to confront her boss. Pelosi did not have as strong a racial prejudice as his female clerk. War had taught him the qualities of black soldiers and their value to the country.

Charlie was not witness to the confrontation although learnt about it from amused workers who had seen the fireworks.

'Mr Pelosi, what's goin' on here? There's one nigger boy sittin' in the office. I ain't going to work in the same office with any dirty nigger!'

Jack Pelosi, who had faced German mortars and machine-gun fire, was not intimidated by the likes of Doreen. He had already started to tire of her continual complaining about any small matter.

'Miz Brown,' Pelosi drawled. 'This here is one free

country. If y'all don't want this job, y'all is free to find another one.'

Eventually she backed down and wobbled back to the office. She desperately needed her job. It would be difficult to find another part-time, easy, well-paid one like this near to home. Pelosi had already discovered he had made a good decision to employ Charlie in the office. In just two days it had never looked as tidy and well-organised. For her part, Doreen took to door-slamming and engaging in pointed phone conversations with her friends when Charlie was in the office, making remarks about "dirty, uppity niggers". She ignored Charlie and would not speak to him.

Doreen could not fault her colleague's politeness in the face of her continual rudeness. She had never had to deal at close quarters with a black man, particularly as a fellow worker and an educated one at that. Charlie knew he had a challenge to overcome her antagonism. Luckily, two weeks later he discovered an ice breaker. He learnt from overhearing her on the office phone that the following week her small son Peter was having a birthday party.

Doreen arrived in the office on Peter's birthday to find a neatly wrapped package on her desk. The label read, 'Happy Birthday Pete'. She forced herself to address Charlie.

'Where did this come from, boy?'

'It is from me to Pete. I hope he has a happy day today. He is a lucky boy to have a caring mommy like you, Mrs Brown.'

He was laying on the compliment thick without finesse. Would it work? Doreen's immediate instinct was to throw the package in the bin but she hesitated. She doted on her son. Would a caring mommy throw her son's birthday present in the bin? That morning she had had a particularly vicious fight with her husband, one of many such fights. Nobody in her life had called her caring, no matter their colour. Unused to the milk of human kindness, Charlie had caught her at a vulnerable moment.

'Thank you,' she grunted, turning to avoid Charlie seeing her eyes fill with tears.

Thereafter, a form of peace existed in the office. Doreen actually started to speak to Charlie and one day, trying to catch his attention, she used his name rather than the more usual white to black form of address of 'Boy' or 'Nigger.' Charlie was unfailingly polite and would open the door for her or employ other little courtesies.

Doreen struggled with deep-rooted prejudices to admit to herself that Charlie was a better person than his white predecessor, or indeed many white men that she knew.

Charlie was a passable mimic and back at home old man Fraser slapped his knees and rocked with laughter with the rest of the family at Charlie's descriptions of Doreen and her behaviour.

Two weeks after starting work Charlie found himself enjoying his role and responsibilities. These included checking time sheets were completed properly and checking deliveries. He taught himself to use the office typewriter and liked typing reports albeit slowly with just two fingers. He took pleasure in working with the other employees, although some of the whites seemed to resent seeing a black man doing a white man's job. The novelty of working and being accepted as part of a group was rewarding in itself. Receiving his pay at the end of each week was also most satisfying. He felt properly valued for the first time. He was not paid at Tori's patrol office, just receiving 'native' rations. One day foreman Pelosi summoned Charlie to his own office on the site.

'Sit down Charlie,' he began. This was the first time he had addressed Charlie by name. 'Y'all is doing a good job here and the big boss is happy too. Dunno what you bin doing but even Doreen is not her usual bitchy self. There's a job here as long as y'all want it. From now your rate is two fifty.'

'Thanks, Mr Pelosi. I like working for you. I appreciate you giving me a job and now a raise.'

A dollar an hour raise was exceptional. He was now one of the highest paid black employees on the site, alongside the skilled tradesmen. He knew he was going to miss his job when he had to leave for Stanford. Moreover, he felt at home living with the Fraser family, not to mention some mutual interests shared with Victoria, an attractive twenty-year-old daughter of one of their neighbours in the black neighbourhood. A romance was blossoming quickly. Evenings were often spent walking under the moon alongside the river that runs through the town. Victoria's mother, Mrs Wood, known as Mama Julie, was encouraging the affair. This 'nice, educated, black' foreigner with a good job was becoming the talk of the community. He was often invited for meals and fussed over. Occasionally, Mama Julie would pointedly leave

Victoria and Charlie in the house alone. Victoria was freer with her charms than any of Charlie's previous amours. PNG village society had strict taboos about premarital sex, but here it seemed that these didn't apply. At least not in Mama Julie's or her daughter's books.

Charlie was starting to feel he was taking advantage of Victoria as his time in San Antonio was coming to an end. He would lie awake at night with the similar feelings as he had when he left Beida back in Tori. He had intense feelings for Victoria and was starting to think about abandoning PNG and his education to make a life in America. He was happy being part of the black community, with whom he was popular. Most of all Victoria had become the centre of his life. He was faced with a huge and unexpected decision.

Tempting though it was, Charlie knew he could not let Mr Nevern and the Foundation down. After all, they had made it all possible. He knew Tom Paul also would be disappointed. Only later did he realise that even more important was a sense of destiny for his future in PNG.

On receiving Charlie's notice Jack Pelosi tried to talk him into staying. He talked of a further raise and more work when the current hotel project was complete.

His last day at work was marked by handshakes from Jack Pelosi and other well-wishers. Doreen was not at work that day and Charlie wondered whether she could have brought herself to wish him goodbye. On leaving the Fraser family Charlie was overwhelmed with sadness. Hugs from Victoria and Mama Julie made for even more emotion.

'Charlie, promise me you'll write,' sobbed Victoria. 'Maybe you can find me work near your university. I am sure there is work here for you with Mr Pelosi during your summer vacation. I am already missing you so much.'

She ran off in a flood of tears.

His time in America seemed destined to leave a trail of broken hearts. Joseph left him at the Greyhound terminal after a brotherly embrace. As the bus rolled out through the suburbs of San Antonio en route to California, Charlie felt a sense of belonging not experienced since leaving Tori village over two years ago.

CHAPTER 26

Charlie found himself at Stanford, considered to be one the country's leading seats of learning with a highly regarded school of humanities and social sciences. He learnt that he was a freshman and if he proceeded to a second year, he would become a sophomore. He had eventually settled to the idea of staying in the USA for a further year before returning to PNG at the ripe age of twenty-two. He was now harbouring thoughts of taking Victoria back with him.

Life at Stanford was unlike Osterley. He seemed to be one of only a few foreign students and in his department, the only black. He was a subject of curiosity and spent much time explaining his origins and situation. Nearly all his fellows were from well-to-do families, the only exceptions being a few other scholarship students who were funded by some benevolent institution. During his time in America, apart from the out and out racists, he had found most Americans to be open friendly people although friendships often seemed superficial. Overwhelmingly, they seemed to find it difficult to relate to foreigners whose countries didn't have supermarkets, cars, televisions and all the accoutrements of a consumer society. He was amazed to see hundreds of fellow students arriving at campus in cars laden with racks of clothes, record players and every conceivable item imaginable for a luxurious university life. He had arrived with one small, well-worn backpack. Stanford was a very insular world – a western, Californian one that seemed to be made up of top achieving students from every high school in the state.

Charlie was allocated a shared room on the first floor of Roble Hall, a student hall of residence. Along the same corridor was another scholarship student, José Cerda from Miami studying medicine. Charlie and José quickly formed a bond. Dark-skinned José, who had spent his early years in Cuba, had more of an understanding of Charlie's feelings of foreignness. His father had been teaching law at Havana University until six years earlier. He then came with the family to the United States under an exchange programme as a visiting professor at Miami University. During this time the revolution occurred against the corrupt Batista regime. Although Professor Cerda's sympathies were with the revolution he decided to stay in the US and successfully applied for citizenship. The eldest of his four children, José, enrolled at a state school and proved to be an exceptionally able student. A contact at Stanford had recommended José apply for one of several hundred need-based scholarships, in the same way Mr Nevern had used his influence for Charlie. In addition to tuition fees, Charlie received a small weekly allowance from the Foundation. He also had accumulated some savings during his time in San Antonio.

Apart from sharing similar outlooks on life Charlie and José found themselves in comparable financial circumstances, unlike many of their fellow students whose lavish lifestyles included cars and seemingly limitless cash. Shortly after meeting when they arrived in the fall for the first semester, the two friends swapped with their allocated roommates to share the same room. Charlie realised he found something in common with Latin culture, with the importance placed on family values and personal relationships. Later this feeling was reinforced when José invited Charlie to stay with his family in Miami during vacations.

Charlie found his psychology studies relatively easy and he achieved good grades at the end of the first semester. The works of Freud, Jung and their contemporaries were challenging but interesting. Nevertheless, he kept privately questioning the relevance of them when he would return to life in PNG. He was starting to wonder if he should have chosen some other course of study. Certainly, life in America seemed infinitely more involved with all that it had to offer. There seemed to be so many options in the way one could lead one's life which did not exist in PNG. Existence there was circumscribed by the basic need to survive, together with an ingrained culture and taboos.

Charlie was amazed at the comfortable life where all the needs of student well-being were taken care of. Academic aspects were catered for with a huge, impressive library and quiet study rooms. He had his own departmental mentor with whom study difficulties could be discussed. Personal problems could be taken to a resident counsellor. The dining hall served wide choices of delicious food. Charlie felt as if he was staying in a first-class hotel. Stanford was overwhelmingly male and white. He felt like a spot of soot on a layer of snow. At first, he was aware of the looks he attracted. Mostly they were curious but a few were hostile. Eventually he grew used to the attention and stopped noticing it.

Sport was a big thing with every conceivable game or activity on offer. At Osterley Charlie had become a reasonably accomplished basketball player, the first time he had participated in sport. To a PNG native, the whole concept of sport was quite strange. One got all the exercise one needed by the simple acts of hunting food, felling trees, building huts, walking between villages and very occasionally defending one's village against a warring tribe. Charlie had acquired good playing skills and enjoyed the camaraderie of belonging to a team. He found that sport was one area where colour differences seemed to be mostly overlooked. One was judged on skill rather than skin colour. End of game socialising centred on beer for which he had found a taste earlier in his travels. He was always called upon to describe life in PNG, not to mention his adventures since arriving in America. He noticed that boys from the southern states were cooler and tended to stay silent when he was recounting episodes in New Orleans and San Antonio.

He was constantly surprised in America at the general ignorance of the world outside of the country. This seemed true even in the educated environment of Stanford. It was assumed by most that he came from a southern state with the inference that he was descended from a slave. Any knowledge of or real interest in world geography was unusual. Ignorance of the existence of a wider world was not unlike that which one would have encountered in most PNG villages. Geography was often not included in the curriculum of many American schools. It seemed that curriculum subjects were determined locally and standards uneven. Once in conversation with another undergraduate, the topic of Indonesia came up. 'Is that in Africa?' was the question.

Chapter 27

At the end of the first semester Charlie accompanied José to his home in Miami for the Christmas break. Here Charlie met José's parents and his siblings – sister Consuelo and older brothers Javier and Pablo. José's mother had been a university lecturer of history at Havana where she met José's father.

While at Osterley, Charlie's time with Maria had stimulated an interest in the Spanish language. Maria and he often spent evenings at a local coffee shop where she would coach her amante in basic grammar, phrases and vocabulary. The abrupt ending of their relationship left Charlie with some limited understanding of the exchanges over the Cerda dinner table. These exchanges were terminated by a stern rebuke from Papa to use English in the presence of their guest.

'Charlie please tell us all about yourself and your

country,' asked Señora Cerda over dinner. Charlie had lost count of how many times he had told his story.

'Fascinating,' was the reply some half an hour later.

'And what do you think of America?' asked Jose's brother Javier. Charlie hesitated for some time before framing his reply.

'I am constantly fascinated by what I have seen and experienced so far. I see the acquisitiveness that seems to dominate the country. It seems to be the main driver of many people's outlooks and ambitions. This motivation sometimes seems to create a reason to commit crime and the need to have a large police force. It is true we have some tribal warfare but we do not have crime to the same extent. People have little by way of personal possessions, except what they need to sustain life. We do not have big cities, just very many small villages where people are dependent on one another. Village community spirit is strong because it has to be to survive. We do not have the wide divisions in our society created by the gulf between rich and poor. I am shocked by the way many old people are cast aside into homes to be cared for by strangers. I notice—'

'But are there any positive aspects?' interrupted Papa.

'For me personally, yes. I have had some wonderful experiences, met many kind and generous people. If I had never met some of your countrymen, I would have been ignorant of so much and maybe I should not be making these unfavourable comparisons. I was sent here to be educated and to take home the best of American culture. Maybe I am being over critical. I have met some of the best and worst of people, but one can do that in my country, where there is also greed and ignorance. Maybe people are the same the world over.'

The dinner time extended late into the night, with discussion of subjects ranging from literature to American foreign policy. Charlie found his three weeks with the Cerda family most stimulating. He had never before met an intellectual family with deep and eclectic interests.

José and his brothers along with their girlfriends, took their guest to a local Cuban nightclub where the clientele were almost all recent immigrants from Cuba who had fled Castro's new communist regime. Charlie was captivated by the atmosphere and exuberant rhythms. He threw himself into dancing, finding willing partners to teach this curious man some basic steps. One such was Eva, a pretty brunette and natural dancer who reminded him of Maria. He knew if he stayed here in Miami for long, he would soon be in love again.

'Say Charlie, the girls were fighting to teach you Cuban dances,' laughed Pablo. 'I don't know how you do it.'

The Christmas and New Year holiday was over too soon and the two friends prepared to leave for the flight back to California. Javier worked in Pan Am's engineering department at Miami airport and had managed to obtain cheap flights for the pair.

'You will always be welcome here,' said Papa with a hug. 'We are so pleased you are José's friend.'

With more warm words and hugs, Charlie left with a lump in his throat. Such was the welcome atmosphere he wished he could stay forever as part of the Cerda family.

They were similar feelings to what he had when leaving San Antonio. He was still missing Victoria.

At the end of the second semester Charlie saw a small card on the crowded student union noticeboard advertising a forthcoming civil rights demonstration. It was organised by the Ad Hoc Committee to End Discrimination, essentially part of the Berkeley campus of the University of California student body. He immediately found himself in tune with the agenda of the demonstration.

'Hey José, shall we go?'

José looked doubtful. 'I've an anatomy test coming up and can't afford the time. You shouldn't go my friend. You could be arrested and that could mean the end of your scholarship.'

The protests were in response to the racially discriminatory hiring practices used by the luxurious Sheraton Palace Hotel. The protesters sought equal treatment for all and the hotel to have black individuals in supervisory positions rather than just as porters, waiters and menial workers. A high percentage of individuals involved in the protest were members of the student population of the Berkeley campus. To Charlie it sounded exciting and challenging. Although maybe José was right. His funds were running low and maybe he could find a job during the Spring Break when traditionally students would leave for holidays, often in groups heading for beaches. He could not afford such frivolity. What he did not realise at the time was that if he had joined the Berkeley demonstration, he would have witnessed the start of a widespread disobedience movement.

The noticeboard was also a place where one could find holiday jobs advertised. He called ahead to two restaurants wanting part-time waiting staff. After lengthy bus journeys on each occasion, he found he had wasted his time. His problem was his colour. One manager told him 'we don't hire niggers.' The other said he could be a dishwasher at a dollar an hour – just below the minimum wage and barely enough to cover his bus fares. In San Antonio he had enjoyed two fifty an hour.

As he lay in bed that night Charlie was still in a state of outrage at his treatment. The speeches of Malcolm X and Martin Luther King now seemed ever more relevant. This was not his country but he felt a kinship with its black population. He understood and sympathised with the revolutionary ideas of Malcolm X but as he calmed down, he realised they would cause bloodshed and leave the white majority further entrenched in its views. He thought the Reverend King's peaceful approach would take forever for black men to gain equality. Thank heavens he would be leaving this blighted country before long, never to return.

He rarely saw another black face on campus. When he did, they would stop and exchange stories. On one such occasion he met Jack Childs, an electrical engineering student from Cleveland.

'Jack, I've a big problem trying to find vacation work. I've wasted hours and money going after jobs, only to be rejected because I'm black or offered slaving for slave wages.'

'I can probably help you, Charlie. I'm under final year exam pressure and have to give up a great job as a weekend and vacation time yardman and handyman in Palo Alto. I don't want to give it up.'

'How much does it pay?'

'Three bucks an hour and you get great food. I'll take you up there this weekend and introduce you as my replacement.'

'Wow, sounds fantastic. You're a real pal, Jack.'

CHAPTER 28

The following Saturday, Jack's rusting Chevy pickup pulled up outside some imposing gates. At the front door the owner of the huge mansion, a white man somewhere in his late fifties, attired in tennis clothes, looked over Jack's proposed replacement. Jack made introductions. His employer was a Mr Donald Way. Mr Way held out his hand. This is a good sign, thought Charlie.

'We've been very happy with the work Jack has done for us. He's a difficult act to follow.'

Charlie realised he had no relevant experience. 'I understand sir. I have worked with tradespeople in San Antonio for a contractor and can give you a work reference if you wish. I can also give you a character reference from a board member of the Valodis Foundation. I understand this is Jack's last weekend and I could work alongside him to learn what is needed.'

'OK Charlie, we'll give it a try.'

Mr Way had a great interest in people. He realised from Charlie's appearance and accent, not to mention his offered references, that he had a story to tell. He would find out more in due course.

For the rest of his time at Stanford Charlie worked in his spare hours for the Way family. He found he had really landed on his feet. Not only was he earning a top wage but was brought nice lunches by Dolores, the black maid. Dolores took an instant shine to the exotic new gardener but Charlie found that he was not such an instant hit with Arthur, the family's black chauffeur. Arthur had designs on Dolores and had noted the shine in her eyes when talking about the new man. Arthur need have had no concerns about a love rival appearing on the horizon, Charlie felt no attraction to Dolores whom he regarded as something of a gossip and a busybody.

Summer loomed at the start of the third semester and Charlie started to review his original decision to attend only one year at university. Despite his earlier resolution to leave America as soon as possible there was no doubt he was enjoying himself. He appreciated the company of friendly, intelligent fellow students and stimulation from his lectures. He liked the warm temperate, dry Californian climate. During his time at Osterley, he could not get accustomed to Ohio's very cold winters. He now had a great, well paid part-time job. He had acquired a good friend in the form of José and had loved visiting José's family, receiving invitations to go back to Miami during vacation breaks. He found his studies easy but thought he would find more interest in history than psychology. Since his early days with Mr Smithson's encyclopaedias, he was intrigued by the wider world. In particular, he wanted to learn more of its past and what brought about the devastating conflicts that dotted human history. He couldn't get away from the fact that one such conflict was indirectly responsible for him being here in America. He resolved to speak with his faculty advisor to explore changing to a major in modern history and extend his stay at Stanford to three full years to obtain a BA degree.

On a social note, he was starting to get invitations to a few student parties. At one such party he was given a small square of paper with a tiny substance adhering to it.

'Take it Charlie. Put it on your tongue, it's better than beer,' said Dave, a fellow basketball player majoring in psychology and one of his new friends. Charlie had heard about LSD 'trips' and how they were wonderful 'life-enhancing' experiences. He could not imagine anything, apart from a reunion with Victoria, that could improve his life.

Nothing happened for half an hour but then he felt a need to sit or lie down and he crept away to a corner of the room and collapsed into an easy chair. With his eyes closed he was suddenly confronted with an extraordinary scene comprising radiant colours, objects and coloured patterns on surfaces appearing to ripple or breathe. Charlie Kikira vanished; he was looking in from outside at a world in which he did not exist. But above all he felt sublimely happy and all powerful, excited and ready to take the world by storm, righting wrongs and solving problems.

A few hours later he came to in his room, feeling sleepy with slightly blurred vision. He wondered how he had got there. José woke to see his friend stretched out on his bed, looking extremely relaxed.

'It's 5 a.m. Charlie. What have you been doing?'

'I've been on a trip. Dave gave me some acid. I ruled the world for a while. Got rid of all sorts of bad things. It was marvellous though right now I don't feel so good.' José, the medic, looked concerned.

'Don't do it again, my friend. LSD works on your nervous system and could have serious side effects.'

Charlie recovered sufficiently to attend lectures the following day but resolved to follow his friend's advice.

Charlie was enjoying his work at the Way home. Jack Childs had been helpful in guiding him through the weekly routines of grass and hedge trimming, pruning, watering and general plant care. He knew nothing about gardening or plants and could be found perusing illustrated books on Botany, taking an interest in the subject and starting to identify some of the items in his care. He found his work enjoyable having spent most of his life among the trees and plants of PNG's jungle environment. Mr Way had a great interest in tropical orchids and occasionally Charlie could recognise a familiar species in his greenhouse.

Donald Way was a research chemist who, early in his career, had worked for a major pharmaceutical company until starting his own patent agency. He had found a niche within his field and his business grew rapidly to become highly successful, generating an impressive income. He and his wife had three adopted children, all away at university.

One day while trimming the edge of one of the many flower beds, Charlie rounded a corner to find Mrs Way sitting reading in the shade of a wisteria-covered arbour. His employer's wife was a tall, youthful forty-five-year-old woman who previously he had only seen at a distance.

'Sorry to disturb you ma'am,' he said respectfully, withdrawing.

She smiled. 'You are not disturbing me, Charlie. Please call me Pat. Come here and sit for a moment and tell me about yourself. My husband tells me you are from Papua New Guinea and with Jack at Stanford.'

It was unusual to find himself talking to a mature white woman, the last being Mary Holden in Osterley. He did not count Doreen Brown, his co-worker in San Antonio. Pat Way and Doreen could have been different species as far as Charlie was concerned. Mrs Way in fact was Canadian and had met her husband at university where she was studying linguistics. She was absorbed by Charlie's accounts of his American adventures but even more so about his homeland. She was interested in a country with its diversity of cultures and over eight hundred separate languages.

'You know Charlie, your country would be fertile ground for a study of its linguistic complexity. You are making me think how I would love to visit to study. We could co-author a dissertation for our doctorates!' She laughed.

'Pat, that sounds a wonderful idea, but the practicalities would be almost insurmountable. We have virtually no roads, maps are incomplete and some tribes are hostile to neighbouring tribes, let alone foreigners. I can't imagine the cost. Anyway, I'm not sure you are serious.' Charlie too was laughing. 'I have an obligation to re-join government service on my return. If people found out I was a doctor everybody would be lining up outside my door with their aches and pains!' He laughed again.

Pat Way was so enjoying the company of this unusual young man with the result that, three quarters of an hour later, trimming of the grass edges surrounding the rose beds had not progressed.

'Excuse me Pat, I think I need to finish my work on the yard.'

'I look forward to another chat with you, Charlie.'

That evening Pat and her husband were at dinner. Pat was talking animatedly about Charlie and wondering what they could do for him.

'I can see our new yardman has been a hit,' said her amused husband. 'I admit I like him too, but let's leave him to cut the grass and trim the hedges.'

Back at Stanford, senior history faculty member Taylor McKee took in the appearance of the young man seated opposite him.

'So Charlie, why do want to convert to a history major?'

Charlie had expected this question and explained his lifelong interest in history, starting at the age of eight in Mr Smithson's bungalow.

'My particular interest is in the conflicts that have shaped the world in this century and the nineteenth. Not so much detail of the wars themselves, but the political landscapes behind them. I see America has cast itself as the world's policeman, fighting communism. No sooner has the Korean War finished and now the US is fighting in Vietnam. This is my country's region and naturally I want to understand its implications. Perhaps I should add that it is as a direct result of one incident in World War Two, that I find myself here at Stanford University.'

'Please explain, Charlie.'

Charlie did so, once again having to chart the events from the visit with Bruce Petersen to Hulwari village to here, sitting opposite Mr McKee. The room went silent as McKee digested what he had heard. There was no doubt that he would welcome Charlie into his department. Most meetings of this sort would have him sitting opposite an ex-schoolboy from a nice white middle-class suburb with minimal experience of life. Only a few of these would draw the same benefit from a university education as Charlie. Here was a young man with a wealth of exposure to other cultures and with real motivation to understand his world.

'Welcome to the History Department, Charlie.'

No longer a freshman but now a sophomore, Charlie first had to plan his forthcoming summer vacation. José had said he would be welcome to stay with his family, but this posed two problems. First, Charlie felt that in three months as a guest he would outstay his welcome. Second, he needed money. The Valodis grant was pocket money to cover his expenses when he stayed in Roble Hall with its free food. Roble Hall was great during term time but was mostly deserted in the summer apart from occasional conferences of which Charlie was not part.

Donald Way had said he could work during the summer at his residence. Between gardening tasks, he would be filling in as chauffeur during Arthur's three-week vacation with his family in Cleveland. Charlie jumped at this. He enjoyed driving and had obtained a license in Osterley in order to borrow Ruben Littuma's car.

CHAPTER 29

Arthur looked doubtful at Charlie's promotion, from being a lowly untrained gardener to the prestigious role of driving the Way's late model Cadillac. He also contemplated with concern the thought of Charlie being full-time and living in the servant's quarters near to maid Dolores. Dolores for her part, almost danced with joy. With ill grace, Arthur detailed the duties of his imagined rival. These included keeping the car in immaculate condition at all times, full of gas and to be ready at the beck and call of either the boss or his wife.

Jack Childs had previously primed Charlie about Arthur's jealous obsession with Dolores.

'She's a terrible flirt Charlie, and quite manipulative. Watch out because she can cause trouble. My advice is to avoid her like the plague.'

Charlie decided to deal with the matter head on.

'Listen Arthur, I'm pretty sure you don't want me here. Don't think I'm interested in Dolores or your job for that matter. I'm just here during my time at Stanford and then I'll be off and you'll never see me again.'

Arthur said nothing, but was relieved, although still wondering if he could trust this foreigner.

Mr Way had regular meetings at his offices in San Francisco. Charlie studied maps before negotiating his first drive into a big city. It was quite a challenge after just the occasional drive around Osterley with Maria in her brother's small car. It was definitely a far cry from a drive to the Tori airstrip from the patrol office in an ancient Jeep. He found it a daunting experience at first. His boss helped with directions until they came to a halt in a large underground car park beneath his offices.

'I'll be here all day, Charlie. Be here at five. Go and do some sightseeing. Here's two bucks for lunch.'

In fact, lunch was only one dollar twenty for a calorie-rich burger, fries, cream soda and ice cream at a Woolworth's lunch counter. Charlie was starting to eat the American way. As he sat down at the counter, he was aware that a white woman at the next place got up and moved with her lunch to another seat.

Charlie had read that just a few years previously a segregated Woolworth's lunch counter had been the site of an historic event. Some black students staged a sit-in in a white section in a Woolworth's lunch counter in Greensboro, North Carolina. They refused to leave after being denied service. The sit-in movement soon spread to college towns throughout the south. Though many of the protesters were arrested for trespassing, disorderly conduct or disturbing the peace, their actions made an immediate and lasting impact. Woolworth's and other establishments were forced to change their segregationist policies. Things were changing but public attitudes were mostly still entrenched.

That evening, having successfully navigated city traffic and delivering Mr Way to his front door, Charlie breathed a sigh of relief upon parking the Cadillac in its garage. Who but Dolores was hanging around by the entrance of the servant's quarters?

'Did you have a nice day, Charlie?' she simpered and without waiting for a reply said, 'What are you doing this evening? There's a lovely movie on at the Paris.'

The Paris theatre in Palo Alto had a growing reputation for showing risqué movies which were not without appeal, but Charlie had no intention of going, at least not with Dolores.

'I'm busy with a lot of studying, so I'll be reading. You enjoy your evening Dolores,' Charlie said shortly.

But Dolores did not give up easily.

'Perhaps I'll see you tomorrow then?'

Dolores edged closer to ensure Charlie had a view of her artfully designed, plunging, low-cut, off-the-shoulder dress. He was also getting full benefit of a cloying perfume. Charlie was definitely conflicted. One could cut the sexual tension with a knife. Dolores was not an unattractive woman and he was facing huge temptation. Never before had he been subjected to quite such an outright attempt at seduction.

He had his pledge to Arthur and Jack Childs's words of warning ringing in his ears. He hesitated, but then with iron resolve stepped to one side, and without a word escaped to his room.

He purchased a second-hand bike advertised on Roble's noticeboard. When not working he cycled to and from Stanford to see if there was anybody he knew. He was getting concerned that he had not heard from Victoria for over six months. Several letters awaited him in his mailbox. There were postmarks from New Orleans and Osterley. Sylvia wrote warm, affectionate letters but there was nothing from Victoria. Maybe she had found a new boyfriend. Sylvia hinted she was thinking of looking for work in San Francisco. Charlie wondered if he should write back, encouraging the idea – girlfriends were in very short supply at Stanford. On the other hand, this would signal a serious commitment of which he was unsure despite his fond memories of his short time in New Orleans. He still had a longing for the intimacy of his relationship with Victoria.

Other postmarks were from Washington DC. Mr Nevern had heard from Stanford with a report on Charlie's performance at the end of his first year. His marks were very satisfactory and Nevern was happy to report that the foundation confirmed it would continue to fund his scholarship.

The other envelope from DC contained a stiff, embossed card with raised gold lettering announcing the wedding of Miss Tara Ann Reeves to Captain Thomas Anthony Paul USAF. The event was to take place at The

Hay Adams, Washington DC, on a date following the Easter recess next year.

The envelope also contained a hand-written note.

'Charlie – yes, I'm tying the knot. Keep the date free! Don't worry about the cost – Tara's family are happy to cover it for you. I'll send you air tickets and details later. Maybe you can come a day or two earlier and we can catch up. Very best, Tom.'

In the regular letters between them, Tom had mentioned a serious girlfriend. Reading between the lines it seemed her family were wealthy; Tom and Tara had holidayed on the family yacht. Tom was going to be moving in moneyed circles. Charlie penned a congratulatory reply, accepting with great pleasure at the thought of seeing Tom again. His brotherly feelings for Tom had grown over the years. Despite their physical separation they had kept in regular touch by writing. Charlie felt as if he was going to acquire a sister-in-law. Tom was the only American he knew who had seen him in his home environment in PNG and had an understanding of the gulf between their cultures.

The remainder of Charlie's days as Mr Way's chauffeur were drawing to a close. Arthur would soon be returning from his vacation. Charlie was occasionally asked to drive Mrs Way to visit one of her friends. One particular occasion was an event in Oakland organised by the Daughters of the American Revolution, known as the DAR. He learnt that membership is lineage-based for women who are directly descended from a person involved in the United States' efforts towards independence. Mrs Way's claim to membership was accepted. Though she was Canadian, Mrs Way was descended from a Frenchman, a soldier who fought the British. Private Bisset was wounded at the decisive battle of Yorktown.

On such outings, Mrs Way sat in the front of the car alongside Charlie. She loved to chat with him, finding out everything about his life and aspirations. She warned him that she had informed their host at the meeting that she would be asking him to say a few words about his country and his presence in the USA. She was fiercely opposed to the prejudices that existed in the DAR and was aware of the embedded attitudes of some of its members. Past controversies had even caused Eleanor Roosevelt to resign her membership. Mrs Way hoped that Charlie would feel welcome.

On this trip he found that racism was still alive and well among some members of the California Highway Patrol. Conversation with his employer was interrupted by the sound of a high-pitched wailing siren. His mirror showed flashing red lights behind. Was he speeding, he asked himself, what could this be about? In his rear-view mirror, he saw a policeman dismount from a large motorbike and stride up to his window. The stony-faced man was in a black uniform, glossy knee-length boots and shiny white helmet with a pistol at his side. Charlie had seen members of the California Highway Patrol before but at a distance. Close up he found this large man with reflecting mirrored sunglasses aggressive and intimidating. The man rapped on the window.

'Get out of the car, boy. Let me see your license.' He

looked at the Ohio license, issued in Osterley, 'Place your hands on the car roof and spread your legs.' Charlie was then roughly frisked.

He lent inside the car.

'You alright ma'am?'

Mrs Way saw the name badge on his uniform. She wasn't going to let this pass.

'Officer Johnston, what was the reason for you interrupting our journey? Had we broken any laws?'

'I saw you being driven in the front seat with this nig – man, and I was concerned for your safety.'

'So, you were concerned because he is black and I am white?'

Johnston couldn't find a reply. Mrs Way warmed to her theme.

'In these circumstances, I suggest you address citizens by their name or 'sir'. Has the Highway Patrol heard of the Civil Rights Act? This outlaws discrimination based on race, colour, religion, sex or national origin. This gentleman is a guest of this country from overseas. I cannot imagine how his impressions of the treatment he has just received will play back home. My husband is a member of the Law-and-Order committee, reporting to the Governor. He will learn of this incident.'

Johnston realised he had met his match and it was time to retire quickly.

'Sorry ma'am.' mumbled Johnston. He held the door open for Charlie, handing back his license.

Johnston walked back to his bike. 'Uppity bitch.' he muttered to himself.

Charlie relished the thought of Officer Johnston being hauled over the coals.

Shortly afterwards, the Cadillac smoothly drew up outside the imposing home of Mrs Humphrey, Mrs Way's hostess and friend. A black maid admitted them. She glanced at Charlie in surprise. She could not recall ever having seen a black man enter through the front door, let alone visiting the house as a guest. Charlie perfectly fitted into one of Mr Way's many expensive suits. He cut a rather fine figure and very cute, the maid thought.

The room of some thirty expensively, immaculately dressed and coiffed women appraised their unusual fellow guest. They had previously been briefed by Mrs Humphrey that they were to be addressed by a black male speaker. This had caused some of the more prejudiced members to be absent. Charlie sat silently in the back of the room, while the group went through what seemed tedious formalities of reading of financial accounts, lists of donations, past minutes, prayers and so on. It seemed that this was a small, local chapter of the DAR, whereas membership of some big city chapters numbered many hundreds.

Mrs Humphries announced, 'Finally ladies, before tea, it gives me great pleasure to introduce you to Mr Charlie Kikira from Papua New Guinea. He is going to tell us a little about his country and what brings him here.'

After about twenty minutes, Charlie ended on an upbeat note by admiring America as a wonderful country with its friendly people and opportunity for learning. As a guest, he could not get into his negative feelings about the common effects endured by black people. He was still seething about the incident with the California Highway Patrol. He invited questions. He could see he had engaged the interest of most of the room, although two elderly dowagers were quietly dozing.

Some of the questions were quite insightful, others less so. One of the latter was a query about supermarkets in PNG. Among the former, a lady asked him,

'What lessons about life have you learned that you can take home with you to your country?'

Charlie hesitated before answering.

'Ma'am, that is a question I have asked myself many times. I think I have learnt that people are the same the world over. The important things in life are family, friends and community. There is a danger that these values can be lost in the middle of an affluent society and some of the ills this creates. In my country, we are fortunate that we don't have these pressures to resist, not yet at least.'

When he thought about it later, he realised that this was a somewhat veiled criticism of America. Despite this it attracted a positive reply.

'Young man, if only people here could realise the wisdom of those words.'

Over dinner that evening with her husband, Pat Way described the day.

'Not everybody seemed to fully understand Charlie's presentation. Afterwards one actually asked me if he was an actor from Hollywood. Perhaps she thought he was an extra with Bogart in African Queen! Old Mrs Lawrence and Mrs Albertella fell asleep and Mrs Jameson kept looking at the tea table with its cakes. She was the first on her feet and to the table when Charlie finished. On the other hand, I think he made a deep impression on some. He certainly has an extraordinary maturity for his age. The meeting was a great change from lectures on quilt-making!'

'Looks as if you need to start a Charlie Fan Club with you as president!' joked her husband.

CHAPTER 30

Like his fellow students, life for Charlie revolved around daily and weekly college routines. Events outside Stanford did not arouse great interest. Available newspapers and radio stations mainly reported on local or State matters. There were usually accounts of the progress of the war in Vietnam. National news only occasionally made the headlines, although at present the forthcoming presidential election dominated the media.

Charlie made an effort to understand US politics. His often tried to imagine a system of governance that might work in PNG, but he did not relate to a system dominated by just two parties with an elected President. At election times, he witnessed the political passions that seemed to be aroused in some fellow students.

It was a Friday during the first semester of Charlie's second year. During an afternoon break from classes an event occurred that shook the whole country. Over coffee with a fellow basketball player, Charlie was dissecting Stanford's performance in a recent match against Berkeley. The next lecture that afternoon was to examine the background to the American Bill of Rights. Professor Harvey Kenton, an ageing, bald and quietly spoken mid-westerner was to conduct the last session of the afternoon and the week. Charlie was not looking forward to it. He found Kenton's monotone delivery dry and tedious. Besides which, the subject matter did not hold great interest for him. He wanted to get away to put in a couple of hours work at the Way's garden. Years later, he vividly remembered Professor Kenton bursting into the room full of students.

'The president's been assassinated, Kennedy is dead,' he shouted.

The normally unemotional man burst into tears and hurried out. There was stunned silence. The room stood still, digesting the enormity of the news. There were a few quiet sobs. Charlie was staggered to think that in a civilised country an apparently popular president could be killed, presumably for some political reason. Debate over the reasons and consequences continued for weeks afterwards dominating conversation throughout the country. The day following the assassination Charlie and José were in their room. As usual the radio was on in the background. It was playing sombre music when interrupted by a news flash announcing the shooting of the man who had been arrested for Kennedy's murder.

'What's the matter with this country?' exclaimed José. 'So much violence in its history. JFK is now the fourth president to be killed. And others have been attacked. And the police cannot even protect the murderer.'

Charlie didn't know what to say. It was all quite incomprehensible, making him feel even more alienated from America. He had been brought here to learn the benefits of so-called civilisation. As time passed, he was counting the months before he returned to PNG but he still had over a year to gain his degree.

Eventually, the day came for Charlie to fly to Washington for Tom's wedding. Fortunately, he and Mr Way were of similar height and build and Mrs Way again lent Charlie one of her husband's many suits, having once more prevailed on him to loan one for Tom's big day.

Thus attired, after Easter Charlie stepped off his flight at Washington National Airport. Waiting in arrivals to greet him with a brotherly hug was Tom Paul, in uniform, sporting an extra shoulder pip denoting elevation to Major. Over beers in Charlie's hotel near to the Hay Adams, the pair chatted about events in their lives since they last saw each other.

'So Tom, you're joining Washington's high society.'

'Charlie, you know I'm not that sort of a guy. I've been happiest doing what I did when we met. The Air Force has me flying a desk at the moment, which doesn't suit. I'm thinking of setting up a flying school in Florida with Tara's Dad's help. She's very enthusiastic and tired of the DC scene. That is to say unless you, as a big wheel, can find me something to do in PNG after your return!' Tom laughed.

'The Australians are probably already wondering how they can find somewhere to lose a Tori native with a history degree. I'm certain they're hoping I won't come back!'

'It's about time you found a nice girl to settle down with. Reading between the lines of your letters, you left a few in your wake down south.'

'Tom, Stanford is a female desert!'

Tom changed the subject, becoming serious.

'Charlie you've been over here for four years. How do you feel about America now?'

Charlie sipped his beer, not replying immediately.

'That's a difficult question. If I hadn't come, I wouldn't be here right now with you. I've acquired a brother and that means a lot to me. But I can't wait to go back to where I belong. I hate the treatment of blacks that seems to run through large parts of the country. As a white man you see it from the side lines, but as a black man, I feel it in the background every day of my life here. Sometimes I get quite angry. I wonder if America will ever change.'

'I'm sure it will, but maybe not in our lifetimes.'

The pair exchanged banter for the next hour until Tom took his leave. Charlie would not see him again until the day of the wedding and reception. On that day, he could not conceive of anything more unlike a traditional PNG wedding. He had attended one in his Tori village. The bride was to be the groom's second wife. The women were separated from the men. Like the other men, Charlie wore much face and body paint and a lap-lap of leaves and colourful armbands of shells. His headgear contained bright bird of paradise plumes. And now here he was in a tailored, dark-coloured suit. Wistfully, he wondered if he would ever attend his own wedding, hopefully in PNG.

Tom and Tara looked an impressive couple, thought Charlie. Tom was resplendent in his major's dress uniform, and slim, blonde Tara in a beautiful, all-white, flowing dress. Looking around him at the expensively dressed congregation, everyone and everything glittered under the huge chandeliers of the hotel's ballroom. He certainly felt no sense of belonging and was slightly uncomfortable in this sea of whiteness and extreme formality. Afterwards, at the reception, a familiar face approached him.

'Hey Charlie. Tony Oakes, remember me?'

'Tony, how could I forget that friendly face from our expedition to the crash site outside Hulwari village? Still in the air force?'

Tony was now a civilian, happy and fondly remembering his visit to PNG.

'That was one of the best experiences I had during my time in the service. Tell me what you are doing now? Tom and I have kept in contact and he's told me something of your adventures. Say, you are looking pretty sharp.'

'I've got a great boss who lent me one of his suits.'

Seeing Tony produced an overwhelming sense of nostalgia. Charlie just wished at that moment he could be back in Tori village. After exchanging reminiscences, he bade Tony goodbye and wound his way through the crowd to congratulate Tom and Tara on their marriage before escaping. He wondered if he would ever see Tom again.

CHAPTER 31

Charlie began his final year at Stanford. He realised he had made the right choice in switching to a history major. For his last written assignment, he had chosen a dissertation on the political history of the British Empire. He was curious to learn how the influence of such a small country had shaped the modern world. African countries were starting to become independent. India had done so over fifteen years previously. He realised he was witnessing the beginnings of the end of the old-world orders and wondered when autonomy would come to PNG.

Although enjoying university life, he was desperate to return home. Still working at weekends for Donald and Pat Way, he no longer needed to fend off the attentions of Dolores as she had been fired for misbehaviour. After a weekend, Charlie would often spend the first part of Monday morning in the library. On one particular day, there was no lecture scheduled until the afternoon. He tried to catch up on work he should have completed the day before, but had been playing basketball in an away game at Pepperdine University in Malibu.

'Hello Charlie,' was the friendly welcome from Janet, the history department librarian.

Her colleagues had noticed that middle-aged, bespectacled and normally taciturn Janet always brightened when Charlie appeared.

'Hello Janet, how is my favourite librarian today?' flirted Charlie with a grin.

'I'm fine Charlie,' she blushingly replied. 'Today's New York Post has just come in. I think you will want to see it.'

She handed him the newspaper which he took to a study desk. He was shaken to read the headline – 'MALCOLM X SHOT TO DEATH AT RALLY'. He sat still for several minutes after reading the report. His thoughts immediately went back to the evening with his Haitian friend, Maxime. They had listened, spellbound to Malcolm X's oratory. Malcolm was raging against the injustices suffered by black people at the hands of whites. The newspaper story said that he had been killed by black men. Charlie was incredulous and again troubled by the violent undercurrents in American society. It reinforced his wish to be in the relative peace of PNG.

He spent his last Easter recess with the Cerda family. He had become attached to each one and believed they enjoyed his friendship. He felt as if they were his family just as three years earlier, he had become attached to the Frasers in San Antonio. He had a longing to leave this itinerant existence and acquire a feeling of permanency surrounded by friends and a family of his own.

He sat opposite history tutor Taylor McKee. Taylor was encouraging his star student to stay to study for his MA.

'You are a born historian, Charlie. Your interest and insight into the subject are impressive. I could write to the Foundation recommending you stay for one more year for your Master's.'

Charlie couldn't think of anything he would less rather do. Politely declining, he thanked Taylor for his support. He had enjoyed his time at Stanford but privately longed to reconnect with the real world – his world of PNG.

Once final examinations were over, party time started. Charlie succumbed to pressures from his basketball playing pals to join them. These were riotous affairs in which alcohol flowed freely and joints were passed around. Charlie recalled his one encounter with drugs in the form of LSD in his first year. He remembered it as pleasurable, but also the dire warning from José about possible side effects. He knew about the various drugs circulating around Stanford's student community. Marijuana seemed the least harmful. Maybe he'd try some. At one such party, Lizzie, a philosophy student he knew from his first year, sat beside him. Lizzie had always fancied Charlie but until now had not an opportunity or the courage to approach him. Giggling, Lizzie offered him a joint. Drawing deeply, his immediate reaction was desperately trying not to cough until he could hold it no longer and spluttered, his lungs burning. This rapidly passed as he was overcome with a powerful sense of euphoria. Suddenly, he found himself sitting in close proximity with the most glamorous, voluptuous, sexy woman he had ever seen, quite unlike the skinny, pinch-faced, bespectacled one that was beside him moments earlier. He leant close to her and said with a loud conspiratorial stage whisper, 'I'm so high!'

He then erupted into a long fit of laughter, before melting back onto the couch unable to move. His euphoria continued as he contemplated his tiny presence on the planet, all his worries disappearing. With the creature on his left, he started to engage in an intimate discussion on elephants and the merits of having them as pets. And so it went on. He woke with the midday sun pouring into his room. He had no recollection of how he got there. He felt totally relaxed, remembering little of the last evening except having experienced what seemed a pleasurable and exciting adventure. He now understood the addiction that could follow such an experience.

Two days later, walking up a path to Roble Hall, he saw two girls approaching. One was Lizzie. He was immediately embarrassed, looking for an escape route, but there was none. He had no idea what had passed between them and didn't know whether he would be ignored or get his face slapped. Lizzie ran up to him and flung her arms around him, kissing him on the lips.

'Oh Charlie, what a wonderful evening that was. I shall never forget it,' with which she ran off to join her friend.

At the end of the degree award ceremony, he said his farewells to the fellow students who had become friends in the last three years. He hugged José Cerda.

'You've been a true friend, José. The way you and the family have befriended me is something that will stay with me forever. When you graduate think about coming to PNG, we'll always need medics. Wherever I am, come and be my doctor!'

CHAPTER 32

Unexpectedly, he did see Tom again that last summer before returning to PNG. He had become friendly with Richard Grayson, a black American student of political science, a rare animal. Richard could trace his family history back to the last century, when his ancestors were slaves on a plantation in Alabama. He was a member of the NAACP and a passionate activist for human rights.

'Hey Charlie, are you coming to Washington in August to join the march for jobs and freedom for black people? I know you're not American but it's about the repression of black people the world over. Transport is free – we'll be on a bus paid for by the NAACP. We can bunk with my cousin in DC. He'll feed us. Martin Luther King is the main speaker. Come on, Charlie.'

'I'll think about it Rich. I'm returning home soon, then it's goodbye to Stanford.'

A week later he received a letter from Mr Nevern asking him to come to Washington for a debriefing at the end of his scholarship. He wanted to introduce Charlie to other Valodis board members who had expressed interest in meeting one of the foundation's success stories.

Perfect, thought Charlie. He could join the march and fit in a visit to see Tom. Mr Nevern would be paying his travel expenses for his flight back from Washington to PNG. Ever short of cash, he could fit in some work for Mr and Mrs Way for the last time before flying to Washington. He had made a long-distance call to Tom to see if he could invite himself to stay.

'Charlie this is a lovely surprise,' chirruped Tara. When Charlie explained the reason for his call, she replied without hesitation, 'Tom isn't home at the moment. He won't let you leave Washington before seeing you. When the big event is over, he will come and pick you up. We'd love to have you stay with us until your flight back home.'

He found Richard Grayson the following day in the Roble cafeteria.

'Hey Rich, I'm coming to the Washington march but don't need the transport, my sponsor is flying me up.'

Richard was impressed. 'How the other half lives! Maybe I'll see you there.'

Charlie arrived in Washington for his meeting with Mr Nevern and his colleagues. His transport to the Valodis Foundation offices had been arranged. He was met at the airport by a uniformed chauffeur who looked askance at his casually dressed young black passenger as he led him to a large limousine with darkened windows.

He was more used to driving expensively suited white businessmen.

A beautifully dressed blonde secretary welcomed Charlie to the opulent offices of the Valodis Foundation.

'Please be seated, Mr Kikira. Mr Nevern will be with you shortly.' She smiled. Charlie detected a hint of expensive perfume.

He sank into a sumptuous leather chair and looked around him. Hanging behind the secretary's antique desk, was a large oil painting of a grey-haired man whom Charlie took to be Caspar Valodis. The thickly carpeted, wood-panelled reception area spoke of money – lots of it. It struck Charlie that the sums spent on him must have been a drop in the ocean of the Valodis millions.

Mr Nevern appeared, shook hands and ushered Charlie into the boardroom where three other men rose to greet him. Each looked to be of a similar age to Nevern, also expensively dressed. After introductions there was a moment of silence as they appraised him. Charlie looked at them, aware of the total contrast he represented in this formal setting, young, black, casually dressed in T-shirt and jeans.

One of the men, silver-haired with patrician features and manner spoke, 'Charlie we have heard so much about you and as trustees of Mr Valodis' benevolence, wanted to congratulate you on your success before you return to your homeland. We would appreciate your views on the value of your time here in America.'

Charlie had been expecting this question. Should he be frank or just say what they wanted to hear? If he was frank there would probably be no other Papuans invited to the USA for education. To be fair to the Foundation, nothing was going to prevent the cultural invasion of his country. He was quite sure he knew the answer to the question. He had started to realise it during his early days in their country. He knew that the traditional lives and values of his countrymen would be dramatically changed and almost certainly not for the better. But could he say this? Would it cause offence and serve no purpose?

'Gentlemen, let me say how immensely grateful I am to have had this quite extraordinary opportunity. My life has been enriched in so many ways. To answer your question, it has been of great value to me personally.' He paused. 'My country has changed little for many thousands of years. The population is mostly uneducated in western terms. It is a tribal society fragmented over a large area, much of it mountainous and forested, with some of it inaccessible and unexplored. There are around a thousand tribes speaking over eight hundred separate languages. There is little infrastructure in terms of transport, education or medical services. I cannot say it is without problems. There is occasional inter-tribal warfare but for the most part we live peacefully in harmony with the environment. International agencies are pushing for us to be given independence. This will undoubtedly cause upheaval as we try to find our way in the modern world. I am anxious that we may be exploited, with destruction of our natural resources. If I have any role of influence when independence comes, my time here will have given me insight on how to make the best of the challenges we will face.'

Charlie realised that this was all a bit vague, but would hopefully make these men feel that the Valodis money had been well spent. Mr Nevern had heard Charlie's views before and was concerned that he would deliver a negative message about his sponsorship. He breathed a sigh of relief.

After a half hour of further questions, Charlie left to find his way to Tom's home in the North Potomac suburb. In his pocket were his airline tickets all the way to Port Moresby.

Two days later, he found himself with about three hundred thousand other civil rights supporters, mostly black, who had come from all over the USA. Standing beside the Lincoln Memorial Reflecting Pool, he heard what turned out to be an historic event. It was peaceful, confounding the authorities' predictions of violence. Dr King's passionate oratory was spellbinding. In later years Charlie came to realise he had attended a milestone in the fight for real human rights for the American negro. Several in the crowd around him were in tears at the end of Reverend King's 'I have a dream' speech.

Charlie spent his last night in the USA with Tom and Tara, before Tom dropped him off the next day at Washington's Dulles Airport to catch his flight to Sydney and then to Port Moresby. He could not help feeling envious of the married bliss and excitement at the news of Tara's pregnancy. His relief and anticipation of returning home was tempered by the prospect of never seeing Tom again.

At the kerbside, the two friends faced each other.

'Tom, you have been such a good friend. We have to

meet again, I don't know how or where or when, but let's keep in touch.'

They hugged in silence then Charlie picked up his well-worn backpack and disappeared into the terminal.

PART THREE

THE RETURN

CHAPTER 33

He gazed at the coastline below. Port Moresby was coming into view and a rumbling sound signalled that the captain was lowering the aircraft's undercarriage in preparation for landing. Charlie was thinking about the role of chance in life. In the normal course of events, by the age of twenty-five he would be living in Tori village, married to Beida and maybe another village girl, with children and chickens running around outside his hut. He would have a smallholding where he would be growing some mangoes and sago, have a pig or two and spend evenings with fellow village men putting their world to rights. He might never have left Tori.

Fate had intervened. Years earlier, after his return to the US, Tom Paul had written and sent him the team's report covering the story behind the B-25 crash near to the Hulwari village. The fact that no fire had taken place indicated the cause of the crash was probably due to fuel shortage. Existing USAF records from the Henderson base showed the B-25 had been refuelled sufficiently to reach its destination. The crash had occurred at a location many miles off course due to a serious navigation error. Some unknown factor had caused this unaccountable mistake on the part of an experienced crew. Fate had intervened with that error. It had completely changed Charlie's life and that of others.

As the aircraft door opened, Charlie was hit with a blast of hot, humid air. He had quite forgotten the climate in his homeland. He had become acclimatised to the dryer, more temperate weather of California. After descending the steps to the tarmac and reaching the passenger terminal his shirt was sticking to him. The Australian immigration official at Moresby's airport had never seen a passport like Charlie's. He noticed the US entry stamp.

'Where you going? To your village or back to the States?'

'To my village, as soon as I can after reporting to my department here in Moresby.'

A few days later, he was still waiting to be called to the headquarters of the Department of Native Affairs which he learnt had recently been renamed as the Department of District Administration, or DDA. He supposed that such changes were to keep government bureaucrats busy. Or maybe, dropping the term 'native' was more acceptable to the outside world. He had already learnt that Australia was coming under increasing pressure to loosen its hold on its colonial possession. Given a bunk in the police barracks, he was becoming increasingly impatient to know his future. Once back in his homeland he sensed that he had disappeared into obscurity. He was now just one of five million. In America, he was something of a celebrity – not always welcome, but at least people noticed him. He was a subject of curiosity, interest or unpleasant prejudice. Here, he just faded into the background.

At last, he received a reply to his request to be able to travel to Tori pending advice on his job with the administration.

The DDA were in no hurry to see Charlie, for them his presence back in PNG was unwelcome. As he himself had once laughingly predicted, many had hoped never to see him again. The colonial mindset was slowly changing but mostly still entrenched. The powers in Port Moresby had been quite unable to reconcile themselves to a 'bloody native' being in any sort of position of responsibility or authority in government service. There was a minority of more insightful members of the administration who realised that Charlie was the thin end of a large and inevitable wedge. They advocated that he be given a role in government. It could use his knowledge of native culture, valuable in forming policy during a transition to independence. Despite this, they were shouted down in deciding Charlie's future in his homeland. After numerous meetings and arguments, it was decided that Charlie's future lay as an APO, Assistant Patrol Officer, at remote Duro Island in the far west of PNG. He was granted one week of leave in Tori before taking up his new post.

After six years in America, he landed back in Tori. He walked from the airstrip, calling to see Uncle Paru. His father's brother, who had visibly aged, was sitting outside his hut. He struggled to his feet to embrace his nephew. One of Charlie's cousins was dispatched to find other family members. Soon, a sizeable crowd gathered around them. Charlie found himself using Tori dialect that he had not spoken since leaving.

'So uncle, tell me everything about the village since I left.'

Paru started to detail the minutiae of village happenings, aided by interjections from the crowd who had settled on the ground around Paru's hut. To Charlie it seemed as if he had never been away. Day-to-day life had continued much as it had for centuries before. The track to the airstrip had been improved. The Hulwaris were their usual objectionable selves, but there had not been any serious violence. Other than that, there was a recounting of births, marriages and deaths. Charlie's first love, Beida, was married with three children. Masta Bruce had been replaced by three kiaps in succession, none of whom warranted much mention.

'Nephew Charlie, what are you going to do now? Are you going to stay and find a wife? Your father's land waits for you to build a hut.'

'Uncle, one day I will, but now the government wants me to be an assistant kiap in Duro in the west.'

The crowd listening to this were murmuring in puzzlement. Why would anybody want to live anywhere but Tori?

That evening and in the following days, Charlie would sit among the men of the village where his attempts to describe life in America were received with incredulity. It was clear to most that although fascinating, these were just fairy stories.

At the end of the week Charlie left his village, wondering when he would return. He realised that Tori had not changed since he left it for America, whilst he was not the man who left five years ago. The truth was that he wasn't sure where he belonged now, except perhaps as a citizen of PNG, then of the world.

CHAPTER 34

At first, Charlie was not a success in his new role. The creation of the rank of APO had been made with him in mind. As an assistant kiap he would be buried away in a remote posting where he could hopefully be forgotten. Duro's waters were alive with crocodiles, not to mention hostile tribes inland who with luck could take care of the problem. Duro was seen as ideal for Charlie's first posting. The only way there was by boat, in this case a cramped government launch whose crew viewed their passenger with some curiosity. Local natives in any position of responsibility were almost unknown.

The new APO was viewed with incredulity and suspicion by his boss, Duro's resident patrol officer. Max Gillespie was a weather-beaten forty-year-old with a Fosters habit. Gillespie had been a kiap for nearly fifteen years, moving from station to station between leave in his home state of Queensland. Fifteen years without promotion marked him as something less than a rising star. His record was tarnished by a number of failures to spot and report unrest. He had also made some bad decisions when dealing with day-to-day problems, causing resentment towards the administration. At a previous posting, this came to the notice of his DC, who arrived for a routine inspection visit, only to beat an undignified retreat from a shower of rotten mangoes hurled by disaffected villagers. This was a rare event in a local population who normally treated a visiting white bigman with respect and deference. Gillespie had wrongly adjudicated in favour of a known philanderer, rather than the headman's son, the aggrieved husband. The DC's subsequent report recommended a desk job for Gillespie in Port Moresby, although the shortage of patrol officers resulted instead in a posting to Duro district, to the misfortune of the local population.

Charlie found himself not only having to overcome his boss's deep prejudices, but to cope with the incomprehension of the locals. To Duro's population, it seemed Charlie had a position of authority normally attributed to white men. He did not speak their local language, had dark skin and looked the same as them. He was obviously another foreigner, albeit an inferior one. He was generally ignored or treated with rudeness and contempt. He was reminded of some of the prejudice he had encountered in America.

Charlie set himself the difficult task of gaining acceptance in his latest world. His first weeks in Duro were marked with bouts of homesickness for America and longings for the warm embraces of Victoria in San Antonio. He had not heard from her now for three years. He now felt he was better understood in America than in his homeland. All manner of inner conflicts were contributing to this crisis of identity. While in America he had started to idealise his country, becoming a proud advocate for PNG and its way of life. Now he started to see PNG as a collection of narrow, inward-looking tribes riven with xenophobia and suspicion. To compound his unhappiness, he had to deal with Gillespie who had none of Bruce Petersen's generous nature.

In his darker moments, Charlie was entertaining thoughts of somehow finding a way back to America and settling for life. San Antonio beckoned. He had no close family in PNG.

Why not? he asked himself. Overcoming these negative ideas with difficulty, he decided he could not face anybody, let alone himself, if he ran away from this situation. He would stay in Duro and somehow make the best of it.

Charlie was housed in a hut formerly allocated to Duro's policemen who had been moved to make room for him. This did nothing to endear Duro's two constables to the new APO. Neither did it confirm Charlie's authority in the eyes of the villagers. If he was important, surely he would be housed in a bungalow like Mr Gillespie? For the most part, Charlie was ignored. To combat this, he recognised he needed to become fluent in Kiwai. In a country of five million, although only spoken by around twenty thousand people, Kiwai was a major language.

He needed to find someone with whom he could form a relationship and practice. This was unwittingly solved for him by Gillespie.

'I want you to go on a tour of all the villages under my jurisdiction. You will update the population record for each village, report on the state of government property and adjudicate on any disputes. I'll need a full trip report on your return. Take as long as you need.'

'OK, boss. Will do. When shall I start?' asked Charlie, his mood immediately improving at the thought of getting away from Gillespie.

'As soon as you like, after you've drawn from stores whatever you need for the trip.'

Duro was on an island. A government boat was allocated to visit the mainland and inland rivers for the trip, calculated to take several weeks or more. Forever, if Gillespie could have his way. The boat was a small launch, with a tiny cabin and an outboard motor. The sole crew, a grizzled old man named Yauwii, would also act as Charlie's assistant. At first sight, Yauwii was not an appealing companion for the next few weeks. He was very small of stature, with a disconcerting squint, one eye being directed outwards and slightly upwards. He was also a man of few words. Tok Pisin was universal and Charlie's starting point to their relationship.

'Yauwii, yume makim tok tok Kiwai – savvy?'

Yauwii's grunt was his standard reply to anything Charlie tried and not an encouraging start. This grunt was evidently to say his role was driving the launch, not teaching languages. A combination of his body language and apparently permanent look of misery made Charlie wonder whether his companion for the next few weeks, was clinically depressed.

A lucky break occurred at the end of the second day, when Charlie despairing of attempts to engage with his assistant, took to casting a baited line over the side of the boat. After twenty minutes a violent tug signalled a bite at which Yauwii gave a yell of delight, leaping forward to help his new boss land an exceptionally large yellowfin tuna. Evidently anybody who could land a meal of that size in such a short time was worth knowing. With the ice, now broken, Charlie could start acquiring Kiwai. His very first words were 'yellowfin tuna'.

Over time during his posting to Duro, Charlie became quite close to Yauwii. He often wondered why the simple act of fishing could have such a dramatic effect on the man's behaviour.

The therapeutic effect of landing a fish seemed somehow to dispel Yauwii's depression for the entire trip. By the end of their time together, Charlie's aptitude for languages enabled him to start limited conversations with other residents of Duro. In his various postings as a boy with his uncle and Mr Smithson's household, he had acquired a working knowledge of several PNG languages and dialects, one of which was in the adjacent Gulf region. This helped Charlie as the local syntax in Kiwai was not dissimilar.

The field trip with Yauwii comprised sailing up the coast until they met the mouth of the great 1,000 kilometres long Fly River. By volume of discharge, the Fly is the largest river in Oceania and the largest in the world without a single dam.

Charlie and Yauwii were to call on riverbank villages and stop to collect the census and other data required by PO Gillespie. Charlie considered his best approach to the tasks in hand. He realised that he needed to assert his authority to gain the cooperation of each village headman. Not an easy task. The slightly comical figure of Yauwii would not help the matter. Charlie would have preferred to have as company at least a uniformed policeman as an identifiable representative of government and authority.

The Western Province was mainly a collection of small riverbank villages, some with only forty inhabitants and rarely more than a few hundred. Charlie's first stopping point was a small settlement on a tiny island near the mouth of the mighty Fly. Inevitably, the arrival of the government launch aroused interest and a small crowd gathered at the ramshackle jetty. Charlie left it to Yauwii to announce their arrival. This announcement in Kiwai seemed to go on for a while. Yauwii later explained that he was telling the inhabitants that not only was Charlie an important government official, but a highly accomplished fisherman. Apparently, the latter carried more weight in impressing the locals than his official position. The headman was in some ways not unlike Yauwii – small, wizened and of few words. Charlie had to rely on pidgin with the headman, who found it strange that any apparently important person could have any interest in numbers of people on the island. He seemed more interested in Charlie's fishing skills.

Charlie expected that collecting data on the village could be accomplished in a couple of hours, however it was soon clear that the headman had other ideas. After a lengthy evening meal surrounded by almost the entire the population with interminable speeches by village dignitaries, Charlie managed to address those assembled. With Yauwii translating he could not assess impact of his speech. It was received mostly in silence with occasional grunts, which Yauwii assured his boss were positive. He requested certain information that he needed for his report to Gillespie. On satisfactory receipt of this the following day, Charlie promised to give out some hints on fishing techniques. Of the latter he knew nothing, but felt he could embellish the obvious with some pseudo-scientific facts on favourable moon phases, water temperature and so on – impressive but difficult to verify. He spent the night in the decrepit hut used as a rest house for visitors. He made a note to request Public Works Department visit to repair the jetty and rest house, both looking in danger of imminent collapse. He left the next day with the required numbers entered into his census book and the island's fishermen scratching their heads, pondering the usefulness of Charlie's fishing tips.

The data collecting expedition continued in a similar vein for the next few weeks. Many villages seemed willing to help as the word spread up the river that a foreign fishing guru was to honour them with some pearls of wisdom.

Some weeks later, on return to Duro, Charlie felt a glow of accomplishment. He was doubtful as to the usefulness of the data he had gathered, but the expedition had enabled him to acquire greater insight into his country, its diversity, culture and human values. He had been vaguely conscious of these before leaving for America but now he had seen them in their stark contrast to western society. For the first time he had a position of authority which he realised he enjoyed.

On Charlie's return, Gillespie was surprised to see that he had not only completed his tasks but seemed happy to be back. Yauwii evidently spread the word that the new APO was to be respected and together with his rapidly acquired basic Kiwai, Charlie found new warmth from Duro's population. Some two months after arrival back, HQ requested Charlie return to Port Moresby by the next government boat visiting with supplies. A situation had arisen in the Madang region requiring urgent attention from a significant government presence. Every available officer was needed to address unprecedented unrest and even violence in a normally peaceful area. Charlie's language skills had been noticed and thought to be an asset.

CHAPTER 35

Charlie found himself leaving Duro with a regret that he had not anticipated. He would not miss Gillespie, but had formed a bond with Yauwii and started to gain a perspective of his homeland, confirming the need to protect it from some of the changes in store from western influences.

A week later, he found himself in Moresby attending a meeting alongside others including patrol officers and senior policemen. Charlie was the only non-white face present. They were addressed by a Mr Conrad, DC from the Madang province. It seemed that his problems sprang directly from the presence of 'cargo cults' in the region under his administration. Charlie knew about the cults and had witnessed them first hand in his youth. Conrad gave a brief talk on the subject and its history that originated from the time of the arrival of white men throughout the Pacific islands.

During World War Two, the Allies set up many temporary military bases in the Pacific. These introduced the isolated people of PNG to huge quantities of highly desirable manufactured goods. Charlie's superstitious fellow PNG inhabitants and other Pacific islanders thought that these must have come from some distant ancestral world. They believed the source of these riches were controlled by a mythical figure known as 'John Frum'. This name was possibly derived from the name of an American serviceman. One theory was that one of the first Americans to arrive announced himself as 'John frum America'. A 'cargo cult' was formed worshipping John Frum with the belief that riches from his distant world would accrue to his followers. The people of the Madang region of New Guinea were only one of the many Melanesian islands of the Pacific to be gripped by a religious cult frenzy awaiting the return of Frum with unlimited 'cargo'. To encourage John Frum to return, islanders indulged in practices aping the American military activities including marching with wooden rifles with 'USA' emblazoned on their bodies. Mock airports and airstrips were constructed. This was all difficult logic for the western mind to follow, but very real to the believers.

The heart of the problems in Madang was conflict that had arisen between the believers in 'John Frum' and converts of the local Presbyterian missionaries, whose god was not disposed to religious opposition.

The resulting unrest had culminated in violent clashes, burning of villages and serious injuries to both sides. The administration was becoming alarmed that such events might spread to other areas. The local officers were appealing for help. A battalion of the Papuan Regiment had been dispatched and achieved a standoff, but a lasting solution was needed to put an end to the serious unrest.

A few days later Mr Conrad, APO Charlie and two Australian POs arrived in Madang. During the journey they decided to split up with Conrad and Charlie talking to the leaders of the cult people and the others to the church leaders. The plan was then to have a summit, bringing both factions together to come to some resolution of the situation. This would take place in the various areas up and down the coast where the trouble had occurred.

It seemed to Charlie to be a challenging problem, trying to achieve change in people with two deeply imbedded, yet totally opposed, beliefs. In their first meeting, he and Conrad found themselves facing a large meeting of John Frum followers. Using halting pidgin, Conrad started by saying that the government wanted it understood that the violence had to stop and there would be severe penalties for those who indulged in it. This had a negative effect on the audience and there were murmurings and scowls. This 'bigman' didn't understand anything about their problems with these god people and their white missionary leaders. The mood of the crowd was becoming more antagonistic by the minute. Conrad had clearly started on the wrong foot. He looked at Charlie who knew he had to get on the same side as the audience. There was no point in trying to preach common sense or rational thinking. Cargo cults were here to stay for now. Education and time would eventually take care of the problem. Charlie started in his fluent pidgin,

'Olgeta man na Gavman save John Frum he gutpela, no ken mekim nois, he laik gutpela taim, he belisi.'

Charlie's praise of John Frum as a good man of peace, known to be a nice guy by everybody including government, immediately produced silence and nods from the audience. Conrad caught on and joined in the nodding. Charlie went on at length about how Frum would not want to hear that his followers had been fighting with the Christians who were also good people, just misguided with strange ideas. The Christian god also did not like his converts fighting and Charlie's colleagues were telling them so right now.

Conrad and Charlie's colleagues had insightfully taken a similar line with the Christians and their missionaries but surprisingly found a less tolerant attitude to those they saw as dangerous pagans. Conrad later had some harsh words for the white missionaries who he put on notice that their residence visas could be revoked if they didn't preach love and peace rather than fire and brimstone. There followed a summit between the leaders of the two factions at each location. Conrad extracted promises of future good behaviour which, if maintained, would see the government pay for repair of damaged property.

It seemed that the expedition to Madang had been a success. Although it was an uneasy peace there were no further reports of unrest. The Papuan regiment had been withdrawn. Conrad put in a report including high praise for Charlie for his part.

With his star in the ascendant Charlie was promoted to Patrol Officer to be sent to his own area. This was a signal moment in the territory's history – a PNG native being entrusted with a white man's job.

On his return to Port Moresby, as he awaited his next orders, he found a bundle of mail waiting for him that had accumulated since leaving the USA. Mostly there were envelopes bearing stamps with images of American presidents. A wave of nostalgia swept over him as he sorted through them seeing postmarks marking his travels and friends made over the last five years.

Halfway through opening the envelopes, he selected one with an eight cent US stamp with a picture of Amelia Earhart and her plane in the background. It was postmarked San Antonio. He slit open the envelope, the contents of which were destined to dominate his life for years to come. His happiness at his promotion and anticipation of his posting to his very own area disappeared in an instant.

CHAPTER 36

The letter was from Mama Julie. Not long after Charlie left for Stanford, Victoria missed her period. Her pregnancy was soon confirmed and some forty weeks later she was delivered of a bouncing boy, clearly a mix of Charlie and Victoria's respective heritages. Victoria resisted her mother's demands that Charlie be informed immediately. He later learnt that her response was along the lines:

'Mama, I loved that boy but I will spoil his life if I make him come back. He always told me the only thing he wanted was to get some education then go back to help his people. No way would I go and live with him in that wild country and its cannibals. I'll be happy to bring up Li'l Charlie here. Besides, after Charlie left you know I started seeing Vern and he says he don't mind being daddy to my baby. Vern is a good man, I love him and he wants to marry me.'

Mama had reluctantly agreed. She would have preferred Charlie to Vern as a prospective son-in-law and thought Charlie should be made to contribute to his son's upkeep. But Victoria would have none of it and forbade her mother to contact Charlie. Later she had a daughter by Vern, whom by then she had married.

The letter was posted three months ago. Two weeks before that, Victoria and Vern were in Vern's pickup when it was hit by a sixteen-wheeler truck travelling at speed at a crossroad. Both of them were killed outright. Mama Julie was struggling looking after Li'l Charlie and his sister. She felt he should know. Could he help?

Charlie was devastated by Victoria's death. His instinct was to return immediately to the USA and shoulder responsibility for his son. Reviewing the reality of his situation, he had very little money, certainly insufficient to fund even a one-way flight to San Antonio. His bosses would not allow him to leave PNG so soon after returning. They would fire him if he left without permission. He had to find a way to bring his son to PNG. He would not let him grow up in bigoted America. From now on, this was his priority in life. He immediately wrote to Mama Julie saying he would see what he could do to help. He would definitely come to San Antonio, but it might take a year or more before he could get leave and save enough to fund his trip. He promised to take responsibility as a father and would meanwhile send whatever money he could afford each month. Victoria had named his son Charlie. He asked for regular news of Li'l Charlie.

CHAPTER 37

Charlie found himself posted to the Obura-Wonenara District in the Eastern Highlands. Here, he was in his own little kingdom. A new patrol office had been built at Okapo, more or less central to a number of smaller villages. No kiap had been stationed in the area before. Infrequent, fleeting visits by a patrol officer from a neighbouring area were the only times a government presence was felt in Okapo. Charlie's arrival was viewed with some curiosity, as apparently, he had a white man's powers, but without the white aura. He was allocated a policeman called Peter, whom he initially found uninspiring but who later proved himself in a most unexpected fashion.

Overshadowing each day were Charlie's thoughts about his son and the death of Victoria. He found himself anxiously looking forward to the weekly flights with mail.

He found a useful ally at the local London Missionary Society school in the form of a teacher, John Edwards. Edwards had been in PNG since the end of the war nearly twenty years ago. Edwards was an affable, single, grizzled, fifty-year old Australian.

'John, something I'm going to need here is an assistant, got any ideas?'

'There's a local lad who's just finished at the school. He's bright, personable and confident, with a reasonable grasp of English. He wasn't too interested in Christianity but I can't hold that against him. His name is Samuel Pulu. I'll get him to come and see you. See if you like him.'

John and Charlie chatted for a few hours. John was interested in Charlie's American adventures.

'They call themselves Christians, but I can't imagine what Jesus would make of their behaviour,' commented John. 'Mind you, we Aussies aren't any better in the way we treat the aborigines.'

The following day, Samuel Pulu presented himself to Charlie at the patrol office. Dark as Charlie, Samuel was shorter by a couple of inches with a muscular frame. He was wearing a T-shirt with a large American flag on his chest.

'Samuel, I am going to teach you how to be a patrol officer's assistant. You will watch everything I do and how I do it. You are going to teach me how to speak with people in this area and everything I need to know about them and their customs. You will report to me anything that happens that is unusual or against the law.' Charlie was using English.

'What do I call you? Boss?' Samuel replied in English with a grin.

Charlie pondered this question. In local languages it might have been appropriate for Samuel to use 'brother' or 'father' as a mark of respect for an older more senior man, although Charlie was barely six years older than Samuel. Had he been an English kiap, he would be addressed as 'Masta' or 'Mr Charlie'.

'Samuel, when we are alone together you can call me Charlie. In front of others, in English, you use Mr Charlie. In Tok Pisin you use Bos.' Charlie didn't want to be called Masta.

As the months progressed, he found his new assistant to be a quick learner. Samuel's English improved rapidly. Charlie became friends with John Edwards, frequently watching the sunset with beers from the patrol office veranda. Charlie found John to be a very empathetic character and he took the opportunity to unburden himself about his worries following Mama Julie's letter.

'If there's anything I can do to help, just say the word. If you can get your boy back here, he can come to the school. I know any number of village women who could be a housekeeper for you and look after him when you're busy.'

One of Charlie's priorities was to acquire some fluency in the local languages. He knew he had been lucky in Duro, having formed a friendship with Yauwii. He realised that the sheer number of these local languages made it necessary to use Tok Pisin most of the time. This was all that was expected of white kiaps, but Charlie felt he should try to get a good working knowledge of the most used languages in his area. He did not want to be identified as a white kiap disguised in black skin. He knew that he would get greater respect by using a local language. Also, it would be occasionally useful to overhear exchanges when the speakers might assume he could not understand their speech. There was a multitude of local languages used in the villages around Okapo and to complicate matters further, some had dialects spoken by just a handful of people. Charlie concentrated on the Benabena language and its variations used in the area and in the regional centre of Goroka. He was also learning Fore which was mostly used in the area under his jurisdiction. Samuel was a Fore speaker and greatly impressed by his boss's linguistic prowess in just a few months.

Charlie quickly learnt that a major cause of resentment against the government was the imposition of a tax on Okapo and surrounding villages. Unfortunately for Charlie he was identified as part of an unfriendly administration that collected taxes but otherwise had no useful function. His Duro experience had taught him one way of gaining respect would be by finding and excelling at some activity valued by the local population. Another might be by solving some longstanding local problem.

There had been little training for his new job. There had been none prior to going to Duro where, despite his title of APO, he had been sent as a dogsbody to Max Gillespie. After his promotion, the obligatory two-week induction course in Port Moresby was mainly for the benefit of newly appointed patrol officers fresh from Australia.

There was some information about limits of responsibility but Charlie knew from experience that these were largely theoretical. At remote outposts the kiap was virtually king.

As a new kiap, Charlie already had a role model for his new position. It had to be Mr Smithson who had been a father figure, revered by Charlie as a beacon of fairness and humanity. He was unlike many of the Australian members of the administration. Among the latter, there were often those who regarded themselves as superior human beings simply due to their colour. Max Gillespie in Duro was typical.

Charlie found that most of his work was settling land and family disputes. Typically, a kiap would be expected to hear complaints and settle disputes in the patrol office although Charlie usually found it more satisfactory to meet the parties as guests in his house. He found a more informal approach acting as a friendly local mediator worked better. He didn't identify as an official laying down the law from behind a desk.

One day Samuel entered the patrol office looking worried.

'Bos, there is big problem with fighting in the village and I saw blood. Constable Peter has stopped it, but I think it will happen again with killing. It is between two families.'

'Tell Constable Peter to bring the heads of the families to me.'

This was a serious matter as blood had been spilled. Unusually, Charlie decided to have a hearing in the patrol office with Samuel as interpreter. He was not yet sufficiently fluent in the local dialect.

Later, Peter ushered two men into the office. One of them had the unlikely name of Tripp Paiyo and the other Paul Maru. Both barefoot, Tripp and Paul were bearded and had prepared themselves by having impressive amounts of white paste smeared on their faces and bodies. Tripp's sole clothing was a ragged lap-lap. Paul was similarly attired but incongruously wearing red-framed sunglasses. Charlie had noticed some for sale in the village store. Both had red gums from chewing betel nut, homemade seashell ornaments about their necks and bird feathers in their hair. They viewed Charlie suspiciously.

Each was to explain the reasons for this breaking of the peace. This took the best part of a half hour with Samuel providing a summary at the end.

Charlie regarded his two countrymen seated on the floor before him in his little court of law. As a dispenser of justice his mind went back to the total contrast with the trial of his and Maria's kidnappers in Columbus' imposing courtroom. He saw the robed judge, the dark-suited lawyers and the formal atmosphere. For no reason he suddenly started thinking about the fate of the defendants that day. He was suddenly shaken from his reverie by Samuel noisily clearing his throat.

'Bos, these men are waiting for you speak.'

Charlie hoped the miscreants before him assumed he was pondering matters of law, not that his thoughts were eight thousand miles away.

It seemed that the men represented families that had been at each other's throats over the same matter for several generations. This had historic roots over some ancient boundary dispute. Occasionally, a flare-up occurred over some trivial matter but in reality, it was just a symptom of the old problem.

'You and I are of the same people – from different villages perhaps, but the same people. You are here because the law of this village and other villages does not allow grievances to cause the spilling of blood. There is good reason for this and wise men know that our ancestors believe this. When an animal, bird or a tree dies it has no life anymore and it is of no importance. The same is true of old fights about land. They also no longer have importance. Our ancestors knew this too.'

Charlie knew that invoking ancestral beliefs would have more effect than just preaching white men's laws. He knew that he was assigning previously unknown attributes to ancestors, but who was going to question them?

'From this day on, there will be no fighting between your families. If I learn of fighting in the future, you will both come here and I will use white men's laws and I will not listen to any of these complaints about each other that I have heard today. You will both be sent away from the village to work in a government prison. You will suffer. Your families will suffer. Your ancestors and I will be unhappy that you think more about fighting than the lives of your families and the shame you will bring upon them. Go back to your families and tell them what I have said and live in peace in this life.'

Samuel translated Charlie's homilies and threats in terms that Tripp and Paul would understand and the pair left the patrol office in silence. Charlie doubted that the two men would ever be friends, but if the long-term hatchet was buried deep enough, he would be satisfied. After the miscreants had left, Samuel spoke up, impressed.

'Bos, that surely stopped them fighting.'

The word soon spread around the village that the new government patrol officer was surprisingly reasonable, but also not to be trifled with. Previously, stories about white kiaps from other districts spoke of harsh summary penalties with little understanding of local issues. Charlie was relieved to hear of a consensus of approval on his handling of the affair which the village had been awaiting with great interest.

CHAPTER 38

One day, Samuel appeared in the patrol office accompanied by Constable Peter handcuffed to a pale-skinned young man. Charlie very occasionally saw the products of liaisons between Europeans and local women. The men were often Australians who worked for one of the foreign timber or other commercial companies in PNG. Some had actually married local girls and gained permanent residence, but most went back home never to be seen again. As in other parts of the world, the resulting offspring from black and white parents were often shunned by both their parents' ethnic communities. The resulting unhappiness gave rise to social problems for the blameless child and they would sometimes turn to petty crime. The fellow shackled to Peter looked unusual.

His appearance struck Charlie as strange. He was less than five feet tall, of slim build and with loose rather than tightly curled black hair. His pale skin colour, high cheekbones and narrow eyes gave an altogether bizarre appearance. While not a pygmy, he was certainly unusually short. Charlie had read of pygmy tribes in other parts of the world and wondered if this man could be related to one of them. There were several tribes yet to be contacted by the PNG administration.

'I don't understand his language,' said Samuel. 'I've tried everything I know, but his language is not from anywhere around here. He doesn't even understand Tok Pisin.'

'Why is he here? What has he done?' asked Charlie.

'He was caught trying to steal food.'

Charlie tried to remember some of the other tribal languages he had learnt during his younger travels with Mr Smithson.

'What is your name? Where is your village?' He tried several times.

In his days as a lad of ten with Mr Smithson, Charlie spent six months in the Morobe province and while playing with local boys, had learnt a smattering of their local tongue. Although a distant memory, he tried a few words that he remembered. Suddenly, there was a reaction from their visitor. Limited though the communication was, it appeared that the small man hailed from a remote village in the Morobe region. His name was Numu. For some reason Charlie could not fathom, Numu had left his tribe and been wandering from village to village for weeks, foraging to keep alive.

Although the Morobe province was outside his jurisdiction, Charlie was intrigued by Numu and decided he should find out more about him, his origins and his village.

He decided to contact his opposite number in the region to see what light they might be able to shed on his strange visitor. Such contact would be by shortwave radio using the new transceiver box recently installed in the patrol office by a Post and Telegraphs' technician. Meanwhile, he wondered if his missionary friend John Edwards would like to extend some Christian charity towards Numu.

As Charlie expected, John didn't hesitate. 'From Morobe, you say? Strange, he must be good many miles from home. Sure, I'll give him shelter and food in exchange for helping out clearing and extending the mission compound.'

Charlie drew a blank from his enquiries about Numu. He decided to request permission from the Morobe's DC to lead a small expedition into the Morobe province to try establishing contact with Numu's tribe. It was government policy to register and map all uncontacted tribes. Normally, this would have been the task of the local regional headquarters but Charlie knew there was often little enthusiasm for such work which was considered onerous and occasionally dangerous.

He had some leave owing in a few months' time and he had little idea of how to spend it. He could not yet afford to mount an expedition to America to fetch his son. An Australian kiap would have been off to his homeland, paid for by the administration. As a local employee Charlie did not qualify for this benefit. He was still sending an allowance to Mama Julie. Despite saving furiously, and desperate to go to San Antonio to collect Charlie Junior, he could not yet afford the airfare and local travel expenses. He would use two precious weeks of his leave to visit Morobe.

'Go for it, mate,' crackled the voice from the radio from Morobe's HQ in response to Charlie's request to try to find Numu's tribe. 'Check in here and we'll fix you up with the necessary before you start.'

It seemed Numu had settled into John Edward's mission, working hard and even showing interest in John's attempt to introduce him to Christianity. He was acquiring a limited ability in Tok Pisin and able to manage basic communication, but as yet was reluctant to talk about his past. When it was put to Numu that he was to accompany an expedition to his village, he became agitated. He grudgingly agreed that if he cooperated, he would be allowed to return to John's mission. The next day he accompanied Charlie in the short flight to Morobe.

'So, you're the famous Charlie Kikira,' Morobe's DC greeted his visitor with a handshake on arrival.

Being the first native kiap, his exploits since his return to PNG and his education in the United States made for much discussion within the administration. George Burrell, Morobe's DC, had been looking forward to meeting Charlie. George, a jovial, lanky World War Two veteran, now in his fifties had originally emigrated from Britain. He had known Philip Smithson and had served as a patrol officer under him for some years. He himself would be retiring in a few years. He knew more than most about Charlie's background. George was more liberal and insightful than many and could foresee and would accept changes when PNG became independent. He loved the country and its people. He planned to spend his retirement right here in Morobe, taking citizenship when the opportunity arose.

'Charlie, you really are a gift to the administration spending leave time doing their job for them. I've long wanted to contact some of these remote villages. The fact is, I've never had the time or anybody for this work to send up country. Plus, I'll welcome being able to separate fact from fiction in some of the stories I hear. You know the sort of thing – visits by ancestors, magic and all that.'

'Mr Burrell—' began Charlie.

'Call me George,' interrupted the other man.

Charlie recounted Numu's story and two days later set off with him, two constables and two porters. George had generously allocated two of his best policemen who, despite the unpromising names of Dud and Onepis, seemed to be alert and enthusiastic about the mission. Two porters named Yosia and Semu were to accompany the party. Charlie had memories of his expedition with Bruce Petersen to the Hulwari. History seemed to be repeating itself but now he was in charge.

After two days in a valley following the Wiwo River, they started to climb a narrow track under the direction of Numu. The ascent meant cooler air and Charlie started to enjoy the physical challenge. Passing under a green canopy of virgin forest, he reflected on the need to preserve this pristine environment. There had been rumours that foreign logging companies had approached the Australian Government for permission to extract hardwood timbers on a large scale from PNG's forests. If for no other reason, Charlie was starting to realise the need for PNG to determine such matters for itself.

As time progressed late into the fourth day, Numu started to become agitated. He indicated that they were within an hour's march of his village. Charlie decided to halt for the day and make camp.

'What is the problem? Why are you trembling?' asked Charlie using Tok Pisin. No reply came from Numu who was clearly terrified, teeth chattering. Dud repeated the question in a local dialect, becoming angry at the refusal to reply to Charlie, an important government man. Eventually Dud managed to extract a reply to the effect that the area was populated by ghosts and devils.

The following day, the group awoke to find Numu missing. Dud and Onepis set off to find him and appeared an hour later, hauling the fugitive before Charlie. Normally calm, Charlie berated Numu in every language he could summon. Was he a woman, a child, a mouse? Some creature that crawled in the undergrowth? None of this had any effect on the cowed man. Questioning a man's courage would usually sting his pride sufficiently to make him want to prove otherwise. Charlie started to wonder what exactly he was to expect when they found Numu's village. Prodding Numu before them, the expedition continued to follow a barely discernible narrow track, hedged either side with dense undergrowth. Fronds hanging from overhead brushed their faces. After an hour the jungle silence was suddenly shattered by a crack of what sounded like a rifle shot. Numu fell and the party stopped in shock. They crouched down below the level of growth lining the track. Dud and Onepis unshouldered their rifles. Charlie crawled forward to Numu who laid blubbering and groaning with pain. Blood was oozing from his shoulder but as far as Charlie could see it was a flesh wound and unlikely to be fatal. Bravery was certainly not one of Numu's qualities. Remembering an elementary first-aid course he took at Osterley Community College, Charlie bound the wound to stem the blood flow.

Charlie knew everybody was looking to him for directions as to what to do next. Yosia and Semu were frozen with fear. Dud and Onepis on the other hand seemed excited by the chance to use their rifles for the first time in anger since they joined the police. Until now they had only fired them on a range and considered them to be little more than heavy ornaments.

Charlie ordered Yosia and Semu to remain with Numu with dire consequences if they left his side. Charlie would follow the constables who would go forward with their weapons cocked. They were to return fire if necessary. After a quarter of an hour, they came to a clearing. In the centre was a crowd of men, heavily decorated with white paste and adorned with feathers on their arms and bodies in what usually signified warrior status in PNG's remote tribes. Armed with shields and spears, they started to advance. Behind them was a man holding a rifle which he was frantically, but unsuccessfully, trying to reload. Charlie commanded his men to fire in the air.

'Arrest that man. Shoot any man who threatens to stop you.'

The crash of two Lee Enfield .303 rounds caused the crowd to melt back into the huts surrounding the clearing leaving the rifleman alone and still trying to reload his weapon, which was clearly beyond him.

Onepis, using his rifle as a club, felled the rifleman with extreme force on the back of the head. Charlie wondered whether the man would ever get up again. Although he could not fault Onepis for his enthusiasm, this was not quite what he had in mind. Really, he wanted to interrogate the fellow. There were so many questions to be answered. At that moment he could not deal with the matter, although as it happened the man whose name he later established to be Ranby, expired later that day.

At this moment, a bandaged and contrite Numu appeared. He had witnessed the whole episode. As he was the only one of the party who spoke the village dialect, there was an opportunity to redeem himself.

'Numu, I need to know who is the headman here. Tell the warriors to come forward and lay down their spears and shields. The policemen will kill anyone who disobeys.' This was something of a stretch of Charlie's authority and a bluff, but it worked as the .303 volley had had the desired intimidating effect.

Charlie stood before a pile of spears and shields like a conquering general. Behind him, Dud and Onepis with rifles stood ready for further violence. With Numu translating, Charlie addressed the bewildered crowd.

'Warriors of Jivi,' he began. He had learnt the name of the village from Numu.

'I see no headman here. I am here as your friend, not your enemy. I am from the government that rules this land, your land, and the many villages beyond here and across the great seas. This government is ruled by a mighty queen who all men respect. She has many huge fierce armies who help her rule and punish those who oppose her. But she is a kind and generous queen who will send powerful medicine men to her villages to cure many diseases which kill. She will stop attacks from your enemies, who are her enemies also, but she does not allow you to attack or kill others. She will be angry to hear that one of you tried to kill my men.' Charlie pointed at the inert rifleman on the ground.

Charlie could not know the accuracy of Numu's translation, but it seemed to have a calming effect on the formerly antagonistic crowd. It transpired later that there had been a sort of coup d'état by a self-declared headman. This was the rifleman, whose supporters promptly disappeared at Charlie's arrival.

'Numu, take me to Jivi's headman.'

The usurped headman was sick but still alive. Charlie entered the man's hut, but he could barely see in the darkness. Numu knelt at the side of his bed, speaking rapidly at great length in some unintelligible language.

'Bring the headman out into the light,' commanded Charlie.

He was dumbfounded at the appearance of the man lying on a makeshift stretcher. He was definitely not a native of PNG but looked to be from somewhere in East Asia. He was semi-naked, wearing only a woven grass lap-lap on his lower half. He had sunken cheeks with a sickly, yellowish pallor which to Charlie looked like an advanced case of malaria.

The headman looked at the black man in European clothes standing before him. He could only guess that this man was part of the enemy he had fought all those years ago. Charlie looked at the emaciated man in astonishment. The man spoke to him in the same unfamiliar language he had used with Numu.

'My father thanks you for coming to his village and beating off the criminal elements that have brought ruin here,' translated Numu. 'He was an officer of the Japanese army, but now has a new life in Jivi village.'

'Tell your father that the war between Japan and Australia, America and the British, ended over fifteen years ago. The world is now at peace. Please tell me how he is now headman of a remote Papuan village. Your father is very sick and without treatment could die from infection and anaemia. He must take tablets to help him recover.'

Charlie called for his medical kit and extracted some chloroquine tablets. Charlie's team stayed in Jivi village for the next week, during which time the headman recovered sufficiently to tell his story.

CHAPTER 39

Twenty-three years previously, Lieutenant Masayoshi Hamada of the Japanese Imperial Army's 13th Infantry Division caught sight of the tree-lined New Guinea coastline. He was excited. Never before had he seen any land that was not part of Japan. Leaning on the ship's rail beside him was Sergeant Yoshida, a veteran of the battle of Guadalcanal. Yoshida's view of the war was unlike the boundless optimism of his young superior. He had seen the strength of the enemy. What the Americans lacked in battle experience and fanaticism they possessed in a seemingly inexhaustible supply of war materials and doggedness.

Little did either of the men realise that nearly two years later they would find themselves alone on a jungle-clad hillside. The officer and his sergeant were the survivors of a five-man group detailed to report on enemy movements from camouflaged hideouts. As the group retreated before an American advance, their companions had died from disease or enemy action. Hamada, still convinced of the invincibility of the Imperial Army, knew that before long they would be relieved of duty.

The pair were now sufficiently skilled at foraging for food. Yoshida was a first-class marksman and downing a wild boar would sustain them for many days. Water was never a problem with streams always nearby. They had become adept at building shelters with material from their natural surroundings. Hamada decided to keep inland but move westwards parallel to the coast, always looking for enemy activity. Sounds of warfare seemed to have ceased, the only noises being bird calls and rustling in the undergrowth.

One morning, Hamada awoke to find his companion shaking and vomiting with a high fever. He realised that he was witnessing an attack of malaria. Their supply of quinine tablets was long exhausted and several days passed with Yoshida's symptoms worsening. Hamada and Yoshida had become mutually dependent. Over time they had bonded, breaking the rigid taboo that forbids the slightest informality between the officer class and other ranks. They had started to discuss family matters, their plans for the future when the war ended, ignoring the likelihood that they would probably not survive. As Yoshida weakened, Hamada was fearful of not only losing a colleague but a close friend. After ten days of symptoms, Yoshida stopped breathing.

Hamada had never before experienced the turmoil of bereavement and reacted with numbed disbelief. Yoshida had become an older brother figure, wise and dependable. He raged against this war that killed good men. How could he continue alone? After burying his companion Hamada sank into a deep depression. For two days he did not eat and slept fitfully, each time waking with disbelief that he was alone.

Eventually he recovered, resolving to carry on his mission. He moved his shelter nearer to the coast in the hope of seeing naval activity or perhaps making contact with another group with the same mission as his own. After three months he had seen nothing.

'Was the war over?' he kept asking himself as he sheltered from the usual afternoon downpour. This had been a constant question in his mind. He could not believe that the Imperial Army could be beaten in combat. On the other hand, if victorious, surely search parties would have been sent out to find him. At that moment he may have felt alone, but the reality was that he was in the presence of another human being.

As he crouched unobserved, Angu wondered what this light-skinned man was doing near his village. Later, some three miles further inland from Hamada's shelter, the men of Jivi village gathered to discuss the arrival of this strange individual in their area. Angu's report detailed the man's bizarre ragged clothing and his odd possessions that seemed to have no practical purpose. It was important to determine whether the visitor was a good or bad omen. For days there were long speeches and discussions about this amazing development. There were long-held beliefs that one day the Jivi men's ancestors would appear in some form. Was this one of them? The consensus said yes. Was this connected with the movements of huge black boats off the coast? It was decided that the tribe would make offerings to this undoubtedly important arrival from the past.

The following day, when Hamada returned from foraging, to his utter surprise on the floor of his shelter, he found some sago and strips of meat wrapped in leaves. The illusion of his isolation was shattered. He was grateful for this bounty but it highlighted his vulnerability, albeit to an apparently benign force.

'These offerings must be from some local natives,' Hamada concluded, talking to himself.

He must try to make contact with these unknown benefactors. Over the next few days he searched the area but failed to locate the native village. There were further donations of food. Some primitive necklaces of sea shells also appeared overnight.

'How could they do this without waking me?' marvelled Hamada. 'They clearly wish to ingratiate themselves with me.'

He was excited and for once stopped obsessing about his mission and the death of his friend. He had been starting to suffer from the effects similar to a prisoner in solitary confinement. Talking to himself somehow seemed to alleviate his loneliness.

Days passed and he started to become dependent on the food left by his mystery supplier. Like Yoshida, he was starting to suffer malarial symptoms and after a while was unable to eat or leave his shelter. As his temperature increased, hallucinations took him away to Japan, his childhood and strange places. Between unconsciousness and moments of clarity he knew he was going to die. In a dream, he found himself with his family or surrounded by alien faces and bodies distorted by peculiar ornamentation and colours. He had no sense of time. This state persisted for days on end, with him concluding he had already passed into another world to join Yoshida.

His mind cleared and he saw palm leaves and woven straw above. He was not in his shelter. His and Yosida's rifles and meagre possessions were at his side. He was in a large hut which darkened as figures crowded into the entrance. Still confused, he spoke to the figures. He was rewarded by a babble of nasal grunts. He could not see clearly but the figures seemed to be almost naked, smeared with white, some adorned with bizarre headdresses. Desperately thirsty he pointed to his mouth miming drinking. Eventually a gourd was given to him. Slaking his thirst, he lay back, realising he was in the hands of an apparently friendly local tribe. After over two years of roaming tropical jungle, he felt an overwhelming sense of relief and gratitude. Not having the slightest idea of what the future held, the mere experience of human contact and kindness was overwhelming. Over the next few days, he slowly recovered his strength. The village of his hosts comprised a collection of about twenty huts. Each one was similar to the one that was apparently exclusively for him. When he ventured from his hut, he was always followed by what seemed to be most of the village's male population. He rarely saw any women. When he did, they were simply clad in grass skirts in contrast to the men, many of whom had elaborate colourful facial and body decorations. Bones or sticks through noses were common, with little covering the body. Hamada could not comprehend the motivation that drove the villager's apparent deference towards him. Only much later did he discover the cultural mysteries of PNG's ancestor belief.

Months wore on and he wrestled with the need to return to his mission. He was enjoying the peace of this undiscovered world. He was moved by the contrast with his own world that was seemingly obsessed with conquest, economic growth and industrialised killing. He thought about the needless death of his companions. The village seemed to be living in complete harmony with its environment. He would stay a little longer, perhaps until he could be sure the war was over, with the world returning to peace.

The village was spread along a narrow-plateaued mountain ridge with deep, jungle-clad gorges on either side, a location Hamada decided was chosen for defensive reasons. The huts of the village were arranged in a series of rough semicircles. Built on stilts, of bamboo construction with roofs of palm leaves, each seemed to have just one room. Two huts were larger than others. As he learnt later, these were for communal activities and one was a spirit house where teenage boys lived after reaching puberty.

At first, when Hamada saw women, they ran away to hide inside a hut and peer out at him as he passed. Later, when they became used to him, they would be sitting in groups outside huts pounding sago. Others would stop what they were doing and simply stare or giggle as Hamada walked past. Naked children and clucking chickens ran around. Men tended to be engaged in hut-building or repairing or fashioning weapons. These would be wooden spears, bows and arrows, or stone axes. From time-to-time men would be away from the village hunting, sometimes for several days.

Hamada found himself enjoying the simplicity and peaceful atmosphere of his surroundings. He could not face his duty to return to coast-watching for the emperor.

As months passed, he became less of a celebrity but was still treated with great respect. He sat with the men to eat and started to learn their language. It was a slow business, being quite unlike any other he had heard. It seemed that a young man named Eri had been allocated to follow him and see to his wants. Hamada sat with Eri for hours on end practicing the Jivi language. Eri in return was starting to acquire some everyday Japanese.

The day dawned when Hamada was invited to join a hunting party. His military training had meant cleaning his rifle daily. Yoshida's rifle had become rusty and beyond use. This cleaning was a curious ritual to the men of Jivi who had no idea of the use for this heavy piece of wood and steel. They would curiously finger the weapon which they believed must have some magic properties to require such attention including its owner coating parts of it in animal fat.

Hamada picked up his rifle at dawn and joined the hunting party as it left heading further inland. A problem was the state of his five-year-old army boots, which were splitting and becoming progressively more uncomfortable. His companions were barefoot. No shoe could contain their broad, jungle-hardened feet. Hamada tripped over roots and struggled to find toeholds on steep inclines. His fellow hunters had no such trouble; nimble and sure-footed, they never stumbled. Their quarries were either wild boar or deer. These are rarely seen in the open and are difficult to approach due to their keen senses and cautious instincts. Young wild boar were the choice of quarry for Jivi's hunters, being easier to track and slower to avoid a well-aimed spear. The only risk was a possible confrontation with an angry parent.

This was Hamada's first experience of a hunt and he was excited. There was a primeval sensation of being driven by the need of hunting for his food instead of it appearing ready to eat on a plate or from a mess tin. Facing dangers from a wild adversary held no terrors. He felt reassurance for his safety alongside his skilled companions and comforted by the familiar feel of the Arisaka rifle in his grip.

The morning wore on as the party continued through the green canopy of densely tree-covered slopes before coming upon a clearing with water cascading through small pools as it continued to lower levels. They stopped in the shade. Hamada noticed the leader wetted his hand to check the wind direction, signalling all to position themselves close to, but downwind of the pools. A wild boar's sense of smell is very well developed. Its hearing is also acute, though its eyesight is comparatively weak. Over time, Hamada would learn the Jivi hunters' skills, developed through evolution and handed down through generations. He also learnt the importance of extreme patience, when a hunting party could spend days waiting for prey to appear. They settled to wait and after several hours a distant crashing announced the imminent arrival of a family of wild boar.

Four animals suddenly appeared. Hamada was struck by the size of the large, black boar covered in short hair, apparently the mother of the three smaller animals. Her body seemed disproportionally large compared with her short, thin legs.

The hunters stayed still until all four animals were noisily engaged with their snouts in the water. Enthralled, Hamada watched as the leader signalled with his fingers for the spearmen to throw.

A Jivi spear is fashioned by its owner from a carefully selected piece of hardwood from the abundant, tough Kwila tree. Using stone tools, he produces a balanced weapon with an extremely sharp, narrow point capable of piercing the flesh of young boar. Each spear represents weeks of painstaking work. Jivi men knew the limitations of their weapons which would not penetrate the thick skin of an adult boar. Besides, they instinctively understood the need to preserve the lives of adults that produce a source of food. Boys learn the skill of spear-throwing from a young age. The modern sport of the javelin undoubtedly relates back to the primitive but functional use of spears.

Two of four thrown spears hit the nearest piglet that leapt into the air before falling on its side, squealing, with its legs kicking feebly. The young of the boar troupe scattered into the forest while the startled mother stood and peered about to see her family's attackers. Hamada operated the bolt of his rifle, the noise of which revealed his presence to her sensitive hearing. She charged towards him. He hurriedly took aim, but missed his target. The crash of the rifle echoed through the surrounding woods, stopping the disconcerted boar in its tracks before it disappeared into the forest. His companions had no idea that Hamada had aimed at the boar and missed, but were impressed that it ran away.

Hamada became more settled in his new life as he became more integrated in Jivi society, learning their language and forming relationships with his hosts. Jivi's ageing headman, Taviri, saw the foreign white man as having a favourable influence on his tribe. He was believed to have a magic aura, almost certainly a returned Jivi warrior. This was in contrast to his son Ranby who was seen as a lazy, weak warrior and poor hunter. Taviri and most of the tribe did not see Ranby as an attractive candidate for the next headman.

Taviri became obsessed with the idea of Hamada as the next Jivi headman, though fearing that he could depart back to the land of ancestors as magically as he had appeared. One measure that could help cement his presence would be for Hamada to marry one, or for that matter both, of Taviri's daughters. Hamada had become aware of the presence of Loa, one such maiden who served his food. Memories of his fiancée Emiko in Sapporo had long faded. Their relationship had been a formal one in accordance with Japanese custom, where they were always chaperoned when in each other's presence. He had now transferred his sexual desires to warm, smiling, bare-breasted Loa. Occasionally, he experienced a fading sense of obligation to the army and emperor. He told himself that the war was continuing and he would return to normality once sure it was over. His life of conforming to the taboos and restrictions of Japanese life were in sharp contrast to the freedoms and stimulus of this new, simple life. He did not hesitate for long when Taviri put his ideas to him. In a moment, Hamada cast aside his Japanese identity.

As the years passed, Hamada became an accepted member of the tribe, his foreignness overlooked and acquired hunting skills admired. He became a de facto son of Taviri. A light-skinned son, Numu, was born. Then a daughter, Yawena. All the while he had an enemy in the brooding presence of Ranby. On the death of Taviri he became headman, although not without resentment on the part of Ranby and his small coterie of followers. Hamada's natural leadership skills asserted themselves and he found himself increasingly content with his life, always trying ways to win over Ranby. The latter was constantly searching for ways to usurp Hamada. When Hamada was away hunting one day, his nemesis crept into his hut and discovered a small pack of rifle cartridges. Ranby did not know what they were, but felt they had to have some magic properties that could empower him. He extracted three cartridges, hoping they would not be missed, and stole back to his hut to examine his booty. He had seen Hamada's magic rifle and knew it could frighten animals. For months he carried the cartridges with him, hoping Hamada's magic would rub off on him, without success.

Purely by accident, Ranby found a way to harness the power of the cartridges. He and three of his supporters were away on a hunting expedition – on principle they would never join Hamada's hunting parties. Sitting round a fire built to roast the small deer they had killed, Ranby, as had become his habit, was rolling a cartridge around in his hand. He threw it on the ground, needing both hands to pull apart some strips of meat. The cartridge landed near some embers and for the moment was forgotten. Some several minutes later, the cartridge ignited with a fearsome crack, scattering hot embers. The effect on the men was one of shock and terror. Ranby knew at that moment he had found a way of defeating his adversary. Ranby patiently waited for the time when he could launch his takeover bid.

CHAPTER 40

'Amazing, absolutely bloody amazing,' said George Burrell, seated with Charlie on his veranda with several empty Fosters cans between them. It was three weeks since Charlie had set off with his party to find Numu's previously uncontacted village. It had taken nearly two hours and for the dark tropical night to fall while he described the background to the metamorphosis of Lieutenant Hamada into the headman of a primitive PNG tribe.

'So that accounts for at least some of the reported strange stories that have been filtering back from the ulu,' mused George, betraying his British Army background by using ulu for deep jungle.

'I guess, as it's in my area, I need to write it up for headquarters, adding yet more lustre in your ascent to stardom.'

'No need to glorify me George, except maybe say something that'll justify me being away from my office for time that I can claim as duty rather than vacation. I need all the vacation I can get now as I am planning a very special trip to the States. I'll tell you about it one of these days. What do you plan to say about Hamada? I guess it will create a media storm. I can see the headlines now "World War Two Japanese Officer lives in Jungle for Twenty-Three Years." We'll be overrun by reporters. The Japs would probably want him back as a hero. Frankly, I think he'd rather be left alone to carry on with his new life.'

'Don't worry about losing vacation time, Charlie, I'll square it with your DC. Terence is a reasonable sort. I have to think what I'll say about Hamada. He is a foreign national after all. If I don't identify him the word's bound to get out. My police boys and the porters will be dining out on this for months to come. So, this Ranby, what magic did he use to become the new headman, albeit temporarily?'

'It was simple really. He had a stroke of luck in a way – Hamada went down with a bout of malaria. Ranby assembled the village in front of a fire in the centre of the huts and made an imaginative speech, summoning spirits from the forest telling them to give a sign that he was now the bigman of Jivi. He threw a couple of rifle cartridges into the fire. You can imagine the effect on the good people of Jivi. The resulting explosions suitably impressed them and there was a rapid transfer of allegiance. This all happened a few weeks ago and Hamada's son, Numu, ran away to find help. Somehow, he wandered over in our direction but couldn't make himself understood. He was thoroughly frightened by the idea of forest spirits conjured up by Ranby, who was a nasty piece of work. But who would argue with someone who could call up evil spirits from the forest? Your man Onepis put an end to his short reign.'

As Charlie had predicted, word did get out about Hamada, eventually filtering through to a Reuters correspondent then inevitably to the world's media. The authorities in Canberra were suddenly overwhelmed with visa applications from newspaper, TV and film organisations wanting to invade George's Morobe district with the intention of mounting expeditions to Jivi village. Jivi, isolated from the world since time began, started to appear in newspaper articles worldwide. Charlie's prediction of headlines became true.

Canberra and Port Moresby administrations were adamant that there would be no press invasion and George Burrell would certainly not allow media hordes in his district. They could not in any event find Jivi without his assistance. Canberra felt obliged to grant visas requested by the Japanese Embassy. Japan's newspapers carried almost no other news for days. There were features with photos of almost anything relating to Lieutenant Hamada, pictures of his birthplace, the still standing family home, the site of his old regiment's headquarters, Hamada's PNG landing place at Buna and so on. Interviews with survivors of the Buna campaign, distant relatives, his deceased parents' old neighbours, pupils at his old school, even those who did not know him were all featured. After its humiliating defeat all those years ago the country desperately needed a hero. It found Japan wanting to fete Hamada with a triumphant return. They were to be disappointed.

Waiting for Charlie on his return from Morobe was a letter from Mama Julie. Enclosed was a photograph. His heart leapt at seeing a picture of Charlie Junior for the first time. A cheeky grin from a little black face looked at the camera. Feeling emotional, Charlie wondered what reaction he would get from his son when they met. Charlie's dreamy anticipation of that first meeting was disturbed by the crackle of the radio transceiver in the corner of the office. There were scheduled times when he was expected to have the equipment switched on and listening. Days would often pass without contact from the outside world. The voice and sudden burst of static from the corner woke Charlie from his quiet musing.

'This is the Director of District Administration in Moresby.'

A call from such a great height at headquarters was unusual to say the least. Accompanied by more crackling and fading, the voice directed Patrol Officer Kikira to proceed without delay to George Burrell in Morobe to help with a visit by Japanese officials. Charlie radioed Patair for a pickup the next day. He knew the journey well from his Jivi adventure only two months earlier. A two-hour hike to Tuvau airstrip, then a forty-five minute flight by single engine Cessna. Waiting at Morobe airfield, a grinning George vigorously shook Charlie by the hand.

'Welcome back, my friend, to the centre of the world's attention, thanks to you! Your little trip to Jivi has certainly stirred up the bosses in Moresby. Not to mention Canberra, who before this probably couldn't find PNG on the map!' George guffawed.

'Let's go and find a beer.'

Back in the office, Charlie received a brief from George on what followed the Jivi village adventure. Based on his discovery of Hamada, Charlie had been selected to lead an expedition back to Jivi. This time he would be leading a party that included four Japanese. George had spent eighteen months in Japan after the war as part of the occupying forces. He had learnt something of Japanese culture.

'They are absolute racists. Apart from the fact that we were an occupying force they found great difficulty in dealing with foreigners. Black American soldiers were looked upon as if they had just dropped from the trees. I learnt a smattering of Japanese but I'll keep that quiet. It will be interesting if I can hear what they say among themselves. The party will include a senior diplomat from Canberra, Kenzo Fukada, an assistant from the embassy, a man from Japan's government information service and a photographer. They will be flying into Morobe tomorrow.'

The government-chartered Piaggio aircraft, with its unique rear-mounted engines, bumped down on the recently constructed airfield's grass strip, stopping to disgorge its Japanese passengers. Charlie observed that the last two to leave the aircraft looked very pale and unhappy. Patair was renowned for its low-level bumpy flights over PNG's mountainous terrain, unkind to sensitive stomachs.

Diplomat Fukada walked across the grass to where George and Charlie were waiting. He bowed to George, ignoring Charlie. In perfect English he introduced himself and his colleagues.

'Mr Shinkai is my assistant and this is Mr Haraguchi and Mr Miyaki from our information department.'

After much bowing the three functionaries produced business cards for George, and continued to ignore Charlie.

'I am District Commissioner Burrell and this is Mr Charlie Kikira, an important and should I say famous member of my government department. Mr Kikira will manage your visit and be your guide during your stay in the Morobe district.'

Diplomat Fukada hesitated for a moment, then bowed and shook Charlie's outstretched hand. The rest of the party followed suit, reluctantly bowing and proffering cards. It was obvious that the Japanese were disconcerted at having to deal with a black man.

Installed in the government rest house, the following day they were briefed by Charlie. George sat at one side, listening.

Charlie looked at their suits and polished leather shoes and could see they were not prepared for what lay ahead.

'In order to reach Jivi village where Mr Hamada is resident, we will need to walk for three days, stopping to camp en route. We will have porters to carry camping equipment, food and any necessary belongings for the trip. There will also be armed police for security. Primitive tribes in PNG are frequently hostile to intruders and a visit may encounter dangers. Please only carry what is essential. There will certainly be heavy rain, so please make sure you have adequate protection.'

Charlie pretended not to notice the consternation on the group's faces and the whispering between them. They clearly had had no briefing that they would be involved in tramping for days in a tropical climate through inhospitable, jungle-clad mountainsides, swarming with axe-wielding, bloodthirsty natives. He wondered if they even had the physical stamina to survive the expedition. Charlie was enjoying himself. He could see that the Japanese had no idea of what they were getting into. George smiled to himself.

'Finally, I must tell you that there is no certainty that you will be able to meet Mr Hamada. Jivi village has historically been isolated until recently contacted by this administration. I have met Mr Hamada and I had the impression that he has totally abandoned his previous life in favour of one here in an isolated village. He has completely integrated into village society, married with children and is a respected village elder. Of course, I have no idea of whether he will wish to meet with you.'

There followed a long discussion in Japanese. Finally, Mr Fukada rose.

'Thank you, Mr Kikira, for that information. It is clear that my colleagues and I are not adequately prepared for what lies ahead of us. In particular, with the uncertainty of Lieutenant Hamada's state of mind I believe I should consult with my superiors as to the best course of action. My government was under the impression that Lieutenant

Hamada would wish to return to Japan. Indeed, it is anxious that he should do so.'

To Charlie it seemed patently obvious as to the best course of action. It was to send somebody up to Jivi to simply ask Hamada if he wanted to return to Japan. Mounting a large ill-equipped expedition didn't make sense.

George, who had listened to the group as they discussed the trip between themselves, understood enough to realise that Fukada was going to lose a lot of face if he didn't bring Hamada home. All of Japan was in a feverish state of anticipation of mounting a huge hero's welcome.

Fukada's problem was how to extricate himself from the situation. Prior to this there had been great competition to lead the expedition and cover oneself with the reflected glory of a hero's homecoming. How he regretted ever hearing the name Hamada. A decent man would have committed hari-kari a long time ago he thought to himself.

After three days of messages back and forth with the embassy in Canberra and the Foreign Office in Tokyo, it was decided that Fukada alone would visit Hamada and report back. The rest of the party would remain in Morobe, while Fukada and Charlie would go to Jivi with the same team that went the first time, namely Dud, Onepis and the porters.

George kitted out Fukada with some of his own jungle trekking clothes and boots. The Japanese diplomat, at five feet seven, cut a somewhat comical figure in six-foot George's kit.

Fukada was not particularly fit and unused to climbing mountain tracks, sometimes at six thousand feet altitude. His discomfort was compounded by the rain coming down in torrents each afternoon, as predicted by Charlie. Although he slowed their progress, Charlie found himself admiring the Japanese diplomat's fortitude and lack of complaints. Charlie himself was tiring of the monotonous diet prepared by the porters.

On day three they set up camp at the same place as before, about half an hour from Jivi.

They had already been spotted and identified by roving Jivi hunters and reported to their headman. Hamada listened to reports from his hunters, who included his son, Numu. He recognised that the approaching group were the same as before except this time there was a foreigner. The description was almost certainly that of a fellow countryman. Since Charlie's visit Hamada had been having uncomfortable thoughts that his presence would be revealed. His Japanese identity had lain submerged for so many years that he rarely thought about it. He was happy and fulfilled, loving his family and the people of his village. He had completely crossed a cultural boundary. He sent Numu and the men away and sank into deep thought. Only a trembling Loa remained at his side. She had always nurtured a dread that one day her husband would return to his own land without her.

'Master, tell me you will send these men away.'

'Light of my life, do not fear. They are not bad people. I shall listen to them and when they go they will not return. Go to the other women and stay until I call for you.' He rose and removed his lap-lap to find some of the long-discarded parts of his previous life.

Leaving the rest of the group behind, Charlie and Fukada approached the village. As they did so Hamada emerged from his hut. He was wearing the now faded and tattered remains of a dark green officer's uniform and cloth cap of the Japanese Army. At his side was a sword.

He approached Fukada, bowed and handed him his sword and cap. Fukada bowed and tried unsuccessfully to hand them back. There followed dialogue between the two men. Numu was behind his father and later translated the exchange for Charlie. As expected, Hamada was informing Fukada of his decision never to return to Japan, of his resignation from the army and resolution to abandon his Japanese identity. This would be the last day he would wear his uniform.

Leaving a nonplussed Fukada standing, Hamada returned to his hut and several minutes later reappeared wearing a plaited straw lap-lap, his bare chest revealing elaborate black and white designs. His head was adorned with a weave of bird of paradise feathers and he held a spear and decorated shield. With a sign he summoned his warriors to stand with him. Charlie witnessing the whole encounter, realised the symbolism of this act. There was no turning back for Hamada. Nobody spoke and there was silence save the for rustling of trees and an occasional bird call. In the face of Hamada's implacable resolve, Fukada realised he had to abandon his carefully planned speech appealing to a sense of loyalty to the Emperor, the Army and the Japanese people.

'Sir, I believe we should leave now,' Charlie suggested.

A crestfallen Fukada hesitated then bowed to Hamada and his warriors, turned and followed Charlie back to his group. Two days later, after their return to Morobe, a Patair aircraft was summoned to take the Japanese back to Port Moresby en route to Australia. Charlie heard later that Fukada had been demoted and sent back to Japan. The whole episode was brushed over and a communiqué issued that implied that Hamada's precarious health would not permit him to travel back to his homeland. To this day a Japanese officer's sword hangs on a wall in Charlie's home.

CHAPTER 41

Whenever Charlie walked through Okapo village, he always noticed groups of children playing. When will his son be among them? he asked himself.

The day-to-day work of settling disputes was mainly about land. This took most of his time. The least popular aspect of Charlie's work, both for him and the area's population under his control, was collecting taxes. His approach to gaining cooperation was to sell the necessity of taxation to the villagers as the way to get improvements in the area. These included the clinic and water supply, both of which were in poor shape. He also needed a rest house, a standard building at patrol office stations. His constant badgering of Port Moresby was starting to bear fruit when a gang of Public Works Department men appeared to commence on these improvements. The resentful muttering about taxes started to die down.

Charlie knew that PNG might appear to the outsider to be a poor country. He knew however from his reading of government reports that it had substantial mineral wealth. A recent geological survey had identified deposits of liquefied natural gas which could bring in vast amounts of money. It was an anomaly thought Charlie to himself as he collected the trifling sums from villagers. All this and its massive forests of hardwood timber were starting to attract interest from foreign corporations. Sitting on his veranda with John Edwards, they would often discuss this at length. They shared a fear that the country was open to exploitation. A frequent topic was who would defend it?

Charlie was no longer the only PNG native to have received a secondary education. The administration was under pressure to have some local representation in government. It had now inaugurated a Legislative Council in Moresby with members from the various administrative districts. Charlie had turned down an invitation to sit as a member. He had no interest in politics as practised at the Council, which appeared to be a talking shop with no significant powers. These were still retained by the Australian administration. Anyway, he was enjoying his role as kiap in his own mini fiefdom.

A command from DDA's head office required him to attend a meeting in Port Moresby. Once again, he left Sam in charge, while he was away in the capital. He entered a room where sitting around the conference table were two white men he did not recognise. Also present was his immediate boss, DC Terence Chiles, and Terence's boss, Controller Gareth Jones. This must be important, thought Charlie. Introductions were made by Gareth. The strangers were Bruce Hart and John Higgins.

'Charlie these gentlemen are from Pacifica Land Surveys. They have government permission to make geological surveys in the Eastern Highlands. They are working on behalf of their principal, a major oil exploration company. The Department requires you to give them every assistance. A budget has been established for you to use for any expenses in respect of their work. Accompanying them will be a new patrol officer fresh from Australia and the Moresby induction course. His name is Fred Stock. Headquarters have allocated Fred to Okapo for field familiarisation and to act as an assistant to you during the project. Other districts have been informed of this project and their responsibility to cooperate.'

Charlie did not like the sound of this. He could only imagine the consequence of oil being discovered in PNG.

'Why have I been chosen to assist with this?' he asked.

'It is known you have travelled over most of the Eastern Highlands, both in your early years with Philip Smithson and more recently since your appointment with the department. You are probably the best linguist we have and your ability to win trust and cooperation from local tribes has also been noted.'

Charlie knew that gold and silver mining had been carried out in PNG for some years. So far as he knew, little of this wealth had trickled down to the people of the local region, many of whom lived without electricity or water in woven huts with dirt floors. He feared oil extraction might well follow the same pattern. Large-scale operations could result in environmental damage, loss of natural habitats and worst of all, irretrievable destruction of local culture and traditions.

Before leaving for Okapo he sat with the geologists to study maps of the area proposed for exploration. Hart was a taciturn individual whereas Higgins didn't seem to be able to stop talking. Charlie could not tell if they were listening to his precautionary advice about protecting themselves against mosquitoes, sunburn and behaviour when meeting with local tribes. He emphasised that, although he was sending local people to help them, everyone had to pitch in. Most of their work to date had been in the relatively benign environments of South and Western Australia. Charlie took an instant liking to tall, tousle-haired Fred Stock. Hailing from Tasmania, he looked fit, seemed amiable and full of school-boyish enthusiasm peppering Charlie with questions. Initially he would not be of much help, with only elementary Tok Pisin and unfamiliarity with tropical environments.

The geologist's plan was to collect rock and soil samples at various locations in the Highlands. This was a significant physical challenge. It meant a lot of jungle trekking over a few months. Charlie assessed that they had not realised the extent of their ambitions and would require logistical support. Teams of porters would be needed, perhaps with air drops in some of the more remote locations. There would need to be assistance from district commissioners in other areas where they could base themselves. The whole project had not been thought through but concocted on an ad hoc basis. Charlie marked on the map forbidden areas known to contain yet uncontacted and possibly hostile tribes. Charlie told his boss of his fears.

'Terence, they really don't know what they are getting into. They are going to need a lot of help that I can't offer. I'm worried too for their safety. They won't be fighting Japanese but we know what the Kokoda Trail did to both sides in 1942. By the way, I'd rather have a couple of extra police than Fred Stock. I assume the budget will give me a free hand to charter a Cessna to fly them around. I want it placed on record that any such survey needs a lot of planning, funding, equipping and staffing by experienced people. For my part I am pretty busy and can't go tramping around as nursemaid to these two.'

'Do what you can Charlie, if that leaves un-surveyed areas then so be it. I'll make sure everybody at the top understands this. I'll try to send you a couple of PCs to go with them.'

A chartered eight seat Piaggo brought Charlie, Fred, Hart and Higgins to Okapo. Charlie knew inexperienced Fred would be largely superfluous. He decided that he would allocate Sam to be the geologist's gopher, accompanied by Fred. By now Sam had proved to be a very able assistant but Charlie did wonder if he might be asking too much of him.

With its full load, the Piaggio shuddered to a stop before the tall palms at the end of Okapo's short runway. Sam was there with the usual curious crowd to greet his boss and these new white faces. A gang of locals were recruited to lug a pile of equipment and personal possessions the half mile to Charlie's quarters and Okapo's recently completed rest house.

Charlie breathed a sigh of relief when a few days later the geologists, Sam, Fred and the one constable sent from Moresby, marched out with a troupe of porters carrying all the supplies needed for camping for a month. One porter's load seemed to be just cans of Fosters. Sam would be key to the success or otherwise of the expedition. Charlie felt uneasy as he watched them disappear among the trees.

After four weeks there was no sign of the party and Charlie started to feel concerned. A few days later he sent out PC Peter and two villagers with tracking skills as a search party. Three days later they returned, shepherding a silent crowd of hungry, bedraggled individuals. The group looked complete with the exception of Fred Stock and two of the porters. The expedition had been an unmitigated disaster.

'OK Sam tell me what happened, and where is Mr Stock?'

'Sorry boss, but I lost control. They wouldn't listen to me. They wanted to camp in places that were swampy and full of mosquitoes. Mr Stock got sick with malaria and I left him with tablets in Ponari village two days from here. I have a cousin there and he will be OK. They didn't want to help with anything and when I asked for some simple thing, they did nothing – just sat on their camp stools. They thought we were their servants, putting up tents, making camp fires, cooking, everything. Mr Higgins is very demanding and rude. He drank a lot of beer and started shouting. One night some villagers, I think from Hauri village, came into the camp and stole many things including the special tools. The few samples they did collect have been lost. The PC from Moresby was asleep but I don't blame him. We should have had more men to help keep guard at night. Two of the porters from here ran away. I shall deal with them. I am very sorry, boss, I have failed you in this important work.' Sam was close to tears.

'Don't worry Sam, you did your best in a very difficult situation. You are not to be blamed. I asked too much of you. I could have done no better with these very difficult people.'

Charlie radioed his boss.

'Hart and Higgins have just returned. My worst fears have been fulfilled. These people are totally unsuited to working here. They have no understanding of the local environment, the local culture and its dangers. They have been here over a month and achieved absolutely nothing. They act as if it's a simple camping trip for a couple days outside Melbourne.'

He then gave a summary based on Sam's report and finished: 'This was probably the easiest of all their proposed areas for exploration. I cannot accept any further responsibility for their work here in the Highlands or anywhere in PNG for that matter. I propose to put them on the next flight back to Moresby. If the powers that be don't like my role in this they can fire me.'

The radio went silent for a while. Terence came on.

'Put them on the plane Charlie. Let me have a written report. I'll support you – the bosses won't like it, but let me worry about the consequences. Everybody knows you are one of our most capable kiaps. They can fire me too if they want.'

Having unburdened himself Charlie felt relief. He realised what a decent chief he had in Terence Chiles. Terence had been a kiap himself in some difficult areas and fully understood what had happened. Charlie later learnt that Terence had been summoned to Headquarters and there had been some stormy scenes. The two geologists were sent back to Australia and nothing further was heard for a long time about the quest for oil in PNG.

CHAPTER 42

Charlie found his passport to look at his US visa. It had been issued seven years ago and didn't seem to be limited to any number of entries. Since his arrival back in PNG from America he had accumulated almost enough savings to contemplate travelling to collect Charlie Junior from the USA. He wrote the same day to headquarters, copied to Terence, requesting three months leave. He was approaching his second year at Okapo and planning a tour of all the villages within his authority. After this tour, which should complete in about six weeks, he would leave for America. He penned a letter to Mr Smithson to say he would like to meet during a stopover in Sydney.

Such periodic tours were to update a census of each village and an inspection of infrastructure such as tracks or bridges for which the community was responsible. Settling of land disputes always seemed to arise. Charlie had no vehicle allocated to his jurisdiction but even if he had it would have been of limited use in the mountainous region. His villages were linked by narrow tracks which he would walk with his party comprised of Samuel, Constable Peter and a porter called Jonas. Following custom they would be accommodated and fed in village rest houses. Being his second visit Charlie would be spared having to introduce himself and account for the fact that he was black and not white. There had been previous tours by white patrol officers from the neighbouring district. Popular traditional beliefs were that ancestors lived in some far away land and were white. He realised that whiteness carried a certain aura and some felt that he was a second-class kiap. He enjoyed these tours which took up to six weeks and considered them time well spent. What he did not enjoy was compiling the numerous detailed reports for the benefit of his DC's office. Were these reports really important? Who read them? What did they contribute to the life and welfare of his people? Did they finish up buried in a filing cabinet with hundreds of reports from patrol offices in the district? There must be thousands of such reports in offices all over PNG. The whole idea seemed to originate in the western concept of order and control.

Four weeks into the tour the group trudged in heavy rain along a valley entering the village of Indini. The party was met by the headman who went by the name of Laka, a tall thin man with a sad expression and lopsided gait. He conducted them to Indini's rest house. The following day the rains had eased and Samuel was detailed to assemble the village for the population count. There appeared to be only about one hundred souls standing before Charlie. Most of them seemed to be old men and women. He consulted his census book in which he had previously recorded a population of two hundred and seventy-five.

'O Laka, where are all your people?' said a worried Charlie using Tok Pisin.

'Masta, the god man took them,' said a dazed Laka.

Further questioning just produced the same reply. An old man stepped forward speaking at length in the local dialect. Jonas the porter piped up.

'I come from the next village. I speak the same dialect. He said a white man came many moons ago promising the young men, women and family's great things if they would follow him and meet a new white god. He showed them magic things that he said were his god's gift to him.'

Further questioning established that the god man had taken his new flock up the nearby River Asaro. They had gone using their canoes, following his outboard boat upstream.

Charlie was aware of numerous missionaries who over the years had focussed on PNG as fertile ground for converting heathens to some flavour of Christianity. From his basic education with the London Missionary Society, he had never really connected with what he later concluded were attempts at brainwashing His spiritual feelings mainly centred on the importance of his ancestors. During his years spent in America he had witnessed some of the behaviour of a professed Christian society. After this he had become even more sceptical of the benefits of Christian evangelists to PNG. He firmly believed these were acts of cultural imperialism and total arrogance. They assumed that people whose descendants can be traced back tens of thousands of years would enjoy fuller lives if they adopted some foreign god, covered their bodies with clothes and sang hymns. Charlie despaired believing this to be an aggressive and unnecessary pushing of faith to another culture, undermining its people's way of life.

He had encountered a number of Christian missionaries and mostly he hoped they would just go home and leave his country alone. He could make an exception for his friend John Edwards in Okapo. John at least was sympathetic to local culture and open-minded in accepting those who took the benefits of attending the mission, learning crafts and receiving medical attention, but without adopting belief. His assistant Sam was a case in point.

Of the various missionaries he had come across, none had so far adopted as aggressive tactics as the abductor of Indini's people. This would not be countenanced by the administration and Charlie realised his next task was to find the trespasser and if necessary, bring him to justice. The problem was how to get up river to find him and bring back the missing Indini population.

He knew that the nearest boat likely to be available would be downstream at a Seventh-Day Adventist Mission. He did not particularly like the Adventists but would have to swallow his feelings and be pleasant to them on this occasion. The idea that God created the world in six days seemed to him to be totally nonsensical, alongside virgin birth, miracles and other concepts. In Charlie's view these would only be swallowed by primitive, uneducated and vulnerable people. The only redeeming feature of this mission was that it provided a small medical station for the area that should rightly be established by government. Even this, Charlie regarded as a form of bribery to grow the flock.

The only practical way of getting to the mission would be by using the leaking two-man canoe dragged up on the nearby river bank. He set off with Sam, both paddling furiously, pausing periodically to bail out water rising every ten minutes to cover their ankles.

After three hours, exhausted, they pulled the canoe up the bank at the Adventist mission. The sound of singing drifted down to them as they plodded up towards the mission buildings. Pastor Joseph, called Joe by everybody, bounded out of the small chapel building to meet them. Charlie rather regretted being a little cool towards Joe on his previous visit some six months previously to update his census book. The number of souls saved by Joe seemed to be increasing the population at every visit. Joe seemed to forget Charlie's coolness, at least pretended to, greeting him as if he were a long-lost brother.

'Hey there Charlie and how's my favourite patrol officer?' boomed bearded six-feet-four Joe, slapping Charlie on the back. 'And I remember this is the worthy Samuel. Hey Sam, did you know that your name is a surname of Hebrew origin meaning "name of God"? Anyway brothers, welcome to our humble mission.'

Charlie felt embarrassed at this overwhelming show of bonhomie, particularly as he was just there on the scrounge.

'So good to see you again Joe,' lied Charlie. 'To tell the truth we are here to call upon your goodwill.'

'Just name it friend. But first come to my house and rest and take a little sustenance, you both look done in.'

Charlie had to admit to himself that Christian charity seemed in abundance when Joe, over tea and plates of tasty rice and curried fish, readily agreed to lend them his large outboard motored canoe, complete with driver. Joe seemed keen to be helpful and distance himself from the aggressive tactics of Indini's Christian abductor. He felt this was casting missionaries in general in a bad light, not to mention that this unknown god man was not a Seventh Day Adventist. With nightfall approaching it was agreed that Charlie and Sam would set off at first light the following day.

'God be with you,' shouted Joe as the boat was cast off. Paul the driver opened the throttle and they roared upstream with a surging bow wave and white foam trail. Paul, an impassive individual who had an intimate knowledge of the river, first stopped at Indini to collect Constable Peter and the porter, Jonas.

'Go slower now. We must look for a place where they might have stopped,' Charlie instructed Paul.

For several miles thereafter, they cruised through narrow, fast-moving channels with overhanging tree fronds creating an impression of passing through green tunnels. Wider, calmer parts edged with mangrove swamps occasionally had clear areas down to the water's edge where villages would be evident, sometimes with women thrashing, scrubbing or wringing laundry. A stop was made at each inhabited part of the river to enquire if the pursued boat and canoes had passed. Yes, the flotilla had passed many moons before and continued upstream.

Finally, on a wide section, they came upon a number of canoes drawn up on the riverbank. There was a larger one with an outboard motor. It was an unusual scene in that there was an absence of people, even children. Typically, a powered canoe filled with strangers would attract a curious crowd. Charlie's group disembarked leaving Paul in his craft.

'Peter bring your rifle. Everybody follow me,' Charlie ordered.

He consulted his map and knew they must have travelled some miles beyond his area of responsibility. Nonetheless, he realised that there was disturbing evidence that needed investigation.

They continued to walk through what seemed to be the usual village layout with a main avenue leading to a central area surrounded by thatched huts constructed of wood and grasses. Charlie was familiar with such a scene, indeed had lived in similar surroundings in Tori village and elsewhere in his early years. The central area was again typical with a spirit house regularly used for meetings, rites, ceremonies and housing important clan artefacts. One unusual feature was a tall pole topped by a large cross and two smaller poles either side also surmounted by crosses. A murmur of noise came from the spirit house that sounded like the buzzing of insects.

Entering, Charlie saw a grey-haired white man standing at the head of a crowded assembly of villagers on their knees with heads bowed. He appeared to be in some kind of trance with arms outstretched. A monotonous rising and falling buzzing came from a loudspeaker connected to what looked like a portable battery-operated record-player.

Charlie strode to the front, pulled a cord from the loudspeaker and shouted, 'Stop!'

The white man started and angrily shouted back. 'How dare you interrupt a religious service! Who are you?'

'I am a government official from the Department of Territories investigating the abduction of inhabitants of Indini village. I need to see your credentials authorising you to be in the territory of PNG and establishing any kind of religious organisation. Influencing of the local population under any pretext to leave their villages is not authorised. Please come with me.'

'I refuse. Get out of here, 'said the man haughtily.

The crowd at first looked confused at this exchange in English. Charlie sensed a mood of hostility developing behind him. He signalled to Constable Peter to join him. In a rare display of initiative Peter ran forward. He turned to the crowd and using pidgin, shouted. 'Asples bilong yu, Indini bilong yu. koan! koan!'

He had become excited and without warning levelled his rifle. The range of a Lee Enfield .303 rifle is over one mile. At six feet the impact is devastating. The record player exploded into a mass of flying Bakelite, wood, wires and components. The effect on the congregation was equally spectacular as everyone scrambled to leave the spirit house. The white man turned a deadly pale. Even Charlie was shaken at the turn of events but quickly recovered himself thinking there was nothing he could have planned that would have worked so effectively in his favour.

'Come with me now and show me your written authority to be here or I shall order your immediate arrest.'

The man offered no further resistance. It later turned out that the preacher, William Brody, was a religious fanatic who had entered PNG on a tourist visa with the intention of taking over and converting a primitive community into a cult with extreme Christian beliefs. He was funded by a fanatical religious sect in the USA. Charismatic and with use of mass hypnosis techniques disguised as Christian worship together with 'magic' in the form of conjuring tricks, Brody somehow convinced his disciples that evil manifested itself in the form of other missionaries and officials of the Australian administration.

Some weeks later, writing his report of the affair, Charlie happily recorded the fact that the errant population of Indini had returned home. He recounted that during his return to Okapo with Brody under escort by Constable Peter, the prisoner escaped in the night from the rest house of one of the villages enroute. Despite a search by his party and a number of villagers renowned for their tracking skills, he could not be found. Subsequently, no trace of Brody was ever found despite later wide searches of the area on the jungle-clad slopes of the Owen Stanley Range. Charlie's report commended Peter but did not include details of his key role in the affair. The unauthorised discharge of a police weapon would have initiated a formal enquiry and a mountain of paperwork.

CHAPTER 43

Charlie arrived back at Okapo gratified to find the area calm and in good order. He felt confident Sam would manage in three weeks' time during his absence in America. A visit from a kiap from a neighbouring area had been arranged in the event of an emergency. He was becoming alternately excited and apprehensive about his forthcoming visit to America. The patrol office's usual daily routine was interrupted by its radio transceiver coming to life with a call from George Burrell in Morobe. Charlie had not spoken to George since returning home three months earlier, following the Hamada Affair, as it became known.

'Hey Charlie, how do you fancy a few days break down here on the coast next weekend? It'll be great to get together again. I know you never take leave and I've got someone here visiting from the UK I'd like you to meet.'

Charlie had struck up a great rapport with George and really enjoyed his company. He was one of the few people he'd met since his return to PNG with whom he felt in tune. He couldn't imagine who George's visitor might be but the idea of a break from Okapo certainly appealed.

'Great idea George. I'll be there but I can only come for the weekend. I'm leaving in a couple of weeks to travel to the US to pick up my son.' Charlie had already told George of his transformation to fatherhood.

A few days later, leaving Sam in charge, he climbed into a Cessna enroute to Morobe. They circled over the coast and Charlie took in golden beaches fringed with palms. He was thinking that if the region was accessible to western tourists, it would become yet another charming coastline ruined by high-rise hotels, traffic, crime and pollution. All in the name of progress. With such thoughts in his mind, he saw George and a small figure waiting for him as the Cessna bumped to the end of the runway.

'Greetings my friend. May I introduce my niece Eve, all the way from London.'

Eve took Charlie's breath away. Delicately formed, framed by blonde elfin-cut hair, her face radiated intelligent beauty. Set against the wild green jungle at the side of the runway, she seemed almost surreal. He had seen many attractive women in his years in America but none like this. Simply dressed in jeans and a blouse, she smiled as she held out her hand.

Gently shaking it, Charlie lost his senses for just a second. 'Nice to meet you, Eve.'

George smiled to himself seeing for the first time his usually self-confident young friend appear awkward. That evening the three sat on George's veranda which looked out to the ocean and the setting sun. They watched as orange light was cast over the water on the beach, reflecting off every ripple. Charlie took a surreptitious look at Eve whose lips had parted with pleasure. Her face was aglow with the oranges and reds from the sinking sun that had illuminated the clouds and everything around them. The sun was quickly disappearing below the horizon, the sky above turning to a clear, purple-tinged grey but with a ruby-red glow to the west. The familiar evening clicking sounds of cicada bugs in the trees filled the air.

Nobody spoke until the sun had finally disappeared and they were enveloped in velvety darkness.

George broke the spell.

'Eve is a freelance journalist. Tell Charlie about yourself, Eve.'

Eve smiled at an entranced Charlie, as she told of a commission she had received from a travel magazine to write an article about islands in the Pacific. Why not start with visiting her uncle in PNG she explained. He had said she should meet a genuine south sea islander. She had heard something of Charlie's exploits and would love to hear more about them.

George disappeared to the kitchen to supervise preparation of dinner while Charlie told his story to a captivated Eve. She would ask the occasional question.

'What an exciting life Charlie! So what next?'

'If I knew I would say, but for the moment more of the same in my little kingdom in Okapo. I am happy to be back now permanently in PNG. This is where I belong.'

The following day George took them on tour of Morobe where they had a friendly reception from villagers. Later they stopped at a local mission station where a kindly Jesuit priest showed them the mission clinic and some of the converts working in a carpentry workshop. Despite his prejudice against missionaries, Charlie found it difficult to fault. He could see that useful skills were being acquired.

The weekend passed quickly. George lent the pair his Land Rover to go to a nearby beach and take in some of the other coastal villages. They spent several hours on a deserted beach while Charlie set out his concerns for his country and how it would deal with the independence that was surely coming. Eve had taken to the smitten Charlie. He represented a startling contrast to Jake, her boyfriendback in London. Jake was handsome, clever and amusing. A highly paid bank executive, his main purpose seemed to be devising strategies to help his employer streamline its operations, creating efficiencies to generate even bigger profits. Their similarly affluent friends thought he and Eve were perfectly matched.

Charlie was a breath of fresh air. He lived a meaningful life and seemed to have survived the temptations of materialism. She wanted to learn more about him, actually she really wanted to spend a lot more time with him. She found his earthy sexuality irresistible but didn't know how to deal with it. For his part, after just two days Charlie knew that this woman was so special yet probably unattainable. He was in agonies over the prospect of having to return to

Okapo the following day never to see her again.

As they returned from the beach that day they walked back to George's bungalow. Eve slipped her hand into Charlie's. He was dizzy with emotion. Until that moment he hadn't known if any of his feelings were reciprocated.

George saw them walking up the path hand in hand. He hadn't expected to be a matchmaker but realised he had help spark a relationship between two young people that had little prospect of developing. That evening they walked back to the beach and stayed enveloped in each other's arms for over two hours. Charlie kept thinking that he must not let this woman get away.

He slept little that night, concocting unrealistic scenarios of how he would be able to meet her in the future. At the airfield the next day a lingering embrace was starting to irritate the pilot who had kept his engine running expecting a quick turnaround.

'After today we'll probably not see each other again,' said Charlie. 'We live in totally contrasting worlds, thousands of miles apart. Anyway, you have a settled life with a nice man in London.'

He was thinking to himself that she would probably lose interest once she learnt he had a son. He had not been able to bring himself to tell her that part of his history.

At first Eve did not reply, on the verge of tears she just squeezed his hand.

'Let's keep in touch Charlie.'

The Cessna took off. Eve watched it until it became a dot, finally disappearing from sight. Charlie sank into a depressed silence for the whole flight.

CHAPTER 44

Headquarters having given reluctant approval for his leave, Charlie flew to Moresby to catch a connecting flight to Sydney. Philip Smithson had insisted he would pick him up and have him stay the night. He would help Charlie with his onward booking. A good friend of Philip's was a manager at Qantas and helped with a discounted ticket to Los Angeles. Pamela Smithson was overwhelmed and hugged Charlie, the nearest she had to a son. Wondering if the Smithsons might disapprove of his behaviour, Charlie sheepishly told them the reasons for his trip. He need not have been concerned. Pamela clapped her hands with delight.

'So what are your plans for your son Charlie?'

'I will bring him home with me and raise him as a Papuan.'

'Make sure you bring him here on your way back. We'll think of him as a grandson!'

A day later he was on a Qantas flight to Los Angeles. Since getting the news a year ago he had been trying to adjust to his sudden transition from bachelor to father. Most people had a partner and together they would have the excitement of looking forward to the birth and responsibility of dealing with the life of a new human being until he or she became adult. Charlie had no clear ideas on the subject of raising his son. He kept looking at his photo which had been pinned above his desk for the past year. He was going to have to manage the whole business unaided. At Sydney Airport he bought a copy of The Common-Sense Book of Baby and Child Care by Dr Benjamin Spock. This at least had a simple core message: do not be afraid to trust your own common sense. In its pages the worried parent could find help for virtually every problem. By the time his flight reached Los Angeles Charlie had waded through most of Dr Spock's wisdom. At least he was comforted by the fact that somebody else had dealt with the messy side of babyhood. Hopefully Charlie Junior had not been imprinted with any undesirable habits.

He had wrestled with his decision to bring his son back to PNG. He saw that there would be a lot of adjustment needed on both their parts but mostly by his son. He knew he could not condemn him to adulthood in the racist, materialistic culture of America.

A day later he arrived at the Greyhound bus terminal in San Antonio. His arrival triggered memories of six years previously with his reception by the clerk at the ticket window. He had written to Mama Julie to tell her to expect him, without giving a date, which he did not know at the time of writing. He had also written to Joseph Fraser. He had not had received a reply before leaving and did not know if he could expect the previous hospitality and friendship. He was exhausted by the long journey and lack of sleep. He had brought his well-thumbed copy of the Green Book and checked into a fleapit of a hotel listed nearby at which to sleep before facing the results of his previous life.

The next day he called at the Fraser household and received the warmest welcome imaginable. It was as if time had stood still. He could stay with them for 'as long as you want.' Later in the day, he knocked on Mama Julie's door, not knowing what reception to expect. He was greeted with hugs and tears. It was as if his return was that of a prodigal son.

'Li'l Charlie is at elementary school. You'll be seeing him soon. This here is his sister Rebecca. We call her Becky.'

A small, shy face peeked out from behind her grandma's skirts. Charlie bent down with a big smile and a 'Hello Becky' and the face disappeared. A yellow school bus pulled up along the street, disgorging a horde of small, black, noisy children. Watching from the window, Charlie saw a boy detach from the group and come running to the house. Bursting in through the door he stopped abruptly before his grandma and the smiling black stranger.

'Li'l Charlie this here is your real daddy.'

'We share the same name.' Charlie reached out his hand to his son. 'I'm Charlie too.'

'Shake your daddy's hand li'l man,' commanded Grandma.

'He ain't my daddy,' said the confused boy. 'My daddy is in heaven with Jesus. My teacher said so.'

Charlie let it pass. Later around the dinner table, there was a discussion about having two daddies. In the little boy's case, a Daddy Vern and a Daddy Charlie. The latter handed over a small model Jeep to his son. Becky received a cute doll. These Charlie had bought at the LA airport but he had found that only white dolls seemed to be on sale. At age three a delighted Becky would not notice that discrimination even reached down to the toy industry.

'Call me Daddy K,' said Charlie to the still puzzled boy who nonetheless registered that another father who brought presents was worth knowing.

After the children were in bed, the two adults discussed Charlie's plans for his son. Mama Julie treasured the relationship she had with her two grandchildren and, although recognising Charlie's right to take charge of his son, was already in tears at the prospect. Suffering with bereavement at the loss of her daughter this was yet another blow. Charlie tried to utter consoling words, but these felt empty. In a sense he was partly the cause of her suffering. Charlie had been considering offering to adopt Rebecca but abandoned the idea when he realised the effect that would have on her grandmother. That night he found it difficult to sleep with the conflict of emotions in his head. He reluctantly realised that he would deal Mama Julie a further blow by taking away one of her grandchildren, or worse, the effect of taking them both. There was only one answer.

The following day after breakfast Charlie Junior left for school clutching his Jeep. To leave the adults to talk, Becky was sent next door to play with the neighbour's daughter of the same age.

'Mama I am so sorry for the grief I have caused you. I—'

'Son,' interrupted Julie. 'You is a good man and Vicky loved you for that. I'd just hoped you'd stay here, marry and be one of the family. These things happen with young people, I know. But please don't take Li'l Charlie away. Becky would lose her brother and I would lose my li'l boy. Please, please don't do it.'

She broke down in tears, overwhelmed and shaking with emotion.

Charlie put his arm around her, waiting for her sobbing to subside. He realised his mistake for even broaching the idea of taking Charlie away. At the same time, he knew he could not leave his son in America.

'Mama, as much as you don't want to lose Li'l Charlie, I don't want him to grow up in America where he will be a second-class citizen and suffer just for having black skin. I can't stand the thought of him being called "boy" or "nigger". But I have an idea for you to think about.'

Mama, with tear-stained face, stared at Charlie. She wondered what he could possibly be saying.

'You could come back with me and the children and help me bring them up. Already you are like a mother to them. If after a few months you don't want to stay you can come back to San Antonio. I know that with you there they will grow up happy. It is not like America, but they can go to school and have a future where people are not judged by the colour of their skin. I know that Vicky's brother George has moved away up north. If you want to visit him and see your other grandchildren you can come back at times.'

'I don't think I could come to a wild country where people eat each other.'

'Mama, it's not like that I promise you. People respect each other. Certainly, I live in a remote village but it has a missionary school where one of my friends is a teacher. I have a house where we can all stay. Soon our capital is going to have a secondary school where the children can attend when they are older. I can get a transfer to live there. You and the children will have American passports so later you and they can always return if that's what you want.'

This was too much for Mama to take in all at once. After a few questions she needed time to think about this momentous proposition. At that point Charlie had no concrete idea how his proposal could be funded. He had two wealthy contacts in the form of Tom Paul and Pat Way. Could he ask them for loans to fund travel for Mama and the kids? He had another restless night with a dozen questions whirling around in his brain.

Mama Julie was a kindly, matronly, forty-eight-year-old divorcee with a friendly and normally happy disposition, although recent events had affected her badly. Other than short term dalliances, she had been single for nearly twenty years after her husband left her for another woman. Life had been a struggle, having to raise two small children single handed. Having left school at fourteen with only a basic education, she could only find unskilled work in a local factory producing car components for Ford. In common with most of her contemporaries she had little knowledge of the wider world that was an almost blank page for her. She had never travelled outside Texas. She lived on the east side of San Antonio where she grew up. She had friends and neighbours whom she had known for years.

Her world was focussed on her family, now tragically reduced. The idea of travelling to the other side of the world, to a primitive country simply terrified her. She liked Charlie and trusted him and understood his wish to take Li'l Charlie away, but couldn't prevent it. The next day she consulted the preacher at her church. The Reverend Fisher did not immediately reply after she asked him for guidance.

'Miss Julie,' he started. 'You are being asked to make a sacrifice for the good of your grandchildren. Remember Jesus made the biggest sacrifice possible by giving his life for us and we worship him and God for this act. You have to do this, not just for yourself, but for love, the love of your grandchildren. Do not be afraid. God will recognise your fear and the sacrifice you are making. Go with this Charlie. It sounds as if he is a good man. His proposal to have the children educated at a Christian mission is reassuring. When you have gone, this church will pray for you. Write to us with your news.'

When she returned home, Charlie was in the yard playing football with his little boy.

'I am coming with you Charlie,' Mama Julie said simply as he re-entered the house. Filled with emotion, for a moment Charlie could not speak, only to give Mama a long hug.

'I know what this means for you, Mama. You will not regret it.'

CHAPTER 45

There were numerous matters to arrange in the three months before Charlie and the family left for PNG. He didn't know what bureaucratic hurdles he would face in getting the children and Mama Julie into the country. Firstly he needed to get passports for them. The little boy was in practice known by all as Charlie Jackson – Vern's surname. He would have to get used to being Charlie Kikira, like his father. Fortunately, Victoria had registered on his birth certificate that Charlie was his father.

A few weeks after much form filling and many visits to San Antonio's main post office, United States passports arrived in the mail. Charlie also wanted his son to become a citizen of PNG but this would have to wait.

The next task was to find the funding needed for their travel. Charlie had learnt during his time at Stanford the litigious nature of American society. As a result lawyers were one of the highest paid professions. Getting bitten by a dog and then suing the owner for damages would not be considered unreasonable behaviour. A citizen of PNG would simply not comprehend this. Indeed, most of the rest of the world considered it to be an alien concept. Here though, maybe it was the key to solving the problem. There seemed to be plenty of lawyers in town who promised to sue for compensation for injury or accidents on a no win no fee basis. There was an abundance of advertisements in town, on buses, billboards, park benches, on the radio. The truck which hit Vern and Victoria's car belonged to a large corporation.

A smooth-talking lawyer assured Charlie that the family would get a generous settlement, less of course his 40%. But it would take time.

He reluctantly decided to write to Tom asking for a loan which could be repaid out of any settlement. Tom replied promptly with a check for twice what Charlie had asked for. 'Don't worry about repayment if the claim doesn't come through. We've got plenty and your family needs it more than mine. And congratulations on becoming a father,' added Tom in his covering letter. Charlie was overwhelmed by his friend's generosity.

During his time in San Antonio, Charlie spent some time with Joseph Fraser and his family. Apparently, the building project which had employed him had been completed and the workers had moved on to another site. Jack Pelosi was still Joseph's boss as site foreman. Doreen Brown no longer worked in the office, much to everybody's relief. After two months in San Antonio Charlie again started to feel a sense of belonging. His heart belonged both in Okapo and San Antonio.

The time arrived for departure to PNG, a day of high emotion. Mama Julie was nervous. The children were excited.

'Mama, I promise this will not be the last time you see San Antonio. When I can afford it, I'm going to get you a plane ticket to come and visit.'

Once again Joseph took Charlie to the Greyhound terminal but this time with the children and Mama Julie.

Charlie wondered if he would ever see San Antonio again as he waved to Joseph from the bus window. He doubted it. He just wanted to preserve his memories of his happy times there nearly five years ago.

The discounted Qantas return ticket that Philip Smithson had procured for him took Charlie back to Sydney. He was able to buy tickets for the rest of the family using Tom's generous loan. Mama Julie was quite overwhelmed at the whole experience. She loved the luxury of being served food by white stewardesses but the sensation of flying was frightening. She tightly held hands with the children on take-off and landing. On the journey Charlie tried to explain in terms his son might understand, that he was going to a second home. He also decided to introduce the idea that in his new home he would have a new name, Charlie Kikira. The little boy took some convincing, but would eventually accept the change. Life was a lot of new experiences, some exciting, some disconcerting. He and Becky had never before had any contact with white people, mostly just seen them at a distance. Here they seemed to be in a white world. But being in an aeroplane was exciting and they liked the white ladies who were bringing them tasty food and colouring books. For some time Charlie Junior had been pressing his face to the window looking at the clouds. After a while he nudged his new daddy.

'Will I see my other daddy soon? He is up here in heaven with Mommy and Jesus. My teacher at school said so.'

'Well son, heaven is a very big place and in another part of the sky.'

The boy considered this for a moment looking disappointed, then simply said 'OK.'

Little Charlie accepted his father's wisdom without question. Charlie would deal in the future with the whole question of religion. Happily, small children usually accept adult explanations.

They were met at Sydney airport by both the Smithsons. Pamela wanted nothing else but to hug both Charlies but Junior and Becky were reluctant to get near this old white woman. After staying overnight with the Smithsons they boarded a flight to Port Moresby early the following day.

Upon arrival at Moresby the family boarded a connecting Patair flight departing for Okapo. Mama Julie and the children had been admitted on tourist visas. Charlie would need to regularise their status as permanent residents sometime later. The exhausted group arrived two and half months after Charlie had left for the US. Waiting for them at the airfield were Sam, young Fred Stock and the usual crowd of curious villagers who were there whenever a plane landed.

The following day Mama Julie woke to a typical hot and humid Okapo day. Lying under a mosquito net she could not at first place where she was until the last months came flooding back. She heard the children talking excitedly about their new surroundings. Outside, Charlie Junior had been busily exploring with all the healthy curiosity of a five-year-old. It was all a strange dream.

As he made breakfast for them all Charlie was still coming to terms with the fact that his bachelor days were over. He now had a family. Later he must discuss Mama's future with her.

'Mama, let's talk about your life here. You have come to care for the children, just as you were doing back home in San Antonio. Maybe later, when you have spare time, you'll find a part-time role helping out at the mission. I'm going to try and find a local lady to help with the household chores.'

Mama firmly defined her role as she saw it.

'Charlie son,' she started. 'Of course I'm going to help bring up the children. At the same time, I kin look after you doing the chores that a wife would do, until you find one, that is!'

She laughed, something she hadn't done for a long time.

Charlie had been thinking about his son's education and reluctantly decided that there was no alternative – he would enrol him in Okapo's London Missionary Society school. He had survived an LMS school and like his assistant Sam, hadn't engaged with the religious aspects. He would speak to John Edwards about Charlie

Junior that very afternoon and would introduce him to Mama.

On his return Charlie quickly scanned the pile of envelopes that had accumulated. He first opened one bearing a London postmark. Ever since that meeting last year in Morobe he had not stopped thinking about Eve, and it seemed she had not forgotten him either. They wrote periodically, their letters warm but platonic with the latest news of their very different lives. It seemed as if they were now just pen pals although Charlie still harboured romantic feelings. Since her return to London, she had stopped seeing her banker boyfriend. Her travels, not least after meeting Charlie had left her thoughtful about her future. Still a travel writer she had been visiting North and South America and wrote entertaining accounts of times in various countries. Charlie in turn had written back about his adventures. So far, he had been put off telling her about finding himself a parent. He felt sure that would destroy any lingering romantic feelings he hoped she might have for him.

Charlie was impatient to be briefed on happenings in his domain during his absence. It seemed that Fred Stock had been making great efforts to improve the Tok Pisin he had learnt on the Moresby induction course, plus useful phrases in the local dialect. Sam expressed admiration for his progress. It seemed that the two men worked well together and Charlie was gratified to learn of the mutual respect that had developed. Unlike many new kiaps, Fred was not burdened with the colonial white superiority complex. He was eager to learn as much as possible of the local culture and customs. Charlie felt he would be an asset to the administration with the makings of a talented kiap. Next month he would send Fred and Sam on the next inspection tour of villages to collect outstanding census data with the usual report on infrastructure and other government property.

After a while, life at Okapo developed a new routine. Mama took Charlie Junior to school which was a few minutes from Charlie's bungalow. Becky accompanied her grandma everywhere. Mama liked the early start when the day was at its coolest. She became friendly with Jasmine, Constable Peter's wife, another mother who helped at the school. Jasmine spoke very little English but wanted to learn as much as Mama Julie wanted to learn Tok Pisin. They would spend many hours together and made rapid progress, talking and laughing in a language mixture of their own. Charlie Junior at first was lost but Mary, a little girl in his class at the school, adopted him. In a surprisingly short amount of time, he started to acquire not only Tok Pisin but sufficient of the local Fore dialect. He was quickly accepted by his schoolmates as one of them. They started calling him 'CK'. Charlie had wrestled with what name to use with his son. Charlie Junior was a bit of a mouthful, so he decided within the family he'd simply be called 'Junior'.

Charlie was happy to be back in his little kingdom. But at the same time, he hankered after female company. He realised that he would not find this in Okapo and his career seemed to be condemning him to permanent bachelorhood. With them living on different continents, his dreams of a relationship with Eve were clearly unrealistic.

CHAPTER 46

The Post and Telegraphs department is located in Port Moresby and all post for PNG first arrived at P&T's headquarters. Most of the smaller outstations only received post when a flight was required to drop off or collect a passenger or packages. Post between the smaller outstations could take several weeks to arrive.

A few months after Charlie returned with his new family from America, Okapo's radio crackled with a message that a consignment of medicines ordered by John Edwards' mission clinic was arriving the following day.

Charlie opened the post bag containing Okapo's mail. There was the usual routine correspondence, official forms, notices and latest headquarters' policies. Charlie noticed a large envelope for Mr Samuel Pulu. It had been posted in New York. Later Charlie found out that Sam had enrolled in a self-help correspondence course which promised the guaranteed benefits of financial success, personal popularity and career advancement to those who finished the course. Unsurprisingly this was linked to regular subscription payments for each month's mailings. Charlie decided to have a serious talk with Sam about this course before he spent more of his meagre earnings on it.

There were several envelopes for Charlie. He saw an envelope with a US stamp with a New Orleans postmark, which could only mean he had not been forgotten by Sylvia. He had not forgotten her but his affections had been totally submerged by memories of Eve. He had hoped against hope that Eve might have written but months had now passed without a letter. He was still fantasising that they would meet again. He had her London address and toyed with writing to her about his feelings but had no idea what to say. He knew he would sound like a love-sick teenager. There was a letter from José to say he was now Doctor Cerda and Charlie was surprised to hear from Pat Way with her chatty letter. After all, he had only been the family gardener. It seemed that he had more friends in America than in PNG.

Sam appeared at his door.

'Bos, there is a white man here to see you. He came on the Patair flight which delivered Mr John's medicines.'

A lanky, red-haired man in his fifties bustled into the room.

'Jack Williamson from the Sydney School of Tropical Diseases,' he announced himself. Charlie looked surprised – visitors to Okapo were few and far between. 'Sorry to thrust myself on you, but I thought the fellas in Port Moresby had told you I'd be here for a while.'

Williamson turned out to be an Australian doctor conducting research into tropical blood disorders. He produced a letter of introduction from his department requesting Charlie give him every assistance with his project. Charlie groaned to himself, he had enough to do without being lumbered with some itinerant academic.

Happily, his visitor stayed just long enough to borrow some camping equipment and supplies and trek off on a tour of the villages under Charlie's jurisdiction. At each village he would take blood samples from villagers. Charlie decided to send the long-suffering Sam along to translate and hopefully ensure Williamson didn't go astray in the manner of the recent geologists' saga.

'Sorry Sam, you'd better go with him. Take a couple of porters and see he doesn't get into trouble.'

'See you in two or three days,' said Williamson, cheerily waving goodbye at dawn the next day.

To Charlie's surprise, two days later a dishevelled and shaken Dr Williamson and his party emerged on the path from the dense green jungle surrounding the patrol office. Breathlessly, Sam recounted what had happened at the first village they entered.

Sam had gathered the villagers together and explained that each person was required to give a sample of blood to the doctor. The men went into a huddle outside of Sam's earshot. It was after considerable discussion that people reluctantly consented to the procedure. Their concern had been that witchcraft was in play but Sam's persuasive speech won the day. When finished, Williamson had some eighty-odd phials of blood stowed in his sample box and prepared to leave. It was at this point that Williamson removed his large, floppy bush hat and wiped his brow.

This caused immediate consternation and uproar among the villagers. As the party prepared to leave men with shields and spears surrounded the doctor, Sam and the porters. An ugly mood had developed. Their anger was clearly directed at Dr Williamson.

It was a widespread belief in most tribes that white men were from a land of ancestors. It seemed that Dr Williamson had been identified as some form of ancestral spirit. He must belong to a race of sky beings, ancestors not of the tribe but of its enemies. It was widely believed by most tribes that evil spirits existed that were responsible for all sorts of malicious activities including accidents, injuries, misfortunes, and even deaths. The village had had little contact with white men, let alone one with red hair.

It seemed that the villagers, on seeing Williamson's red hair, assumed he had drunk some of their blood, colouring his hair and resulting in him absorbing powers from them. The only solution for the villagers was obviously to kill Williamson and reverse the process.

Once a frightened Sam had understood the situation, he tried to explain that the doctor only wanted to look at their wonderful blood and would not drink it. He pointed at the box of phials. The headman looked dubious.

'He must have drunk some of our blood to get power from us. It is in his body. It has gone to the hair on his head. We can only get it back by killing him,' he said, as if a matter of fact.

Sam had to think on his feet. Rational argument would not work here.

'That is true. But what would be better for the tribe is if he gives you his magic hair, which has special powers,' adding as an afterthought, 'He will lose his powers to you and his hair will not grow again. Also, Mr Charlie the kiap, will be very angry if you kill a white man.'

The headman then discussed all of this with the men of the tribe at great length. Dr Williamson sat trembling, awaiting his fate.

As Sam finished his tale of events, Dr Williamson entered the office removing his bush hat to reveal a very closely cropped head of hair.

'Mr Kikira, I'd be obliged if you could arrange for me to be picked up by the earliest flight to Port Moresby. I shall not be returning.'

CHAPTER 47

The day came for Fred Stock and Sam to start on their inspection tour. Fired with his usual youthful enthusiasm Fred had been looking forward to this day. It was a real demonstration of confidence from Charlie in appointing him to lead an expedition. Charlie for his part had been wrestling with his decision to entrust Fred with this responsibility. Charlie knew the native mind and its unpredictability and wondered how Fred would cope with the unexpected. With some misgivings he watched Fred, Sam and the rest of their party disappear into the trees.

A month later headman Tokeru of the Habogabuna tribe sat sharpening his axe. He looked pensively at his young son playing with some seashells at the mouth of his hut. He had called the men of the village together and they were starting to assemble in the central clearing. The space was ringed by thatched huts, outside of which women were pounding sago, children were playing and chickens were pecking at the dusty ground. Tokeru stood before the assembled men.

'Warriors of Habogabuna. We know our enemies the Kanabo are stealing our land. They did this during our fathers' time'.

There was murmuring, nodding and some stamping. Their headman was confirming the rumours that their neighbours, the Kanabo, were clearing fertile land for planting crops at the no-man's land halfway between the two villages. This area had been in contention for generations and caused the occasional flare up. There had been an uneasy peace for several years with confrontations mostly confined to hurling insults rather than spears.

Tokeru warmed to his theme.

'Warriors, do we allow the Kanabo to steal from us?'

This was received by shouts and stamping.

'Warriors, do we allow the thieving Kanabo to insult us? Are we women or are we warriors?'

He had worked up his audience who were now ready to be led against their neighbours.

'We will show the weak, stupid thieves that we are to be feared. We shall leave with our spears as the sun rises tomorrow.'

What Tokeru did not know was that Fuifui, the wife of Paiyo, one of his warriors, had heard everything. She was her husband's first and oldest wife, barren after eight years of marriage. She hated Paiyo for beating her almost daily and lavishing all his attention on his younger wife who had borne him two sons in the last two years. He now treated her as a slave to both him and his young wife. Headman Tokeru showed no interest or sympathy when Fuifui complained to him.

Here was her opportunity for revenge, both on her husband and Tokeru. The distance between the two villages was no more than five miles and Fuifui ran as fast as she could down the tree-shaded track. After an hour she met two Kanabo hunters.

'Where are you going Habogabuna woman?' They spoke in a dialect of Benabena, a language common to the area. She explained her mission to warn them of tomorrow's planned attack. They looked sceptical. Was this some trickery on the part of their traditional foes?

'Why should we believe you from a tribe of liars and thieves? Come with us to speak with our headman.'

Sitting before Kanabo's elders she again explained her mission.

'If you find I am lying you can kill me,' she said simply. 'I have no wish to live anyway.'

She was dismissed but put under guard in one of the women's huts.

The tribesmen of fighting age then debated at great length their strategy to meet this apparent threat.

Fred was enjoying the autonomy of leading his party. He felt he had been following the footsteps of some early twentieth-century explorers who had first contacted these remote highland villages. He knew that even now there were uncontacted tribes who had never seen a white man. How he would love to be part of an expedition to the parts of PNG yet to be explored. As these thoughts ran through his head, the party entered the village of Kanabo. This was the last stop before returning to Okapo. They stopped in the central clearing and looked around. There was neither sight nor sound of the human population, just the pecking chickens and snuffling pigs in a corral at the back of the huts. Smoke rose from smouldering cooking fires.

'Where is everybody, Sam?'

Sam scratched his head and shrugged. The others had been looking inside the huts. Constable Peter came up to Fred and Sam. He was roughly pulling along a small, wizened woman. She was shivering and seemed frozen with fear.

'She was tied up in that hut, Masta,' said Peter pointing. 'She will not speak to me.'

Sam addressed the woman in several of the local dialects but elicited no response. All at once the group became aware of men holding spears, bows and painted shields emerging from the trees surrounding the village. Each man's face and body were painted in vivid colours. Adorned with elaborate headdresses and wearing grass and feathered bodies, the effect was intimidating. The men had stopped at the edge of the clearing, not expecting to see a white man with a policeman and party of other men not from the area. One of the bowmen suddenly shouted in anger and plucked an arrow from his quiver. He strode up to Fred's group and aimed at the silent woman still being held by Peter.

'Stop,' shouted Fred, who ran towards the man as he released his bow string. The arrow struck Fred in the chest and he fell, impaled. Sam went to his side, pulling the arrow out. Blood gushed from the wound.

Peter rushed at the man, pulling him to the ground and pummelling his head with his fists. When the man stopped resisting, Peter summoned the porters to stand on him as he secured him with handcuffs. As this was happening, the painted warriors melted back into the forest and disappeared. Meanwhile, Sam tore off Fred's shirt using it to stem the blood flow. He found the first aid kit. He had seen minor injuries dressed by John Edwards at the mission but nothing as serious as this. He smeared antiseptic cream on the open wound and did what he could with bandages. Fred was awake but in pain.

'Don't worry boss. We'll get you back to Okapo and you'll be OK.' Fred nodded.

'Send a runner to tell Charlie,' he rasped.

Sam dispatched Kemai, the fittest porter, to run the fifteen miles to Okapo with a scribbled note. Kemai had never run so far and so fast in his life. Four hours in fading light after the dramatic events at Kanabo, a breathless Kemai burst into the patrol office. It was late afternoon and Charlie was finishing his monthly report to headquarters.

Charlie scanned the note with a sinking heart. He radioed Moresby to urgently send a doctor. It was obviously serious, but how serious? Would it be dangerous to move him? The new Okapo clinic was still awaiting a local nurse to be trained. John Edwards had a Fijian trained nurse in the mission clinic. He wrote a hurried note to John and handed it to Kemai.

'Kwiktaim bringim leta long masta john long misin,' he commanded.

Kemai ran off. Half an hour later John Edwards appeared with a young man named Joseph.

'Mr Charlie I will go to see what I can do for Mr Fred. I think I can tell if it is safe to move him. Mr John says I can take our emergency medical kit. It has morphine for pain. For infection we can give antibiotics. The mission has a stretcher we can take. It is too dark to go now, it is a very difficult path to Kanabo. We can start at first light tomorrow.'

Charlie reluctantly consented to wait until the following day before sending Joseph with a team of porters to Kanabo.

The following day Patair delivered a young Australian, Dr McKenzie. The aircraft remained on the ground for the return journey with Fred. Later in the day Sam emerged from the trees followed by the stretcher party bearing a heavily bandaged and unconscious Fred.

After examining the patient McKenzie spoke to Charlie. 'Your Joseph has done a good first aid job but well-meaning Sam should not have pulled the barbed arrow out as it enlarged the injury and caused more bleeding. I'd say he has a collapsed lung. He has lost a lot of blood – we need to get him to Moresby PDQ. My worry is infection and shock in his weakened state.'

Fred was loaded into the Piaggio and accompanied by McKenzie, the plane took off for Moresby. Charlie interviewed Sam for a briefing.

'Bos, I am so sorry. Mr Fred is my friend. I should not

have let him jump to protect the woman. I did not know I should not have pulled out the arrow.'

'Sam, tell me, who was the war party? Tell me the whole story.'

'They were from the Habogabuna village. The headman is Tokeru and he is known to be a very jealous and aggressive man. Apparently, he found some excuse to attack the more peaceful Kanabo people. The woman is from Habogabuna and had informed the Kanabos of the plan to attack. They deserted their village before their enemies came. The man who injured Mr Fred is tied up in the storeroom. He is a Habogabuna, husband of the woman. We brought her back here for her safety.'

The storeroom doubled as a prison cell and this was the first time it had been used in this role. Charlie listened in silence.

'You are not to blame for what has happened. We will visit this Tokeru who is responsible for these events.'

Fred died that evening.

Charlie was devastated and filled with guilt, feeling responsible for his young assistant's death. If only he had listened to his earlier worries. Sam had developed a close affection for Fred and was inconsolable, angry and vengeful. Charlie consulted DC Terence who was matter-of-fact.

'Poor Fred's murderer must go to Moresby for trial, as must this nasty Tokeru. I'll arrange transport. I'll send you a couple of capable extra constables to help with the arrest and escort these scoundrels to Moresby. Sounds as if this Habogabuna needs sorting out with a new headman. I'll leave it to you to calm the area down.

These things happen, don't feel bad about it. Send me a full report.'

Charlie did feel bad. He was tormented about it for a long time afterwards.

CHAPTER 48

After writing his report on the Kanabo Tragedy as it became known, Charlie wrote to Fred's parents. He had never written a sympathy letter before, but could not do other than express genuine admiration for their son and the sadness, not only his own but that of everybody in Okapo. 'The passing of a more worthwhile human being was hard to imagine' he wrote. 'His loss was not just of a talented government officer, but an asset to the people of Papua New Guinea.'

Fred's body was repatriated to Tasmania, and after his funeral his parents wrote. They said how they had heard from their son saying how he loved his posting to Okapo and working for Charlie. Fred had said Charlie was an inspirational boss whom he wanted to emulate.

Mama Julie had been disturbed at the events, particularly in the light of Charlie's assurances when he had asked her to come with the children to PNG.

'Mama I am so sorry that this has happened but I can tell you that nothing like it has happened before in my life.'

'Son, nobody talks 'bout anything else. I cried when I heard the news. He was such a nice respectful young man. Both Junior and Becky is asking where is Uncle Fred.'

Charlie's urgent task was to visit Habogabuna to arrest their headman and see him replaced by a more civilised leader. Together with Peter and two constables sent to assist, Charlie set off, leaving Sam behind. Sam had wanted to come but with his calls for revenge Charlie felt he might be disruptive to the cool dispensation of justice.

Tokeru had been warned by one of his hunters of the approach of Charlie and his party. After the injuring of the white kiap, news from his spies that the man had died made him apprehensive. White people were popularly supposed to be spirits returned from the world of the dead. Killing one had unknown consequences. He shivered at the possibility of receiving a visit from unfriendly spirits. Habogabuna village looked peaceful as Charlie entered with his policemen. He had ordered them to cock their rifles and be ready for violence. If anybody so much as raised a weapon they were to be shot.

He ordered Peter to find Tokeru and bring him forth. The headman ambled out of his hut and followed Peter into the central clearing. Charlie had met him a year earlier when collecting census data. On that occasion he had found him grudgingly cooperative.

Villagers were starting to emerge from their huts.

'Ho Tokeru. I have your man Paiyo and he tells me you

ordered war against the Kanabo. So now a white Masta is dead. What do you say?'

'My warriors and I went to the Kanabo for a peaceful palaver to talk about their stealing our land.'

'Do you go to peaceful palavers with war paint and spears? You lie. You know that war is forbidden. You will answer to the government lords for this. There will be a new headman of the Habogabuna.'

Charlie motioned to one of the policemen who advanced with handcuffs. At this Tokeru turned, ran to his hut and emerged with a spear, drawing it back to hurl at Charlie. Both Peter and the other constable fired at once and Tokeru staggered back falling lifeless. The crash of the two rifles produced a cry from the startled population who had witnessed the whole episode. Silence followed for a minute, then a shaken Charlie turned to the fearful faces.

'Tokeru broke the law of this land. All men know this. Tokeru has paid the price. Paiyo will also be punished. I will speak with the elders of your village and you will have a new headman.'

Charlie had the elders, comprising about a dozen men assembled before him. He addressed them in Tok Pisin.

'Speak among yourselves and tell me the name of your new headman. Give me the name of a wise man. He shall be a man of peace having respect from all. If this new headman is as foolish as Tokeru, he too shall die like a dog and I shall return with soldiers and there will be terrible punishments for every living Habogabuna man.'

This produced much murmuring from the old men. This was not the diplomatic approach that might be taught on a Port Moresby induction course but Charlie knew he had to make a dramatic impact. Had he known, he would have found his threats were unnecessary. There had been much resentment of Tokeru and his methods for years. He had ruled as a despot and would not be missed. The village was ready for change. After two hours the elders' spokesman came forward to where Charlie was seated with his policemen.

'We are decided,' he said simply.

'Bring him to me.'

'It is I,' said the spokesman. 'My name is Boassi. I will be headman.'

Charlie regarded him quizzically. He looked to be in his mid-forties, with a gentle manner. At forty a man would be considered old in a PNG village. Charlie called the village together.

'Boassi is your new headman. You will respect him and accept his wise judgement and that of his council of elders.'

There were murmurs that Charlie sensed to be of approbation. Afterwards, back in Okapo, he thought about his appointment. It was of course a pretty arbitrary choice. In his Stanford studies of history there were many examples confirming that power corrupts. He made a note to periodically call in at Habogabuna to check on Boassi.

CHAPTER 49

A month elapsed after Charlie's promotion of Boassi and so far, he had heard nothing to suggest that his choice had not been a wise one. The whole area had been unsettled after the news of Fred's death but was now returning to normal.

Charlie entered his office, seeing envelopes on his desk that had been awaiting his attention for the past two days. Important communications were via radio, resulting in his desultory approach to mail that was normally dominated by bureaucracy from Moresby or from religious organisations soliciting donations. The only real items of interest for him were letters from friends in America.

Sorting through the post he found an envelope bearing a stamp with the head of Queen Elizabeth II in the corner. The address was handwritten. The postmark showed the envelope was posted over six weeks ago.

This envelope was addressed simply to 'Charlie'. The contents caused his pulse to quicken. Eve hoped he had not forgotten her; she hadn't heard from him for several months. Her time in PNG since meeting him had made her re-evaluate her lifestyle. Would he write to her and keep in contact? It was signed, 'With warmest regards, Eve'.

That night, unable to sleep Charlie started to reassess his life. He would be twenty-seven years old in three months. He craved female company. He loved his work but life seemed incomplete not to be able to share it with somebody. Would he end up like some of the crusty middle-aged bachelor kiaps he had met at departmental meetings in Moresby? He had fantasised about Eve ever since that weekend in Morobe. Her letter reawakened that desire. Was he being irrational though, he asked himself? He knew almost nothing about her. His affairs in America had never aroused the same personal chemistry. He decided to write to keep the friendship alive. He would tell her that he had a son although realised that would most likely end any future contact from her.

Three months later, the day dawned of the annual inspection by the area's district commissioner. DC Terence Chiles' large frame squeezed out of the tiny Cessna opening to full height rather as a butterfly emerges from its chrysalis. He was greeted warmly by Charlie who had always enjoyed the company of his boss. This being a visit by an important bigman, there was a large turnout of villagers on the airfield. The pair had now known each other for two years since Charlie's appointment to Okapo. Terence had a full appreciation of Charlie's competent administration and the annual visit was little more than a formality. He gave a cursory examination of record-keeping and inspected the buildings and equipment. He had brief chats with key staff including Sam and Peter. He congratulated them both on the favourable reports he had received on the performance of their duties. He knew of Charlie's transition from bachelor to parent and the story behind his leave in America. He was introduced to Mama Julie for whom he turned on his usual charm.

'How nice to meet you Mrs Wood,' he beamed.

'An' nice to meet you sir. An' call me Mama,' she giggled.

'And please call me Terence. I've met your lovely grandchildren – you must be so proud of them.'

Mama giggled again. She almost wanted to curtsey. Never before had she received this level of interest from a white man, let alone an important one.

That evening the two men sat outside watching the sun disappear below the treeline. Cicadas and other nocturnal insects in the trees started their usual night-time chorus of chirping and clicking.

'You know Charlie, big changes are coming to this country. Your compatriots are already talking about independence. As you know, there is now a House of Assembly being set up in Moresby, although power still rests with the Australian administration. Australia is under a lot of pressure internationally to let PNG go its own way. There is a dearth of educated locals and you might want to think about putting yourself forward to be part of a new PNG government. The Aussies are keen to promote people like you, rather than see some power-hungry hot-heads running things.'

Charlie listened in silence.

'I hear what you say, Terence, but I'm really not interested in becoming some big-time politician. I'm very happy here – the kids have settled in nicely and Mama Julie is happy. I was worried about how they'd cope with the transition. Most of all, I enjoy running my own little world. I love the people and feel I'm doing some good, helping to solve their problems.'

'Charlie there are some much bigger problems facing PNG that you could a have a hand in solving. I'll be going back home in the future, but I feel great affection for PNG and I'm troubled by the prospect of a premature grant of independence. Think about it.'

After Terence left, Charlie looked through the correspondence that had arrived on his flight. He quickly opened the envelope with a stamp bearing a London postmark.

Dear Charlie,

I think about you a lot. Your news about having a son and your decision to bring him up with his sister touched me. By coincidence, the magazine has asked me to do a series about Australia. Next month I shall be in Queensland. I've a generous travel budget. Could I come and visit you? I leave in four weeks, so write soon.

Yours, Eve

Charlie could not wait to reply that he would love to see her. The platonic tone of their correspondence since their meeting in Morobe made him wonder if his fantasies were ever going to become real. He dictated a telegram over the radio to the telegraph office in Moresby. The other thing occupying him was the previous evening's conversation. It would stay with him for years. As he would find out, Terence's prescience was justified.

Eve came home in the evening to her Earl's Court bedsit from her office in London's West End. She couldn't wait to escape from the daily crowded tube journey full of other commuters. In two weeks, she would leave for her Australian assignment. The landlord left residents' post in the entrance hall on a table. Every day she looked anxiously through her mail, hoping for one with a PNG stamp. There wasn't one. Unusually, there was a GPO telegram envelope. The pink form inside simply read:

HAVE TOLD KIDS THEY HAVE AUNTIE EVE COMING FROM ENGLAND STOP SEND TELEGRAM WITH ARRIVAL DATE STOP CHARLIE

In the following week Charlie had a summons to attend a departmental meeting in Moresby. A car was waiting for him on arrival at the airport. There were about thirty men seated in the large conference room. Charlie recognised Controller Gareth Jones from the meeting with the ill-fated geological survey team last year. The other white officials were also heads of various administration departments except one who was introduced as Bill Woods, Deputy Minister of Territories from Canberra. A very big shot, thought Charlie. The remainder were local men most of whom he did not recognise.

The deputy minister spoke at length. The purpose of the meeting was to inform regional leaders of a decision to grant independence to PNG within the next decade. The House of Assembly would be the core of a new government and those present were being urged to submit themselves for appointment. Those from the regions would continue to reside and function in their present areas. Terence's words were ringing in his ears. Maybe there was little commitment at this stage, so he decided to register his interest in being the Assembly Member for his district. In reality, at that moment, his mind was more occupied with the prospect of Eve's impending visit.

PART FOUR

AFTERMATH

CHAPTER 50

Fifteen years later Charlie sat in silence with Junior on the veranda of the family home, overlooking Port Moresby bay and harbour. Sunset was approaching and the pair were becoming bathed in orange as the sun sank below the horizon. In the distance they could see Gemo Island, a leper colony shortly to be closed following the virtual elimination of the disease. A dark shape just visible above the waters of the bay was the remains of a ship bombed by the Japanese in World War Two. Sight of the wreck always turned Charlie's thoughts to the discovery of the crashed bomber near Hulwari village. The events that followed had shaped his life in a way he could not have foreseen.

The following day Junior was due to fly to Sydney for his first year at university to study aeronautical engineering. His father broke the silence.

'I want to say something that I'd like you to bear in mind while you are away. We've talked about my experiences, but now you'll be facing this prejudiced world as I did at your age. Here in our country, you and I as black men don't have to think about it. You don't think about your skin colour or racism until it hits you in the face. It's often going to be the elephant in the room from tomorrow. Racists are ignorant, small-minded people but unfortunately there are a lot of them. Ignore them, they are to be pitied. You'll find out who your real friends are. Don't get drawn into violence, walk away from it unless you physically need to defend yourself. Model yourself on Martin Luther King or Gandhi rather than Malcolm X. It won't happen in my lifetime or possibly yours, but the time has to come when people no longer notice skin colour. So, deal with it.'

Junior did not respond immediately.

'OK Dad, got it. Any other words of wisdom before I set off tomorrow?'

'Son, wisdom is something you have to learn from your experiences in life. We could sit here for hours with me telling you my life story again and the lessons I learned along the way.'

'How about a few highlights that maybe I haven't heard before?'

'You've heard the story of the B-25. Those young men in the plane, just hours before the crash, would have thought of themselves as immortal, before fate suddenly overtook them. Just to say there are no certainties in life. Live life to the full. Try to make the best of it whilst you can. You simply don't know what's around the corner.'

'Have you made the best of it Dad?'

'Good question. Though others will have to make that judgement.'

'Dad that's a real politician's answer. Evade the question at all costs.'

Charlie laughed and then thought for a moment.

'All right then. I've tried but I know I've made mistakes. When I was younger, I suffered from the arrogance of youth, not thinking of the hurt I might cause. When I was older, in a position of authority, I made an ill-thought out decision which resulted in a good man losing his life. It was an accident I could not have foreseen, but I have been haunted by it for many years. I guess the lesson here is always try not to do or say anything that you might later regret. So, to answer your question, I've certainly tried to make the best of life but I've not always succeeded.'

Charlie had not expected to be baring his soul but for many years he had been troubled by sending the inexperienced Fred Stock on tour to his death.

Junior lapsed into silence, admiring his father's honesty. At that moment he felt close to him as he had never felt before. They stood and hugged for a few moments.

'Let's go and find Mum and dinner.'

CHAPTER 51

Two weeks later, after Charlie and Eve waved Junior off to Sydney. It was the anniversary of their life-changing meeting in Morobe. They were celebrating the date and remembering the events that followed.

Two years after they first met in Morobe and within two days of Eve's arrival in Okapo, Charlie proposed. Six months later when Eve had completed her Australian assignment, Charlie travelled to London. In the presence of her parents and friends they married in her local registry office. Charlie insisted that they could only be properly married in PNG. Accordingly, they returned to Okapo for a traditional Eastern Highland wedding. Among the guests were Philip and Pamela Smithson, Eve's parents and her Uncle George from Morobe, who had been the architect of the couple's meeting. In keeping with local tradition, Charlie had to pay her family for Eve's hand. It was decided that Eve's bride price was six pigs – an absolute bargain, thought Charlie!

On the day, surrounding the bride were maids of honour – a group of painted, bare-breasted women dressed in grass aprons. Eve's face was painted according to local tradition – white with yellow streaks, her hair adorned with feathers. She also was dressed in a traditional grass apron open at the side. Eve drew the line at being bare-breasted and wore a bikini top. The wedding of a local bigman was an important occasion attended by a few hundred, some of whom had trudged from outlying villages. John Edwards and the entire population of the Okapo mission joined in. Mama Julie, Junior and Becky were present also traditionally dressed and painted. The children thought they had never had so much fun. Bridegroom Charlie, his face also painted white and yellow, wore a specially woven lap lap together with armbands and was adorned with feathers, shells and grasses. An elaborate bird of paradise plumed headdress befitted his status. Painted and plumed Okapo men were dressed for the occasion carrying spears or bows and arrows. Arranged in two lines, with the men facing the women, dancing with rhythmical swaying, chanting and much stamping took place. This was followed by the important handing over of the bride price. After the pigs had been inspected and pronounced as meeting his approval, Eve's father donated them to be roasted for the wedding feast. The day ended with more dancing.

A year later, Eve gave birth to a daughter and eighteen months after that another daughter. Eighteen months following Charlie and Eve's marriage, Mama Julie and

John Edwards announced they were to be married. Junior and Becky were to gain a grandad. The wedding took place at the mission officiated by a fellow missionary. A happy but sober affair, thought Charlie and Eve, compared with their own ceremony a year and a half earlier.

With the coming of independence, the post of kiap no longer existed and Charlie reluctantly left his Okapo home to serve in government.

Chapter 52

At his desk in the Ministry building Charlie sat reading an indictment. Apart from minor offences disposed of in magistrates' courts, as Justice Minister he saw all impending prosecutions heard in the country's higher courts. This case was against a Hulwari tribesman who had been arrested for the large-scale killing of birds of paradise, a long-protected species. The accused had been sent up to the Assizes in Moresby. The unfortunate man now languished in the capital's newly built gaol in Bomana. The even less fortunate birds had been slaughtered for their feathers, not to decorate Hulwari wigmen but to sell to someone in a criminal chain for illegal export to a fashion house in Europe or the US. Genuine feathers were greatly prized and highly valuable. On the face of it, and in any other country, killing a few wild birds for their feathers would not seem to be a sufficiently grave offence to warrant a hearing in a higher court. But in PNG there were two aspects to the crime. First, there were the practical effects on the environment and the economy. Ornithologists and tourists with their valuable hard currencies were drawn from around the world to see these unique and wonderful creatures. Second and perhaps more important and emotive, is the fact that the bird of paradise is the national symbol of PNG. It even appears on the national flag.

Sadness filled Charlie at this moment. His nostalgia took him back to his early days and the simplicity of tribal life. His sadness was not so much about the crime per se, but what it represented. He cast his mind back over twenty years when the crime was virtually unknown. At that time the Hulwari certainly killed the birds for their feathers for personal ornamentation but once his wardrobe requirements were satisfied, a Hulwari man would have had no concept of killing these gifts of nature for further personal gain. The buying or selling of objects was unknown to him. The crime just highlighted to Charlie the fact that the ills of western society, had now reached remote villages in his country. He lamented that hitherto almost unknown crimes of violent robbery, rape, corruption, drug abuse and trafficking were now endemic to certain parts. Sometimes guns were replacing spears. The problems were worse in the rapidly expanding urban areas of major towns. Murder, although previously linked with emotive causes, now took on a more gratuitous form and was frequently to do with robbery or drugs.

The habit of betel nut chewing had been part of PNG society for thousands of years, just as the Greeks had a special contaminated barley brew, which produced a similar effect to LSD. Long before that, the opium habit was very much a part of Chinese culture. In all these cases the habit remained relatively harmless, not fuelling a crime wave as in western society. What had gone wrong?

The entrance of his assistant Brandon, interrupted his thoughts. Brandon was one of the up-and-coming civil servants who had been to university in Australia. He tended to model himself on the latest youth culture there in appearance, language and taste in music. To Charlie, Brandon was yet more evidence that the native lifestyles and cultures of PNG would eventually all be overwhelmed and succumb to alien values. These seemed to place little emphasis on anything but profligate consumption.

'What's the matter boss? You look worried,' Brandon said.

'It's nothing,' said Charlie. 'I want to visit the Hulwari fellow in Bomana, you know – the one who was caught selling feathers to the Dutch trader.'

'OK, I'll arrange it for Friday morning, how's that?'

Charlie consented and dismissed his assistant. They had conversed in English. Brandon came from outside Madang and his native tongue was not one that Charlie spoke. Educated men used English between themselves rather than Tok Pisin. At his age, it was something of a rarity for a Highland native to speak faultless English. Indeed, Charlie was unusual on many counts. At over forty he was also the oldest Minister in Government. He had stayed a member of the Assembly through several elections. Politically, he was allied to the dominant political party although his election to the National Assembly was more a measure of his popularity in his constituency, than any real interest by the electors in party politics. PNG politics are highly competitive, with most members elected on a personal and ethnic basis rather than as a result of party affiliation. Members of Parliament are elected on a 'first past the post' system, with winners often gaining less than 15% of the vote. Charlie bucked the trend with over 60% at the last election.

The following morning, Charlie's official car pulled up at the prison guardhouse receiving a smart salute from a policeman, who then conducted Charlie to the governor's office. The governor was an Australian who remained after independence like a sizeable number of foreigners who had taken PNG nationality. Jack Heathcote and Charlie were not close but maintained a polite, cordial relationship. After independence, Charlie had managed to win over the resentment that some Australians felt for their new masters. Heathcote wondered why the justice minister could possibly want to visit a small time criminal. He knew PNG law took a serious view of bird of paradise killing whereas in Australia a similar offence might warrant a fine at most. Charlie himself, was starting to wonder why he was there. He had instructed Brandon to arrange the meeting, remembering his past involvement with the Hulwari tribe. It had been a highly significant event in his life that culminated with him meeting Tom Paul, and all that followed.

'Yuorait', said Charlie in pidgin on entering the cell, then repeating the greeting in Hulwari. Puka, who was maybe in his early twenties, was startled at hearing his native tongue in this alien environment. He realised this older man, dressed in western clothes was important but not of his tribe. Charlie could see a confused, frightened man trying to maintain his pride with an air of youthful arrogance.

'What do you want?' was the rude response.

Charlie responded gently and politely. 'Puka, I want to know what made you commit this crime and I want to know what you were going to do with the money you made from killing the birds. I want to know why it was worth the disgrace you are bringing on your family and your tribe and I want to know why you do not seem to care about the beauty of our country? I know your tribe and its proud tradition. I know your headman and I knew his father. Tell me why did you do this?'

The young man was taken aback. He shifted about in his chair, looking uncomfortable and avoiding eye contact.

'This foreigner offered me a lot for the feathers and it was simple, easy money. In the village everybody knows I'm the best with bow and arrow and know more about the birds and their habits. I didn't know I would be in prison. I wish I had not done it.'

Charlie tried to explain the reasons for the law, the protection of creatures which were part of the magnificence of the Hulwari forests. The man should be proud of the fact that foreigners travelled from all over the world to see these birds. He should see himself as a protector not a destroyer of such beauty. Charlie thought the man was touched by his gentle sermon and felt sorry that he had been corrupted by western values.

'You could serve yourself, your tribe and your country by using your knowledge and guiding those rich foreign tourists who want to do nothing other than see and photograph birds. Puka, do you promise never to repeat this foolishness? Will you try to make your time on this earth one to be proud of and to be a credit to your tribe and your country?'

Puka promised, but at that moment felt he only wanted to do these things if it helped to get him out of jail. All he could think of was the impending trial and punishment. Who was this man anyway?

Charlie bid farewell to Heathcote on the way out. On returning to his office, he called the circuit judge who would hear Puka's case, also the state prosecutor. He spoke to a local solicitor who owed him a favour and explained the case and asked him to represent Puka on a pro bono basis. Much to everybody's surprise, Puka was only released on probation so long as he fulfilled certain conditions. One of these was to present himself to the justice minister.

Suitably awed by his surroundings, Puka was ushered into Charlie's presence. He instantly recognised the Hulwari-speaking man who two weeks ago had visited him in his cell.

'Puka, you must promise me that when you return to your tribe you will tell everybody you have agreed to never again kill these birds. I will speak of you as a clever forest guide to a local tourist agency which organises ornithological walks for foreign tourists. Puka, I am putting trust in you.'

Charlie knew he was taking a risk in promoting Puka's welfare, but had a sense that this was not misplaced. All his life's experiences told him that dialogue and compassion intelligently applied, often worked better than harsh punitive measures. A generation ago, this episode would never have taken place. Why punish Puka for a crime that had almost been foisted on him by the lure of money?

His assistant Brandon was extremely sceptical.

'Say boss, why did you let off that thieving Hulwari? You should have locked him up and thrown the key away. Before you know it, the whole tribe will be out there trapping every bird for a hundred miles.'

Charlie just hoped Brandon was wrong.

That evening, brooding over the day's events, he watched his two teenage daughters talking with friends at the front of their bungalow. Becky was in her room revising for exams. He related the affair of Puka to Eve who was preparing the family's evening meal. She came and sat beside him, silent for a moment before speaking.

'Darling, I know the helplessness you feel at what is happening in your country. All one can do is try to live by one's own standards and to pass these on to one's children. I know that you want the best for your people and today you did the best you could for Puka. One can only hope that investing trust in people will be rewarded.'

Charlie looked fondly at Eve. Whatever happened in the future, he knew he had made the wisest decision of his life that day on the beach at Morobe.

AUTHOR'S NOTE

C harlie's story and its characters and places are fictional except in the case of historical fact. The description of PNG in the 1960's is formed from the author's memories of his time working in this amazing country. Apart from PNG's major centres, village names are not actual but with descriptions that could relate to hundreds of typical villages throughout the country in the period and probably even today.

The book would not have seen the light of day without the help, patience, many reviews and encouragement from my wife Ann. I also must thank Jill Hackett, my son Graham and his wife Justine and Margo Bekkering for their insightful reviews and to my daughter Lynda for her comprehensive editing and proofing. I am grateful to Mike and Irene of M+IM Frost Design Consultants for their cover design. Thanks are also due to Bill Windred for his interest and practical help.

The reader can find out more about the author and the inspiration for Charlie's story at www.richnyeauthor.com

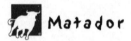 Matador

For exclusive discounts on Matador titles,
sign up to our occasional newsletter at
troubador.co.uk/bookshop